LOVE IN THE TIME OF A HIGHLAND *Laird*

ANGELINE FORTIN

Published by

MY PERS🌑NAL
BUBBLE LLC

ISBN-13: 978-1518612541
ISBN-10: 1518612547

My special thanks to my fabulous critique partners, Jody Vitek, Joyce Proell, and Terri Schultz. Thank you so much for adding me to the group.
And to Esther M. Soto for the endless encouragement she's given me over the past couple of years. It was so great having you just a block away, to pick your brain at any hour. To eat with and drink with... but then you abandoned me to move to Florida. :P

Chapter 1

"Oh, no. Not again."

Allorah Maines gaped in horror as a man—yet *another* man—pitched through the mouth of the open portal. This one was quite unlike the first, wearing the crimson and blue uniform of a pre-Revolutionary British solider. His rows of brass buttons catching the light, he staggered to the side and fell, sprawling facedown on the lab's pristine stainless steel floor. The clatter of his long, bayoneted musket skidding across the floor was audible even through the glass barrier separating the control room from the inner chamber.

This wasn't at all how it was supposed to be. When she'd signed on to work this project with the noted astrophysicist Dr. Roy Fielding at Mark-Davis Laboratories, all she'd imagined was the glory of scientific discovery. Making unprecedented strides in the creation of a stable wormhole.

Making history.

Achieving the impossible.

While they had managed the impossible, it had come with a most unexpected side effect.

1

Often… too often, what was on the other side of the wormhole they'd created found its way through.

"Fuck, fuck, fuck!" Fielding was a bit more vocal in his dismay, slamming his clipboard forcibly against the console again and again. "Shut it down! Shut the fucking thing down!"

Marti and Todd, two of Fielding's other lab assistants, shared a glance before beginning the slow process of safely tuning down the whirling vortex.

Al was too concerned with the man on the floor to be as worried about the success or failure of their project and by extension, their jobs. There was a man in there. Not just a stray animal, but a human being who'd been cast through the portal and was now lifting himself up, his expression one of confusion and horror as he rolled onto his back.

He wasn't the first to look so bewildered.

Nor was he to be the last.

She cried out in shock as another man followed the first, this one not clad in the bright red of the soldier but in a full Scottish kilt. His heavy jacket was torn… no, sliced in several places. Darkened by blood. His leg bleeding profusely.

And he was armed with a wickedly long sword.

Her distress had everyone else lifting their heads as the huge Scotsman lurched dizzily, clearly disoriented. His furious howl echoed through the chamber. Even muted by the walls between them, the sound curdled her blood.

He tripped over the other man's feet and fell on top of him, the sword between them as he collapsed. A muffled scream of pain followed, she wasn't sure from which one.

There was so much blood. Al rushed for the chamber door and lifted the handle.

"Al, no!" both Todd and Marti yelled.

"They're hurt," she shouted back. "We have to help

them!"

"You can't go in there," Marti insisted, grabbing her hand. "The portal isn't closed yet."

"They're *people*." Al shook her off. "I can't just stand here and watch this happen. Not again."

Both of her co-workers appeared startled by her vehemence. Well, why shouldn't they? She wasn't one to ruffle feathers. She wasn't normally the one to bear the standard for revolution but this had gone too far.

She would fight for what was right.

"Ms. Maines," Fielding barked, "I've had enough of your bleeding heart. You go in there and you're fired, you hear me?"

"Then fire me!" she shot back, surprising him and herself. "This is wrong and you know it. You've completely screwed this project up."

Yanking open the door, she rushed into the chamber, ignoring the whine of the alarms and yawning whorl of the still open portal. She dropped to her knees next to the two fallen men. As she did so, the kilted man rolled to the side and heaved himself to his knees.

But for his dazed expression, it seemed like he would live. The red-coated soldier didn't look like he would be so lucky. He moaned piteously, blood oozing around the sword blade embedded in his chest.

"Fuck it all!" Fielding barked from the doorway. "Will someone call security, for God's sake?"

Marti rushed to do his bidding.

The sterile clean-room couldn't be called that any longer. Blood seeped from one while it spurted from the other. Life was doing the same. Cursing under her breath, Al probed the wound, wondering if it would be better to remove the sword or leave it there until he got medical attention.

"Maines, get out of there. That's an order."

Or perhaps it would be better to let him die now than subject him to the fate she knew awaited him. They'd gone from scientists to jailers already.

It tore at her heart every time she had to…

A huge hand wrapped around her arm and with a start, she turned to stare into the bluest eyes she had ever seen. Blue eyes sharp with pain and confusion.

"What is this place?"

"I…"

The maelstrom of the wormhole easing, a security team rushed into the chamber. The kilted man wrenched his sword from the other man's chest and pushed her protectively behind him, as if he sought to protect her from the quartet of armed men rushing them.

But he shoved too hard and the unexpected move sent her stumbling toward the shrinking portal. It was closing but not closed enough.

Her cry of alarm was lost to the vacuum of the black hole.

Chapter 2

The Drumossie Muir
Near Culloden, Scotland
April 16, 1746

Such a bloody waste.

It was all Keir MacCoinnich could think of as he watched the battle from the relative safety of his position on the rise overlooking the Drumossie Muir. A bloody waste of human life.

And there was plenty of blood. The blood of his countrymen, his clansmen soaking into the highland soil. He'd never witnessed anything so terrible.

So pointless.

He was not a religious man. He didn't feel compelled to do anything simply because God or King demanded it. Only his father could have compelled him to take part in such a futile endeavor. He already regretted giving into the summons prompting his return, calling him to this place.

Cannon fire from the Hanoverian army whistled like perverse birdsong through the air before crashing through man and earth alike, raining bits of dirt and body parts down like a burst of fireworks.

The loss of life sickened him As it might in any war but more so when the cause was a fruitless one. The Hanoverian army woefully outnumbered the Jacobite regiments, made up of mostly Catholic Highlanders intent on restoring the Stuart line to the British throne. But whatever support Bonny Prince Charlie might have roused among the Highland chiefs, it obviously wasn't enough to make a successful stand against the Duke of Cumberland's superior forces. Not an hour into battle, and nearly a thousand of his countrymen had already washed the green moors red with their blood.

While he might mourn the loss of life, he felt no sadness at the loss of the cause. In fact, he felt not much more than disgust for that. It was the loss of his people. His clansmen. His countrymen.

Such a bloody, fucking waste.

The mount standing alongside his own horse shifted restlessly and Keir glanced at his cousin Hugh Urquhart, the Duke of Ross, seeing the same impatience in the man as in his mount.

Unlike himself, Hugh was a poet. An idealist. He would view the massacre below with far more passion than Keir. He would hear the battle cry of their clansmen with his heart and soul rather than a logical mind. All he saw were men too tired, too hungry, and too outnumbered to make any sort of impression on the well-rested and well-supplied Hanoverian army.

"Your Highness, we must retreat."

Keir rolled his eyes. Leave it to the Prince's adjunct general, O'Sullivan, to make the plea to his liege to abandon the fight when it was O'Sullivan's fault they were in this position to begin with. It was he who had chosen this wretched stretch of moorland between the walls of the

Culloden enclosure to the north and parkland to the south. His senior commander, Lord Murray, had attempted to protest the unsuitability of taking such an open position on soft ground against the Duke of Cumberland's heavy artillery but the Prince had upheld O'Sullivan's choice.

And look at them now.

For an instant, it had been a splendid visual. The Highlanders charging, banging their spiked shields and shouting out their clan's war cries.

Then their advance was forced to veer to the right around a previously unnoticed bog, leaving the far left regiments under Glengarry, Keppoch, Ranald, and Chisholm almost unusable in the battle.

Leaving the men on the right ripe for slaughter.

He ground his teeth in frustration. Even Hugh's jaw clenched at the words, but he knew his cousin well. Hugh would never give over to surrender, even if it were the only sane choice.

No, Hugh was a romantic. He would take it upon himself to be the avenging angel of his clansmen and swoop in to save them all.

Even as the thought crossed Keir's mind, Hugh unsheathed his mighty claymore and dug his heels into his horse's sides.

"Nae, cousin!" he shouted as the beast surged forward. "Ye dinnae hae tae!"

"Aye, Keir, I do."

"Bullocks," Keir cursed before he, too, drew his sword and followed his cousin into the fray with the battle cry of Clan MacCoinnich on his lips. If a man had to die, it was a fine spring day for it.

Hungry and weary from days of marching without

adequate supplies, the Jacobite army still rallied for this last charge. Into the guns and bayonets of Cumberland's army. Many of them raked by cannon fire and grapeshot before they even reached the enemy. They gave it every last ounce of heart they possessed, taking down as many of the enemy as they could.

Despite his lack of devotion to the actual cause, Keir was intent on supporting his clansmen in battle to the best of his ability. He attacked aggressively, working his way deeper and deeper into the foray until the enemy surrounded him. With a grim smile, he sent redcoat after redcoat to meet his Maker. It wouldn't be enough though. It couldn't be. They were weaker than their enemy, outnumbered.

It couldn't last long.

The scream of a horse drew his attention and he saw Hugh go down, rolling away to escape being crushed by his injured mount. Knowing his cousin had no hope of survival on foot among the overwhelming odds and long reach of the enemy's bayonets, Keir kicked his mount into motion. Slashing his way through a sea of redcoats, he made his way toward Hugh.

Such magnificent valor, he thought with a grin of admiration. Hugh continued to fight the enemy with his every fiber. He towered over them all, twice the man any of them were. Giving twice the fight.

Then one of the cowardly Sassenachs struck Hugh from behind and Hugh dropped to one knee. Fear for his cousin's life surged through Keir. He was just close enough to see that his cousin had been pierced in the leg by a bayonet. Judging by the angry expression on Hugh's face as he turned to face his attacker, the spineless Sassenach didn't have much time remaining in his life. The redcoat turned tail and ran like the coward he was. Despite the injury to his leg, Hugh gave chase, working his way through the battlefield with but one target in mind now.

The fight in the Jacobite army diminished now and their slaughter assured, the horns ultimately sounded for the Jacobite retreat. Still, Hugh kept after his prey, chasing him across the open moors to the south and through the rubble remaining of the park wall, which had been destroyed to make room for the Highland dragoons to advance.

Finally breaking free from the fringes of the fray, Keir kicked his mount into motion to follow, determined to save at least one life that day.

It was with some amusement that he realized his cousin was far more fleet of foot than a man of his size should be. He gained on his quarry far quicker than Keir was gaining on them. Hugh would get his man shortly, then Keir would take him up and together they'd leave this place before the Hanoverians began taking prisoners.

The red-coated Sassenach looked back over his shoulder in terror. Hugh was but an arm's length away, however, before Hugh could grab him, the Sassenach fell out of sight, swallowed by a gaping hole.

He yelled for his cousin to beware. Hugh skidded and stumbled, trying to stop his forward charge, but it was too late. With a shout of alarm, he too fell out of sight.

Shaking off his shock, Keir kicked his horse into even swifter motion but as he neared the breach, the animal spooked and reared, tossing its rider before sidestepping nervously away. Cursing the animal, he scrambled the few remaining yards as the cavity began to shrink. Calling frantically for his cousin through the curious blackness.

He was as spooked as his mount. He'd never seen such an oddity before. A chasm that appeared from nowhere. So black that he couldn't see into its depths. Could not see his cousin below. Or hear him over the whipping wind shrieking around its mouth.

Gathering his nerve, he thrust a hand into the void, hoping a hand might clasp his own, but there was nothing within. He felt nothing beyond an odd tingle stretching up his arm before he yanked it back.

"Hugh!" he called again, frantic now. "Hu—"

He scrambled away from the shrinking precipice when a white bundle sailed from the hollow, landing with the soft thud not far away as the gap closed.

"Hugh!" he yelled one last time, pounding a fist against the now-solid earth. Confusion ripped through him. He fisted his hands in the stiff grass, pulling it from its roots.

What had just happened?

Where was Hugh?

"Oh… Oh, no."

At the soft feminine moan, Keir spun around and gawked at the tiny woman unfolding herself from the ball of white the crater had spewed forth. Light blue eyes blinked up at him.

And widened.

Her surprise could be no greater than his own.

Chapter 3

Rough hands grabbed Al's shoulders and lifted her, shaking her hard. The hard jolt rebooted the slow ebb of the nausea her trip through the portal had prompted. Blinking against the bright sunlight, she glanced up into a blue gaze almost identical to the one she had met moments before in the lab.

But this was not the lab. Nor was this the man she'd seen there, though he was dressed almost identically.

He surveyed her in surprise and glanced down at her bloody hands before shoving her away. His eyes narrowed menacingly as she landed on her bottom. He pointed another of those long swords at her, bringing it closer and closer until Al's eyes nearly crossed.

"Where is Hugh?" he snarled in a harsh brogue. "What hae ye done wi' him, ye bluidy wee witch?"

Speechless, she stared at him, torn between awe and terror. Mostly terror, though he was the most magnificent looking man she had ever seen or imagined. The living, breathing manifestation of the untamed Highland warriors she so loved in her favorite novels. Black hair, a wild mass of tangles and curls, surrounding a granite-sculpted face that one never came across in real life. And those riveting eyes!

But those eyes weren't warm with the desire she'd read about. No, beneath his dark brows, they were glacial with an anger bordering on murderous.

Swallowing hard, she tried to find her voice. He came closer, the tip of the sword touching the tip of her nose.

She could smell of the coppery tang of the blood tainting the metal. Practically feel the frenzied beating of his heart.

"Speak, ye barmy witch!"

She jumped at the command. His harsh voice demanded a response though she didn't have a clue how to answer.

"Where is Hugh? What happened tae him?"

What on earth could she say? She didn't have to think twice about what had happened to him. She knew exactly what had transpired. And how. Fielding's project had been a comic disaster straight from the beginning. They hadn't at all achieved what they had set out to do.

Mark-Davis had taken government funding from UNICOM—U.S. Army Intelligence and Security Command—to develop a way to win the war on counterintelligence and information warfare. Fielding's idea was to create a passage through space. A covert way of traveling throughout the world to reposition troops, spy, or even assassinate without anyone being the wiser.

They had succeeded in generating the wormhole but that was all. Their lack of success in controlling the portal's destination in place, and even more surprising, *time* had Fielding hovering on the verge of a mental break for weeks.

No, she knew *what* had happened.

The only questions that remained for her were where and when. She couldn't get those answers from him any more than she could provide the answers this raging philistine demanded.

"Speak!"

She wasn't sure she could manage that either.

"I-I don't know," she stuttered.

The sword dipped as he neared until his face was just inches from hers. His eyes pierced hers but Al fought the urge to cringe and cower, meeting him steadily.

"Ye lie."

Leaving the grumbled accusation hanging, he pushed away and paced over the place where the churning portal had once thrived. He brought his foot down hard on the spot, even going so far as to stab at the ground with his sword, but that wasn't going to bring his friend back, nor was it going to help her get back home.

The thought brought a sudden rush of reality and for just a second, despair gripped her. Breathing hard, she struggled to conceal her emotions, knowing that any sign of weakness would be a mistake in front of this savage man.

Struggling to her feet, she backed away from the deadly arc of his sword as he swung it around with a haunting howl of rage and despair that exactly echoed the pain in her heart.

Then he turned on her once more.

"Bugger it all," he growled and wrapped his fingers around her neck, squeezing until her face began to heat and her head pulsed painfully. "Where is he? I kent ye did something wi' him. Tell me true!"

Though she had no better response than before, she was spared the need to produce an answer when a shout drew his attention. Loosening his hold, he turned to another kilted man who was yelling from a rise not far away. She couldn't understand him nor could she understand the response of her captor.

But another appeared. Then another. And more until a small army of kilted men on horseback was riding toward them.

"I must be away but I will hae an answer from ye yet, witch," he ground out. "Ye're mine 'til then."

"No, no please?" Ignoring her protest, he grabbed her by the arm and dragged her to where a massively terrifying horse was pawing the ground impatiently. "Y-you *barbarian*," she yelled, trying to jerk her arm back before he freed it from its socket. Her face flushed, not with true anger but humiliation that 'barbarian' was the worst thing she thought to say.

She stared back at the spot where the wormhole had been with pleading eyes. Futile eyes. She knew well enough from dozens of failed attempts that it was gone and that it would never... could never reappear in that spot again.

Her fate in that regard was sealed. What remained of her future would be up to her and the wild man wrenching her arm from her body.

Frustrated, she tried to slap his hand away, swung wide and landed a blow close to his groin.

He hissed at the near-miss and glared down at her. "Hae a care, lass. If ye were tae land such a blow, I'll for certs be showing ye how barbaric I can be."

With the menacing threat ringing in her ears, the brute smacked her bottom hard then gripped her around the waist, lifting her off the ground. He threw her facedown across the saddle and mounted behind her, bringing another hand down with a stinging blow to her backside to defuse any attempts to struggle.

He kicked the horse into motion and the first compression of her stomach against the hard saddle brought a burning lump of acid to her throat.

Oh, God. She fought the nausea the veritable Heimlich maneuver the saddle was generating. This certainly wasn't like it happened in romance novels.

Or at least she'd never read one where the heroine threw up all over the hero when she was in a position like this.

Struggling, Al tried to lift herself into a more manageable position but her captor just shoved her back down with a hard hand between her shoulder blades.

Hanging like that, black dots soon crowded her vision. Before long, she succumbed to horror and uncertainty, losing herself to the bliss of unconsciousness.

Chapter 4

The clink of metal against metal woke her. Lifting her head, Al tried to figure out where she was. Her hair, partially fallen from her now lop-sided bun during her inverted journey, obscured her vision.

The metal clanged again when she lifted a hand to brush the tangled mass aside, and she gaped in horror at the iron manacle around her wrist.

A metallic chill encircled her other wrist, and Al gave it the same appalled consideration as the first before turning her gaze to the huge man clamping her in irons.

"Are you... are you actually *chaining* me up?"

A swift glance took in the dark radius the circle of light cast by a single candle resting on a wooden bench nearby. Thick stone walls beneath her, behind her. The darkness beyond. Was she lying on the floor of a... a dungeon?

Closing her eyes, she inhaled deeply, trying to calm the panic rising swiftly from her gut, but no comfort was found in the stale odors of urine and abandonment.

"Ye're a bright one, aren't ye?" her captor-cum-jailer drawled mockingly, lifting her from the floor and setting her on her feet.

Taking up the length of heavy chain connecting her hands, he attached it to a ring set into the stone wall. Her arms were lifted above her head. Not far. Not painfully. But for a woman who'd never been in a dungeon… or put in chains, it was traumatic nonetheless.

"Aye, I said I would hae answers from ye and so I shall 'ere ye are freed from this place."

Despair clawed at her and Al shivered with dread. A period of unconsciousness had done nothing to make answers any easier to produce. Swaying on her feet, she wondered if another would do the trick. His behavior in abducting her had marked him as a savage, as the barbarian she had accused him of being. There was no chance that any explanation she offered would make him happy. Just as there was no chance he would understand even if she dared to answer with the truth.

Drawing in another long breath, she rolled her shoulders under the burden of the heavy chains.

"Och, lass, dinnae be thinking that heaving a magnificent pair of tits or wiggling a ripe arse will sway me from my course," he growled in a husky burr. "I'll be ha'ing my answers one way or another."

Puzzled, she followed his eyes downward, where her breasts were straining the buttons of her prim, green silk blouse beneath the parted lapels of her lab coat. Then she lifted her gaze back up to meet his fiery one. Her eyes widened at the appreciation she saw there.

She'd been blessed with more tits and ass than any woman of just five feet should have, but her abundant curves draped in a lab coat didn't usually garner the kind of male appreciation she saw in his eyes.

Assuming she was reading him correctly.

His gaze dropped once more before he glanced away and Al shivered, but for a very different reason this time.

Yes, he'd taken note. A man who looked like that.

Looking at her. Like *that*.

Suddenly, the same savagery that had her quaking in her sensible heels and kept her from telling him everything he wanted to know was working against her in a way Al would never have anticipated.

He'd shed the heavy jacket he'd worn before under the length of tartan draped over his shoulder, as well as his scabbard and sporran. She could see the deep tan of his skin straight through the thin linen of his shirt. Could fairly feel the muscles popping and bunching across his broad chest when he crossed his arms and glared at her once more.

Oblivious to the physical awareness now setting her nerves on edge in a much different way than before, he fingered the lapel of her white lab coat then flicked at the edge of her laminated Mark-Davis personnel I.D. as if it would bite him.

"If ye willnae answer one question, then answer me this. What are ye wearing? This outlandish jacket?"

His question hardly registered, though she'd been rendered too speechless to even consider an answer. Perhaps she'd read too many romance novels, but there was just something about him…

She'd always loved tales of hot men with bunches of lovely muscles wearing kilts. And this man was just that.

Those novels were her secret passion. Fantasy and escape from the trials and tribulations of everyday life. But what else was there to do when she lived alone with no one but her cat for company?

Horror struck and washed away the budding desire.

"Oh, my God! Who's going to feed Mr. Darcy?"

"Darcy?" the man repeated, clearly puzzled by her response. The first coherent sentence she'd yet to utter, yet it was all obviously nonsense to him.

"Are ye friend or kin to the Darcy of the West March? Are ye a Sassenach, lass?"

Al had read enough novels to know that when a Scot—if that's what this man truly was—asked you if you were a Sassenach in a tone bearing such disgust, the smartest recourse was to respond with a resounding 'no.' The best she managed was a shake of her head.

"Speak true for I shall ken if ye speak false."

"N-no," she cried, tugging at the chain binding her as if she might be miraculously freed. The fight was as useless as thinking she might find a way home. "No, he's my cat. Poor Mr. Darcy! He's going to starve."

"A cat?" There was so much confusion in his voice, there could be no doubt she'd completely thrown him for a loop. With a finger, he lifted her chin and pierced her with a fiery gaze. "Ye weep for a wee puss? Och, if ye think the welfare of a wee animal is going to gain ye freedom from answering my questions, ye'll be mightily disappointed. There will be nae escape for ye."

No, there was no escape for her. Al knew it without a doubt or a shred of hope. Fielding would never give a minute's consideration to trying to find a way to retrieve her. Todd and Marti would be bound by their nondisclosure agreements never to breathe a word about what had happened to her.

Best case scenario, someone might think to notify her mother of her 'accidental demise.'

But that was it. The most she could hope for. There

20

would be no rescue. No knight on a white charger swooping in to save her.

"No," she said, drawing another deep breath to calm herself. "I know there will be no escaping this place. Or you. I'm a realist." And a scientist mere steps away from a PhD in quantum physics. A depressing combination. Neither allowed for any wiggle room contrary to the facts.

This was it for her. She couldn't replicate the science to get back home. Barring any mystical fairy rings, enchanted Celtic stones or ancient gypsy magic she would never return.

There was no point bemoaning her fate or casting about fruitlessly for a solution to a problem that was beyond solving. Al's future was here in this place and time... wherever and whenever that was.

She was on her own.

It was a terrifying thought, but not a new one. Al had been on her own for quite some time. And had been alone for some time as well.

She was only beginning to understand what being truly alone might be like. "No, believe me, I know I'm never getting out of this."

Poor Mr. Darcy aside, she had to consider her own future and unless she wanted that future to begin and end in a dark, dreary dungeon, she would have to make something happen like the bold, fearless heroines in one of her books.

Though this was not at all what she dreamed it might be like in her own romantic fantasies...

Okay, perhaps the hot kilted man before her.

And perhaps the chains...

Just a little.

ANGELINE FORTIN

Chapter 5

Keir regarded the curious female speculatively.

He knew she feared him—as well she should—but for some reason, he didn't think she was truly afraid of him.

It made no sense as one contradicted the other. And if Hugh's life wasn't hanging in the balance, he might have the time to be more intrigued by this wee enigma. She was a rather fetching lass for all her oddities with her mussed blonde hair and scantily covered limbs.

But he didn't have time to let his baser nature interfere now, for his own life might be endangered as well. Following their victory at Culloden, the Hanoverian army would act swiftly to squash any lingering bravado the Jacobites might possess. They would be prompt in searching out Prince Charlie and taking prisoners of any they believed had supported his cause.

From what he gathered from letters over the past few years, his father, the Earl of Cairn, had been outspoken in his support. They might think to arrest him... and by extension, come for Keir and his three brothers as well. Even if he hadn't been in the country until only recently.

It was an aggravating situation, made all the worse by

Hugh's inexplicable disappearance. All he had to go on was this woman.

Whoever she was.

And she was an oddity. A mystery. From her stumbling speech to her dress, there was nothing about her that made any sense.

Keir hated mysteries. Whenever he came across one, he tore it down bit by bit until it was completely unraveled, comprehensible.

He would do the same with her. The delicate shudders shaking her tiny body told him she was on the verge of becoming undone. He merely needed to push a wee bit harder.

Fear was a strong motivator.

"Ye ken I could beat the truth from ye. Aye?" he said softly, pacing closer and drawing his dirk from his belt. He slid the flat edge of the blade down the side of her neck, pressing the tip lightly against her jugular. Not hard enough to break her delicate skin but hard enough to make his point. "I could torture ye for it."

Another tremor racked her from head to toe but still she said nothing. Had he frightened her beyond words, he wondered? She was a bitty thing for all her bountiful curves. Meek. She might very well be cowed by his size.

Or was it something more?

※※※※

God, she was a hot mess.

On the one hand, wallowing in utter misery for the hand fate had dealt her. The life she had worked so hard for lost. Her hopes and dreams gone. Her academic achievement all for nothing. Since that was where she had dwelt for most of her life, the loss was devastating.

On the other hand there was terror. She had no idea what this savage man was capable of. He could skin her inch by inch with that sharp blade for all she knew. Dissect her piece by piece and have her for dinner. No one would ever be the wiser.

No one was about who might even shed a tear for her demise.

On the third hand—if she were allowed one—she was absurdly tantalized by what was happening to her. Not the potential for death and dismemberment, naturally, but by the far flung fiction of being thrown somewhere in time and landing at the feet of a man like this.

For all his frowns and threats, her captor was dazzling. True, that cold blade across her throat brought visions of her blood being painfully spilt on the hard stone floor. Quivers of terror were winding up and down her limbs.

But... yes, but. But she was also shaken by the thought of his rough fingers following the same trail in a far more tormenting, sensual caress.

It was the stuff fantasies were made of, and being so much more pleasing than the reality of her situation, some part of her wanted to embrace it as such. That she couldn't shake the thought left her on the verge of puddling at his feet.

Not in a mound of trembling lust, but in mortification.

Quaking, visibly no doubt, with that odd combination of fear, excitement, and humiliation, she flinched as his thick fingers encircled her neck once more. When the icy tip of the knife pricked at her throat, fear dizzied her and she might have collapsed into a heap on the floor if he weren't holding her up.

His breath brushed hotly against her ear. "I will hae my answers, lass. By any means necessary, so ye best speak now 'ere something unpleasant befalls ye." The words were a raspy burr but the threat was unmistakable. He was quite serious.

But so was she. There was nothing she could say that would give him the satisfaction he desired. The where's and the how's would make no sense to a brute like this. Most likely she'd be tortured as a heretic for even suggesting such a thing. Though she wasn't sure yet when she'd landed, it all had a very medieval, witch-hunty vibe to it that wouldn't bode well for the truth.

Still, holding her tongue on the matter wasn't going to be enough for him. He shook her hard by the shoulders once more. "Tell me what I bluidy well want tae hear," he boomed, bending her back until he was looming over her.

Al was a petite woman. She'd spent a lifetime looking up at people. But until that instant, she'd never been completely overwhelmed by anyone. He was so massive, so muscular. He could snap her in half with those meaty hands without breaking a sweat.

He could do anything, anything at all to her that he damn well pleased. She'd be but a gnat to be swatted away for all a struggle would be worth to oppose him.

His eyes narrowed as if he could read the thoughts running through her mind. Pushing away, he took a step back and raked his fingers through his shaggy locks. Some, but not all, of the anger in his eyes faded. "Bugger it, lass. Relax. I'm nae rapist if that's what ye're thinking."

Straightening, she shrugged, refusing to acknowledge the truth of her thoughts aloud. The marked violence of true rape hadn't been at all what she'd been thinking. More like the impassioned struggle of an interrogation turned to a thirst for more than knowledge.

Geez, she really had read too many novels.

And a damned good thing he couldn't truly read minds.

"Ye ken, I am nae a barbarian ye think me tae be." He flung the word she had used back at her.

"Are you sure?" she asked, flinging her straggling hair over her shoulder with a toss of her head as if bravado could wash away the unseemliness of her thoughts. "Because it all looks pretty barbaric from here."

At her impudent sarcasm, her captor took a step back, regarding her with astonishment. His full lips compressed. "So, ye do hae spirit in ye, lass. I had wondered."

"There's a whole lot going on here you'd wonder about," Al shot back, surprising them both. In the normal course of her life, she was terrible with confrontations. It wasn't like her to react aggressively in any situation. Especially one where she'd hardly been able to squeak out a word otherwise.

"And I do. Unreservedly." His quiet tone was the most reasonable she'd yet to hear from him. To her further surprise, he unhooked the chain holding her manacled arms above her head and gestured for her to sit on the bench. With weak knees, she slid the stubby candle aside and sank down. He retrieved a wooden chair from the shadows beyond the circle of candlelight and sat as well. "I wonder aboot ye. From whence ye came. Why ye're dressed so... peculiarly?"

He studied her for a long while, leaning forward with his elbows on his knees. "Since ye dinnae respond to threats of violence, I gather 'tis something ye expected from a barbarian such as myself, perhaps ye'll respond tae reason. I am nae a simpleton, whatever ye think. I ken that ye're nae unassuming Highland lass. Something happened out there... I cannae begin tae describe. But ye... ye showed no surprise. Ye kent what it was."

His calm, forthright manner was oddly compelling. He

seemed almost like a normal guy in that moment. An average 21st century guy with at least average intelligence and enthralling blue eyes. Al struggled against blurting it all out. Where she had come from and how. How would he take it?

"I'm asking ye plainly... nay, beggin ye," he continued. "Tell me what has become of my cousin."

Al closed her eyes in a silent plea for help. From anyone. From anywhere. The man who'd come through the portal wasn't just a random acquaintance, he was his cousin? Could this whole situation get any worse?

"Please?" he added. "Hugh is as much a brother to me as my own kin."

Apparently it could. She groaned, stifling the regrets that were not just for herself and her own fate any longer.

"I willnae...nay, *cannae* leave the reason for his disappearance a mystery. Not when there is any chance I might save him."

There wasn't, she knew. Could she be the bearer of such news? Wasn't mystery better than the reality of what might actually be happening to the man who was like his brother right now? Surely telling him the truth wouldn't make anything better for him?

Vacillating internally, Al maintained her silence, but as before, her refusal to answer sparked his unpredictable temper.

"Argh! Ye obstinate witch." He stood, throwing back his chair in a sudden burst of violence. "Just tell me what I want tae know!"

"Please don't yell at me. I hate being yelled at." He stared at her with thinly leased violence, but rather than cower in fear or retreat into silence as she typically might, she continued, "My stepfather was an ugly drunk. He used to bellow like a rabid ape at me and my mom. It was invariably a precursor to something far more unpleasant. And I just can't stand it anymore."

"If ye dinnae want to witness my temper then put an end tae it," he snapped, his burr all the thicker in his anger. It rumbled from deep within him. "Tell me. I beg of ye. Put me out of this misery uncertainty has born."

"I wish I could. I want to." She did, Al realized. The pain in his soulful eyes was so real, she wanted to give him the truth. To let him rest his head in her lap while she stroked his hair back from his broad forehead as she assuaged his fears.

Except she couldn't do that.

It was as much a fantasy as thinking that anything she might say—even if he understood it all—would alleviate his anxiety.

How could she explain that to him?

"I'm afraid you wouldn't understand."

"Try me."

Al chewed her lip. Where to begin in the summation of *Quantum Physics for Idiots*?

"Well, I…" No. "There's…" No. "You see…"

"Lass…"

"Keir!"

A dark-haired young man banged open the cell door and ran in, chest heaving and a panicked expression on his face.

"Nae now, Oran!"

"It's Frang and Father," Oran panted, glancing between them.

"Ah, bluidy fookin' hell!"

Chapter 6

Four days later

Storming into the library, Keir tossed his scabbard and sword on his desk. Four days and still his temper hadn't been relieved. Nor his father found.

Nor his curiosity about his cousin satisfied.

No, all the past four days had brought him was misery. Tragedy. His brother Frang had been killed in the aftermath of the battle on the Drumossie Muir. Killed, not in the blood bath of the battle itself, but murdered.

According to the witnesses he could find, those fearful few running for their own lives but willing to talk, the Duke of Cumberland had ordered his redcoat army to kill every surviving clansman left on the field that day, be he injured terribly or only marginally. Some of the Highlanders had been buried alive in great pits. Frang among them.

His armies had then marched on toward Inverness, raiding homes, searching for other Jacobites fleeing the battle. Any person being suspected of being one of, or even supporting, the Jacobites had been killed by means of musket, bayonet, or left dangling at the end of an all-too-short rope.

Their homes burned. Women, children. It seemed to be an issue of little importance to Cumberland, who had already been labeled 'The Butcher' around the region.

Who knew what other atrocities might be committed in the days to come?

Luckily, his family home east of Dingwall was too far afield, too remote to attract immediate visitation. Though it might very well in the days and weeks to come as the search spread.

Prince Charlie was fleeing to the west Highlands, he'd heard. Perhaps the Isles. The information was sketchy but available. From men still loyal to his cause, eager to salvage what hope they had left in his person and see their 'rightful sovereign' to safety. Nevertheless, for all the gossip and news he'd been privy to, there had been no news of his father's death. Or imprisonment. Nothing.

That didn't mean one or the other wasn't true, however.

He had serious doubts his father would have discovered enough good sense to hide himself away, since most Jacobite supporters were after partaking in such a ludicrous affair to begin with. If he were hiding out, he was doing a bloody fine job of that but a horrible job as a father not to let them all know.

But that was nothing new.

Blast the man!

He could only hope that with the rank of Earl of Cairn, Camran MacCoinnich might have been spared the mass graves on the field of battle. Perhaps he'd been captured, imprisoned with the fifty or more prisoners taken to the Tolbooth gaol on the Canongate in Edinburgh.

He'd sent his cousin Mathilde to find out for certain. She was Hugh's oldest sister but more importantly her husband,

Alexander Kinnoull, Earl of Hawick, was of Clan Hay and a known patron of the Hanoverian King George, making her Keir's best chance at finding out what had become of his sire.

She would come to his aid, he was certain. Though her worries were no doubt focused more on the fate of her brother.

Pouring himself a full tumbler of Scotch from the decanter on the sideboard, Keir dropped into a chair and stared morosely into the cold ashes of the fireplace.

Hugh Urquhart, the Duke of Ross.

Keir's cousin, his brother-at-arms. His compatriot in deviltry throughout his life.

After Hugh's parents died when he was but a boy, they'd been raised as brothers. Of an age, Keir had been closer to him than his own brothers. Fostered together at age eight to the MacDonnell at Glengarry. Reprimanded together for pulling pranks on the headmaster at the University of Edinburgh. Sent off together to sow their oats on their Grand Tour of the Continent.

And now they'd been called back to do their duty together, when Cairn commanded them to take up arms for Prince Charlie.

Keir had known Charlie for years in France. He wasn't worth the effort. The death. Not his brother's or even his father's.

Certainly not Hugh's.

He might not have disappeared directly because of the rebellion but he had been lost because of it. Because Cairn had demanded his presence on the field. Hugh had only been there to fall into that void because of Keir's father and his ridiculous politics.

A fall that still made no sense.

It was time that it did.

Pushing himself from the chair, he grabbed a tasseled rope tucked between the bookshelves and gave it a firm tug. Reclining back in his chair, he downed his Scotch in a single swallow, wincing at the burn as it raked his throat and singed his gut. A sensation perhaps more pleasant than the confrontation to come. Yet come it must.

"Aye, laddie?" Archie, the man who'd come to answer his summons, asked, scratching absently at the side of his thigh beneath his kilt as he glowered out the far window.

Used to the quirks of his father's longtime retainers, Keir instructed, "Hae my cousin—"

"Which—?"

"Maeve," he snapped. Aye, he was too used to his father's men. "Hae Maeve bring our guest to me."

They were an impossible lot, all of them. Doddering fools and abstracted fossils. None who saw him as anything more than a wee lad in a long shirt. All who should have been retired years before.

"Our guest?" Archie scratched at his thigh again, transferring his frown to Keir.

"Aye, Archie." Keir spoke slowly. "The wee lass I put in her charge 'ere I left."

"Ye left?"

Keir merely rolled his eyes, for such a response was nothing out of the unusual at Dingwall. "Just hae Maeve fetch the lass. I'm sure she'll ken which one I mean."

XOXOXOX

Al woke with a jolt when her leg fell from the narrow bench. With a sharp cry, she yanked it back up and curled her arms around both legs until not the tiniest bit of herself dangled over the edge.

There were rodents down there. She'd seen them skittering across the dim field of light cast by her candle. Heard them scampering in the darkness. Little squeaks and hungry chewing haunted her fitful bouts of sleep.

Her overactive imagination had been hijacked by pure absurdity. Fancifully, she'd determined the little rats were taking their revenge upon her for years of being used as laboratory experiments. She just knew it, no matter how many hundreds of years spanned between their times.

"It wasn't me," she'd whispered into the darkness. "I'm not that kind of scientist."

She was pretty sure they knew it, but simply didn't care.

Nonsense was all it was. Nonsense to fill endless days. She wasn't certain how many had passed. Her fears moving from what her captor might do to her when he returned to what might become of her if he never did.

Would the remainder of her days be spent in that dungeon with nothing but conversation with rats and herself to occupy her?

There was no way to know.

She didn't blame Hugh for any of this. He'd been trying to protect her, not throw her into the hole from which he'd come. A chivalrous man.

The same couldn't be said of his cousin.

He'd left her there with nothing but a chair and a narrow bench to use as a bed. It wasn't until hours later that someone had brought her a meal and another candle. Hours more until someone thought to toss her a threadbare blanket that was almost useless in combatting the constant chill of the cell.

And a bucket.

That might have been the kicker. Days without fresh air, without decent food, without a toothbrush, but that...?

The final straw for sending her over the edge.

He'd done this to her. It was proof of his barbarism for only a true beast would leave anyone – female or not – in such a place. Slowly transforming her into one of them.

Barbarian? Beast? It irked Al that she couldn't even put a name to the brute so that she might curse him properly. Carr, the younger man had called him, with a rolling 'R' at the end. Was that his name? Or was it Kerr like Deborah Kerr? She wasn't sure. Perhaps it wasn't a name at all.

Presumably the young man who'd come in was his brother Oran. An assumption based on the reference of 'Father.' Sounded like it might have a capital *F* to it.

Carr or Kerr, it didn't matter which, only that he'd just gone off and left her, obviously without a second thought. And in doing so had provided nothing greater to occupy her mind than such inane debates and conversation with rodents.

For all his fervent questioning, clearly his cousin's fate placed a far second in importance behind his father. It made sense. Most people cared for their sires, though in her experience, she'd found little to appreciate about fathers. Or stepfathers for that matter.

Whatever the reason, he'd left her down in that dank, dark dungeon without much of a word about her to anyone. She might've become a veritable afterthought all around were it not for the ragged boy who showed up twice a day with a small plate of food but offered little in the way of conversation or information. He didn't even seem to speak English, which Al found odd. Even though their accents were thick and often nearly unintelligible, her jailor had spoken English and Oran as well.

"Argh!" Al bit her lip, swallowing the scream of frustration at her tedious thoughts. Banging her head against the hard wood would be no more constructive this time than it had the last. She was just so freakin' bored.

The only things she'd had on her person when she'd fallen into the portal were her phone, her lab coat, her Mark-Davis I.D. and a keycard to the inner lab. She diminished her phone battery straight away flipping sadly through pictures of Mr. Darcy, reading the rest of a novel on her ebook app, and using her flashlight app to light her cell between the burning out of one candle and the arrival of another.

Her I.D. and keycard had provided no entertainment whatsoever. Her lab coat. Well, it had been torn into pieces and sacrificed for a worthy cause.

How could he have left her to this?

Another squeak in the darkness and Al drew her knees even more tightly to her chest. God, she hated rodents of any sort. Now, more than ever.

A key turned with a heavy grind in the door and Al sat up, ready for her breakfast. Or would it be dinner? She'd forgo both for five seconds of conversation. Which was almost laughable, she'd rarely sought out company voluntarily in her life.

To her surprise it was a woman of perhaps forty or so, dressed in a simple brown dress with a long tartan draped around her shoulders. Unlike the dark blues and forest greens of her jailer's kilt, hers was brightly colored with lively greens, reds and yellows. Her rich brown hair was pulled straight back from her forehead, laced with a few strands of silver that glittered in the candlelight.

As she came closer, Al could see the familiar blue she'd seen repetitively echoed in her eyes.

Damn, she was one of them.

Did that make her, too, one of the enemy?

The woman looked her up and down, taking in Al's unwashed body and scraggly hair with what seemed like a gleam of pleasure lighting her eyes. One of Al's verminous roommates skittered along the edge of her long skirts and though she squealed and leapt back, she seemed even more pleased. Her eyes glowed with inner glee as she met Al's gaze.

"*Compordach, tá muid?*"

Al didn't understand the language she spoke, but sarcasm was universal. The facetious drawl and malicious glee glowing in her eyes told her the woman was delighted by what she saw. Why? The eyes marked her as a close relative. Was she a sister? A cousin as happy as Al's captor to see her suffer?

Producing a key, she unlocked the wrist shackles Al still wore around her wrists and turned back toward the door, motioning for Al to follow. "*Tar liom.*"

Wary of both the woman and what might await her beyond those doors, Al stayed put on the bench.

The woman paused at the door and gestured imperiously once more for Al to follow.

"*Tar.*"

Al held firm. As much as she wanted out of her prison, going anywhere with this woman seemed far more dangerous.

"Do ye nae speak Gaelic?" the woman asked with a frown. "I said come wi' me. I am tae take ye tae see Keir."

There is was again, though this time she could make out the burr of the vowels more clearly.

Keir.

Too quixotic a name for such a fierce man.

But it called her involuntarily to her feet, eager to confront him after days alone. She followed the woman down a long corridor punctuated with cell doors, guided only by the candle held aloft by the raggedy boy who led the way. Up they went, the worn stone of the winding stairs cool and smooth beneath her bare feet.

Damn, she forgotten her shoes. There was no chance to retrieve them. A door opened at the top, letting in a blast of heat to warm her as well as a burst of sunlight to blind. Al squinted and glanced around, though it all appeared at first to look like nothing more than an overexposed photograph.

The light dimmed once more as they moved through another door, and leaving the young boy behind, the woman sailed regally through another stone passage. It was cooler again but not as cold as her dungeon. Her eyesight returning to normal, Al could see the improvement in these walls as compared to the ones she'd been staring at. The stonework was tighter. Neater.

Through a kitchen. Another wave of heat. Everyone stopped to stare at her and she returned the favor. It was like stepping into a living museum, reminding her of a trip she'd taken with her parents to Colonial Williamsburg when she was little. The huge fireplace with spits of meat and iron pots hanging over it. Wooden tables and women in caps and long aprons.

Her guide kept moving and Al followed, absorbing the change from rustic to tidy to elegant as they moved from room to room. Frowning, she scanned the space, trying in vain to absorb her surroundings. Grand halls, velvet drapery. Gilded art works?

It was cool, quiet, and calm. Rather like a museum.

The woman stopped in front of a set of doors and an ancient old man dressed splendidly in a neat kilt and blue coat bowed before opening them.

Stepping aside with a smirk, her guide gestured toward the door. "After ye."

Chapter 7

Scratching bewilderedly at her matted hair, Al stepped through the doors and stared up in awe at the room within. It was a glorious library at least thirty feet long with towering bookshelves on both sides. Shelves filled from floor to ceiling with leather-bound books of varying thickness. Dazed, she walked slowly into the room, aware of the thick carpets beneath her bare feet and of the frescoed ceiling high above resplendent with cherubs.

Surely it wasn't *his*. All those books, the elegance, just didn't jive with what she'd seen of her captor. She wasn't even confident he knew how to read.

It must've come with the house.

The candles in the wall sconces and chandelier above were all unlit but sunlight filled the room from the bank of floor to ceiling windows dominating the far wall. Drawn by the light and sun she'd been missing for so long, Al wandered that way. Finding a door in the glass, she passed through it only to have her breath taken away.

Beyond the elegant terrace was the most magnificent garden. Not a garden in the manner she'd ever seen. No veggies for sure and in truth, not an overabundance of flowers either. It was a classical English garden with pathways cut across from all sides and corners of the huge walled-in area. They crossed here and there to create the impression of starbursts and pinwheels. All of it converged in the center where a marvelous fountain spouted merrily.

As if that were not splendid enough, the triangles formed by the pathways and the pristine hedgerows lining each side were filled with more hedges cut into elegant twists and twirls that boggled Al's mind. Sculpted trees rose here and there like classical statuary. And beyond it all, as far as she could see, a wide swatch of trimmed lawn stretched into the distance, separating the woodlands on either side. A body of water filled the picture to the horizon.

She turned back toward the door, her eye drawn up, and then farther upward until she staggered back against the balustrade. Speechless.

It was a castle!

Her dark, dank dungeon had its very own castle. That would mean… No. It wasn't possible. She returned to the library shaking her head. No, there was no chance her abductor and jailer belonged to a place so elegant and refined.

He was a brute. A bully. A sava—

Al stumbled to a halt as she spotted the man leaning on a desk on the far side of the room near the door. She recognized the massive form but could not reconcile what she saw now with what she knew to be true. He was clean-shaven, every plane of his gorgeous face bared to an even more stunning effect. Gone was the filthy shirt. The ragged and bloodied kilt. In its place was an elegant, thigh-length jacket of gray that hugged his broad shoulders, with dozens of silver buttons lining the front edges. Beneath it, he wore a long vest of silvery gray that appeared to be silk and a knotted linen neckcloth. Matching knee breeches, white stockings that hugged his calves, and shoes with silver buckles. He should have looked ridiculous, but he did not.

But for his wild mop of wavy black hair, he looked almost like a gentleman... and a rather dashing one at that.

An involuntary sigh of pure appreciation escaped her.

He seemed as surprised by her appearance as she was by his, which made no sense. She looked exactly as she had when he'd abandoned her to the dungeons, minus her lab coat. But she was suddenly very aware of her dirty silk blouse hanging untucked over her black skirt. Her bare legs and feet tingled under his raking glance and she couldn't help fidgeting, shifting to one foot, chafing one calf with the arch of her other.

His surprise fell away into an expression of shock and disgust. She couldn't blame him there. She was a bit more crusty and far more noxiously fragrant than she'd been before. Then anger descended over his handsome face. It was familiar enough. She'd been privy to that expression before. His eyes narrowed and Al shivered in dread for what was to come next. More chains? Knives? Something worse? Why bring her up here at all and risk ruining the lovely rug on the floor if he could have tortured her with what was available in her cell?

Perhaps he didn't like the stink down there any more than she did.

Abruptly, he turned on his heel and strode to the door, anger evident in his every step. Throwing it open, he bellowed at the top of his lungs, "Maeve! Tae me now!"

The woman who had escorted her through the castle appeared in haste. So quickly, Al thought she might have anticipated being recalled to the room. A tiny smile lifted the corner of her mouth. She seemed as pleased by his reaction as she'd been upon finding Al in the dungeon, not even flinching when Keir laid into her with a rough stream of what Al could only assume was Gaelic, since the woman had questioned her in it before.

Maeve stood her ground against the verbal onslaught, not at all cowed by the harsh words. But, she shifted uneasily as he carried on.

For all he was obviously berating the woman pretty harshly, the guttural turns and burrs of the foreign language had a beauty to it that Al found mesmerizing. Punctuated with a slash of a hand or a roll of his shoulders, she admired the graceful movements though she had to wonder what he was saying.

Then he stopped and turned to Al, holding her gaze until she first squirmed then caved to scratching at the filth that tormented her flesh.

"I owe ye an apology."

Itches forgotten, Al stared at him incredulously. After the tirade he'd heaped upon the woman, the kind tone was the last thing she'd expected. An apology?

"What?"

"'Tis nae excuse, I was exhausted by battle and grief for my cousin when ye... er, when we met so abruptly." He pushed away from the desk and bowed. *Bowed.* "My terrible shock prompted unconscionable rudeness."

"Rudeness?" Al parroted, unable to come to grips with the pure courtesy spewing from a mouth that before had only been prone to incivility. Who was this guy?

"Let's call it barbarity, shall we?" He winked playfully but Al wasn't about to let a bit a charm wash away days worth of misery.

"You *left* me in a *dungeon*."

"'Twisnae my intention to leave ye there." He gestured to the woman, but Al shook her head. Her irritation and voice building in force.

"Don't blame her, you're the one who put me down there to begin with."

"Aye." He nodded, looking a bit taken aback by her heated outburst. "Oot of anger. Mayhap tae frighten ye a wee bit. But I'm nae monster, lass. I meant tae free ye from those bonds straight away but for a miscommunication in my absence. Please accept my apologies and allow us tae begin again."

"Begin again? I had a bucket!"

"Ye've found yer tongue most handily, I see. Much tae my disadvantage now." Though he gave her but a nod, she could have sworn he seemed... *pleased* by her reprimand. "However, I'd like ye tae ken, 'twisnae my intention a'tall. Please allow me to extend the hospitality I had originally intended."

His gaze slid to the woman and Al's followed. Gone was the malicious pleasure that had washed her expression before. She was so taut with anger now, she practically vibrated with it.

"Hospitality?" she spat... actually spat on the thick carpeting, the ugly gesture a contradiction to her regal façade. "Lecture me all ye like, Keir MacCoinnich, but she be getting what she deserves and there'll be more of it if I hae my way."

"Maeve..."

"Nay!" Maeve shouted furiously, spittle flying from her lips. "She killed my brother! She deserves more than a slap on the wrist for it. Mayhap I cannae do it myself, but when Robert returns—"

"Yer husband willnae lay a hand on her." Keir's voice was deadly calm but Al was rattled by the woman's threats.

"Please, I didn't kill your bro—"

The woman pinned her with a look of such venom that Al wondered how such hatred had been contained before.

"Lying witch! All the men are passing stories of Hugh's disappearance. Ye were the only one there. Tell me that isnae the truth of it."

Since it was, technically, Al couldn't exactly argue the point but before she could offer a defense or even the truth of it all, Maeve rained downed a long string of Gaelic on her before she spun away. She ran from the room, slamming the door behind her with a bang.

Silence echoed through the library as both Al and Keir stared at the door before turning to look at each other.

"Did she just *curse* me?" she asked, finding her voice at last.

Keir shrugged. "Dinnae take it personally. Such things rarely come tae fruition."

A squeak of disbelief climbed up her throat and the tiniest smile lit Keir's eyes. "Come, allow me tae right my wrongs and allow ye a chance to change oot of that curious yet distasteful garb."

"A bath?" she straightened with pleasure at the thought.

"Aye, a bath, but then…," the condition rang ominously before he continued, "I'll be expecting ye tae right yer wrongs as well."

He didn't have to explain himself. He'd be wanting an explanation of where his cousin had gone and how he'd gotten there.

Al only hoped the bath might last forever.

Chapter 8

Keir rotated his glass faster, watching the amber liquid climb the sides of the tumbler before he slowed the action and the swirling Scotch settled back into the bottom. Lifting it to his lips, he took a long sip, eyeing the mantel clock over the rim.

Where was she? Surely a bath couldn't last so long. Her water had to have run to cold by now. She had been rather grotesquely grimy though. He shrugged, silently agreeing with that inward assessment. Her blonde hair—at least he recalled it as blonde from their initial meeting—dingy and half-fallen from its trappings, had been matted and tangled when she'd walked past him into the library earlier. The sight of such a mangled mess had stayed his tongue until she wandered far beyond, absorbing the splendor of the room with open awe.

Obviously she wasn't accustomed to the sort of opulence his French grandmother had favored when overseeing the redecoration of Dingwall Castle upon her marriage to the old Earl of Cairn. He might not favor it himself, but Keir was more than familiar with such settings. It made him wonder from whence his prisoner came that she would look upon it all with such wonder. She denied being English but she was no Scot with that accent and dress. No woman of his acquaintance, even in the more risqué courts of Europe, wore skirts above her knees.

She was as much a peculiarity to his eyes as his home was to hers. Staring at her would not provide an answer to his questions.

He needed answers. After a long, tiring journey where none had been found, for his own sanity, he needed some from her.

Or would the answers she'd provide only cause him to sink into madness? He could still hardly account for what he'd seen out there on the moors. These past days, he'd begun to wonder if it had all been a hallucination of sorts. A bit of madness springing from the grief of watching his beloved cousin perish.

That might explain it all.

Though it couldn't explain her.

An odd wee lass with fetching gray eyes and an air of mystery about her. The stuttering miss from his dungeons taken over by a veritable termagant vocal in her opinions. Surely she would find the words now to put him out of his misery.

Her.

Ha, he didn't even know her name.

✗O✗O✗O✗

Her trip through time had become even more surreal since she'd stepped into the library earlier and had her entire perception of this place and her captor turned inside out.

Trying to mesh this new reality with the old had thrown her for a loop. That imbalance had followed her through being scrubbed, dried, and dressed in multiples layers of ivory and blue linen with varying degrees of discomfort... both on a personal and physical level.

Now, Al followed the pointed fingers of the occasional servants she came across as they directed her wordlessly through the castle, still trying to reconcile those two divergent realities. Which of them was real?

The nightmare?

The fairytale?

The savage?

The gentleman?

It was all incredibly bizarre. She was trying to make herself understood to the people in this castle. Some of them, it seemed, spoke no English. According to the young woman who had persistently attended to her while she was bathing despite Al's repeated assurance that she could do it herself, many of the Highlanders spoke nothing but Gaelic.

Others might have been simply refusing to speak with her. The foreigner. The interloper. The killer.

As outlandish to them as all of this was to her.

Rumors must have circulated through the castle over the four days of her incarceration, though, given the dark looks she received. She'd been astounded when she'd heard the time frame. Four. Not ten, not twelve. Just four.

A lifetime. But not.

It made her want to hate the man responsible but after such an eloquent apology in that soft, purring brogue, she'd had a hard time holding on to her resentment.

She'd reserve that for Maeve now. From a distance. Instinct told her to steer clear of the irate woman.

Keir seemed to have relinquished some of his anger toward her as well, though his frustration was still evident. He would want answers now. She only hoped she was brave enough to give him the truth, damn the consequences.

Clearly he loved his cousin. He deserved to know.

Hopefully when he was done with his interrogation she'd be able to deliver one of her own. The wheres and whens of her accidental passage through time were a mystery she'd like solved.

Scientist problems. Al repressed a giggle at the thought. How often had anyone ever been faced with such a setback?

She was still smiling when another servant, a rickety old man in a faded kilt and brilliant blue jacket, pointed expressionlessly at a pair of double doors. She entered to find Keir rising from a chair set at the head of a ridiculously long table.

He was dressed even more flamboyantly than before. This time in a green silk jacket with golden frogging along the edges and wide, turned-up cuffs with lace spilling out over his darkly tanned hands. His mop of black hair was tamed into a ponytail at his nape, sending the sculpted perfection of his facial features into sharp relief.

He should have struck her as preposterously effeminate with all the braid and dripping lace, but again, he did not.

The magnificence of his person sent her heartbeat racing. Any lingering anger she'd been nursing fell victim to a sudden rush of shyness.

"What do ye find so amusing?" he asked, tugging at his cuffs and fluffing the lace of his jabot... playfully? He was becoming more human and less monster by the second. "The barbarian is gone, I assure ye. Tonight we shall dine... and converse like two civilized people. I hae dressed for my part. I see that ye were well garbed fer yers."

Al brushed shaky hands down the fabric reining in her midsection and refrained from indulging in the deep inhale she longed for to calm her nerves. An attempt to do so when she'd first seen herself in a mirror had nearly rocketed her breasts right out of the too-tight bodice. She'd didn't want that to happen again.

Still with his eyes wandering downward as they had days ago, alight with appreciation, the inhale was involuntary. His eyes widened… and warmed. A little tingle ran down her spine that was as inappropriate now as it had been four days ago.

Keir cleared his throat and bowed, much as he had earlier in the library. This time he held out his hand expectantly, and having no other option beyond awkwardly retreating, Al placed her hand hesitantly in his.

He kissed it. Actually kissed it. And Al nearly fainted as his lips brushed over her knuckles. Her knees trembling when he raised his eyes and winked at her.

"My compliments, lass. I'm fairly speechless in awe at the bonny picture ye present."

Damn, he was good. So far he was beating a lifetime of detailed fantasies, hands down.

"Tell me, does such an angelic vision hae a name?"

A name? Oh.

"Al," she stuttered out.

"Al?" he repeated using her same, flat American accent on the short word. He straightened, his brow furrowing as if the name were completely nonsensical. Or repugnant. "*Al?*"

With a grimace, Al tugged her hand away and entwined her fingers self-consciously at her waist. She nodded jerkily. "Yeah. Or a lot of my friends call me Big Al." His brows shot upward and she rushed to explain. "It's ironic, you see? Since I'm so not… in size… but…"

"Al." He repeated her name, testing it on his tongue with far more flavor than the diminutive deserved. It sounded better with a thick Scottish brogue to bring it to life. He must have agreed because after a brief pause, he nodded, looking her up and down. "It suits ye, I suppose, for all it is a masculine moniker. Concise and forthright as ye appeared in yer other garb."

The scrutiny in his eyes changed, becoming more speculative, and Al knew he was going to be changing the subject with that segue.

"It's short for Allorah," she rushed to extend her reprieve. "That's my name. Allorah Danaan Maines. It's ridiculously whimsical, I know. My mom was like that."

"Nae a'tall like ye, I gather?" he said. "Are ye nae given tae whimsy, Allorah? Ne'er?"

Al couldn't help but warm under the knowingness in his eyes. As if he knew every stray thought running through her fanciful mind. If he only knew how prone to fancy she really was, he might be the one blushing.

She'd had a long four days in that cell with not much else to occupy her.

Still, she couldn't have him thinking he was all that. In her admittedly limited experience, men, no matter where or when, couldn't be allowed that much of an upper hand.

"And your name? Keir MacCoinnich, if I heard right."

He frowned at her standoffish tone and stepped away, politely holding a chair out for her near his at the end of the table. "Aye, ye heard it right."

"And just who are you, Keir MacCoinnich?" she asked, taking the glass of wine one of the servants put before her and sipping deeply. For strength of nerve.

Her bold inquiry must have struck one of his nerves because his brows snapped together as he resumed his seat. Tenting his fingers, he leaned forward and spoke. The low timber of his voice holding a note of that old menace she remembered so well from the dungeon.

"Enough. Questions ye may hae but I'll be getting the answers tae mine long before ye'll be getting yers. Or shall we put aside this fine civility and return tae the dungeon?"

Fear renewed, her hand shook as she set her wine glass down on the table.

Chapter 9

Irritation pummeled Keir. He snatched up his own glass, swallowing his Scotch in a single gulp before thrusting it toward his waiting footman for a refill.

Irritation at her... Al, but mostly at himself for being diverted by her.

And for putting forth the effort to show her just how un-barbaric he actually was.

Or at least, could be.

Wearing clothes he'd never touched beyond court, dining in this little used state room. All to impress the lass.

But he was the one impressed. She'd managed to take his breath away the instant she'd walked through the door. Her bonny face clean and warmed with a pink blush. Blonde hair, shiny clean, upswept into a loose knot with a long spiraling curl bouncing seductively on the rise of her bountiful bosoms with each step she took. The low square neckline exposed half of her creamy mounds to his suddenly ravenous eyes. He could hardly stop ogling long enough to appear the gentleman.

He could as yet hardly say what the color of her gown was for all the other distraction she provided.

Distraction from everything but the pleasure of looking at her. Just as he'd allowed himself to be sidetracked by her bedraggled appearance earlier, though his anger over her mistreatment had been real enough. She was too tiny, too delicate to suffer so many days in a dungeon that hadn't been used for that purpose in nearly two centuries.

She was a constant distraction from his purpose.

Anger with her and with himself bubbled to the surface.

"Enough of this toying wi' me, lass." The words emerged coarsely, showing his annoyance with no attempt for courtly manners. "I've played the gentleman for ye. A kind host. But if ye dinnae want tae find yerself returned to the cell below, ye'd best be telling me what I want tae ken."

She gasped at his threat, her fingers rising to the fluttering evidence of her racing heart at the base of her throat. "Well, I... You didn't... Geez, you didn't need to get all..."

Geez?

"I was going... I was planning on... Before you..." Al broke off her flabbergasted sputtering to pin him with an affronted glare quite unlike anything he'd yet seen from her. "I guess you really can't hide a brute in gentleman's clothing, can you?"

Abashed, Keir looked away. Toying with his tumbler, he lifted it to his lips. The liquor mended his fraying mood. "I've a temper, lass. I always hae. Ye've been naught but a spur in my side for days. Ye ken what I need tae ken. It's wi'in ye even if ye want tae speak of it nary a wee bit more than I want tae be hearing it, in truth."

"And I'm building up the nerve to talk about it," she shot back. "You didn't have to be so mean."

She thought *that* was mean? Ha, he could show her a

thing or two. "I've ne'er been the charmer in this clan. I left that for Hugh."

As his cousin's name sprang from his lips, Keir felt a pang of sorrow score his heart. A part of him didn't even want the confirmation that Hugh was gone. Perhaps that was why he'd allowed himself to be so easily distracted. Distracted by his father's fate. By grief for his brother.

By this lass's charms and unexpectedly vibrant character. Along with her other attributes.

He'd let it go, for now. He could wait a minute longer if only to pay brief homage to his cousin. He lifted his glass once more, speaking more to himself than to Al. "Hugh could charm a turtle out of its shell… and more than one lass out of her virtue, if truth be told." He chuckled and caught his companion's involuntary wisp of a smile before it was gone. "We went on our Grand Tour together. We traveled Europe," he clarified, when a crease marred Al's smooth brow.

"I know what it is. I just never heard… Never mind. Go on."

"As I was saying, we traveled the Continent together. He was a true romantic, ye ken? A lover of music, poetry, and philosophy. He studied and studied, thinking all the while that I did nothing but pursue the lasses."

Her lips parted at that but she held her tongue, so Keir continued, "I'm nae like him in many ways but in others we we're fair identical. A love of learning. To him 'twas all that philosophical rubbish, but tae me it 'twas the more practical studies that drew me. Areas where fact and truth told sway. I'll be the first tae admit it. There's naught one thing evident aboot ye that provides me any answers. At least nae logical ones."

Tipping his glass, he drank to Hugh. She lifted her glass and swallowed deeply but he doubted it was in tribute. False courage, more the like.

"How did ye come tae be upon that field, lass?"

She drew in a deep breath. This time he managed to keep his eyes from the distractions trembling below. "I don't suppose I can just say I was in the wrong place at the wrong time?"

"Nay. 'Twould nae do."

"No, I suppose not. But I still feel as though there's no way you'll be able to understand this. Even seeing all this." She glanced around the room. "Though it does give me more hope that you're not going to..."

"What?"

҉҉҉҉҉

Kill me when I tell you.

Al didn't say it out loud. Hopefully there was something truly civilized within him. Because the truth was coming out.

"That wasn't a normal hole your cousin fell into. Or that I came out of."

His brows lifted. "I gathered that much on my own."

Al shook her head, gnawing her lip nervously. "It was a wormhole." He stared at her blankly and she rushed on. "It's a portal across space able to transport something instantaneously from one spot to another. I helped create it along with a group of other scientists."

Keir watched her solemnly, his vivid eyes seeming to pierce the veil of her person and delve into her mind. She was struck anew by the notion that he could read her thoughts. Stupid. If he'd been able to do that, none of this would be necessary. "Well?" she prompted when he remained silent.

"Ye expect me tae believe that a wee lass like yerself is a

scientist?"

Al blinked. "That's it? That's all you've got? No accusations? No fingers pointing to call me a liar?"

"There's much I want tae say, but let's begin wi' that." His voice was calm but the hand lifting his glass once more to his lips was taut, trembling just a bit. In rage?

"Begin with what? Which part?"

"Scientist?"

The nerves that had held her in their clutches since she'd walked into the room fell away. Hadn't she heard that a million times before? From her mother. From her stepfather.

"What? A little thing like me can't be a scientist? I was this close," she jabbed her hand out with her thumb and forefinger just an inch apart to measure the distance, "to finishing my doctorate before all this happened. And my entire academic career has been filled to the brim with men like you thinking I don't belong there."

He slouched in his chair, brows high. Probably as shocked as she was by her rant. Al couldn't say what had gotten into her. She'd spent most of her life shrinking from conflict of any sort but had already berated him more than once.

In the silence that followed, a pair of footmen brought plates of food and set them down before them. She thanked them quietly but didn't touch hers. Despite days of having nothing more than bread and some sort of bland porridge to eat, the thought of swallowing the more exotic fare knotted her stomach. Keir seemed similarly disinclined to partake.

"I'm sorry." Her apology was soft, filled with shame for harping at him so. "I'm not normally so combative. This whole thing has really brought out my... color."

"Is that what that was?" There was a hint of humor in

the words. His surprise faded and a slight smile graced his handsome face, softening him. Making him more human than the more fictional persona he had so far presented. "I ken why some might call ye this 'Big Al' from time tae time. Ye're e'er so wee in stature but ye make up for it in enormous character."

It sounded like a compliment but since she wasn't certain, she merely nodded and studiously straightened the numerous utensils arranged around the gilded plate on the table before her. The salmon on her plate did smell appealing, if she were able to salvage it from the pool of heavy sauce it was swimming in. If she could stomach it at all.

"I do hae many other questions aboot what ye said. Too many mayhap, but the most important... The one I've been most hesitant tae ask..."

Caution was evident in his broken words. Al glanced up. "Yes?"

"Ye sprang forth from this wormy hole hale and hearty. It gives me a measure of hope..." Keir sighed heavily, pressing the heels of his hands hard against his temples.

If she hadn't felt a rush of heartrending sympathy for him, she might have been entertained by his distinct break between the words *wormy* and *hole*.

"Obviously it isnae deadly in its own right..."

Another blast of compassion washed away the amusement. "You want to know if your cousin is still alive?"

"Aye."

Al nodded and saw the gleam of moisture shine in his eyes before he looked away. A stream of Gaelic was whispered under his breath. A prayer of thanks perhaps? Her heart ached for him. Gone forever was the savage she had taken him for. Here was a man capable of genuine caring and feeling.

"Did ye see him?"

"Yes, briefly before I fell into the portal."

He nodded, obviously hesitant to know more. "Will he be able to return to us? Or is the distance too great?"

It was very great.

"No, Keir. I'm sorry."

A moment of silence passed while he digested that.

"And ye?"

"No." Making the admission aloud was like putting the final nail in her coffin. "I wasn't lying before when I said I knew I couldn't go back. I can't. While in many ways our experiment was a success, we weren't able to predict exactly where the wormholes led. Nor could we replicate a destination. The whole project was useless without being able to do that."

Another brief silence. This time she assumed he was trying to make some sense of what she'd said.

"So ye're stuck here?"

"Yes."

"And Hugh is forever trapped there?"

Al winced for him. "Yes."

"Where is that?"

"Halfway around the world, I'm afraid."

Give or take nearly three hundred years.

He grimaced, his grief diminished by her assurances of his cousin's survival but not gone. "Will he be treated as poorly there as ye've been treated here?"

Ouch, that one was going to hurt. For a second, Al considered lying to him. She could tell him that his cousin would be well taken care of. Given the opportunity to live a life of freedom. It would probably be better for Keir's peace of mind that she give him that comfort. But...

"He won't be hurt, but I'm sorry to say he will be imprisoned there in the lab where I worked. He's evidence of our project's failure, you see? Dr. Fielding, one of the scientists I work with, will hide any proof that he can't accomplish what he was paid to do."

His eyes widened perceptively. "Hugh wisnae the first tae wander into yer worm's hole." It wasn't a question.

Al fiddled with her silverware some more, then pushed her plate away. Reaching for her wine, she gulped it down. In for a penny, in for a pound. He hadn't called for a stake to be raised for her burning in the village square yet. Odds looked good that he probably wouldn't. There was no point withholding anything from him now.

"No. There've been a variety of animals, big and small, to wander into it. Dr. Fielding started collecting them in small cages at first. It seemed harmless at the time. Keeping them, I mean. They were just animals. The growing number of cages prompted him to build a room of cages. It was a regular zoo. Then, one day, a man came through. This was our first real clue just how far off target we were. I mean, a Native American... Anyway, our zoo became a prison. Dr. Fielding saw no problem locking a human being up with the animals. As if he were one of them. It was the worst sort of human rights violation."

"*Human* rights?"

"It just means the rights every human is entitled to have on this planet," she explained. "Freedom. Liberty. Dr. Fielding called me a bleeding heart for caring about them but I couldn't stand it."

"Why did ye work wi' him then?"

Al shrugged. "Jobs like that didn't just come along every

day. It was an excellent opportunity. But it hurt to see what he did to that first man and when your cousin and that other soldier came through, I knew he wouldn't hesitate to treat them any differently. He saw them all the same. Animals. Savages."

"Just as ye saw me."

"No, I didn't assume you were a savage. You just acted like one."

Her pert rebuttal brought a slight smile to his lips. But then it was gone with a heavy sigh. "Every word ye speak rouses a hundred more questions tae my mind. Native American? Zoo? This job ye were paid tae do? Yet all of it fades in significance when compared tae what I saw. I ken I saw it, but yet I disbelieve my own eyes. I hardly ken where to begin tae find answers."

"Well, then maybe you could answer a couple for me while you're figuring it out." Keir lifted a brow and nodded, gesturing with a curl of his fingers for her to proceed. It was her chance but Al found herself almost as tentative as he'd been before to hear the answers. "Where am I?"

If possible, that brow rose even more. That hadn't been at all what he'd been expecting. "This is Castle Dingwall, laying at the western end of the Cromarty Firth. Ye may hae seen the water from the terrace."

Al nodded. "So Scotland then?"

"Aye, Scotland."

Nodding again, she chewed her lower lip. "Okay, then second question."

"Aye?"

"*When* am I?"

Chapter 10

When am I.

In three simple words, the lass explained everything Keir had found curious about her. It clarified so much. The perfect answer, but one he instinctually rejected. He was not a religious man, nor a superstitious one. He prided himself on being open-minded to a fault.

Still, he inwardly rebelled against the idea, even reining in the compulsion to cross himself. Witchcraft, sorcery. The work of the devil. If he'd been any other man, he'd accuse her of them all.

Her hesitance in speaking of his cousin's fate made all too much sense now. Most anyone else would have condemned her without asking for further explanation. Keir looked to the footmen not far away, but far enough to have missed Al's softly spoken words.

This time.

"Leave us," he commanded firmly, flicking his wrist at the pair. "I will ring for ye if we need anything else."

"But the second course...," one started to protest before he withered under Keir's sharp glare and disappeared through the door with the other on his heels.

When.

Keir shook his head hard as if the motion could knock the notion right out of his head. It was ridiculous, insane really.

When.

Strumming his fingers one after another on the table, he struggled against the reflexive denial.

Thump, thump, thump, thump.

Logic wouldn't work either. The very idea defied the natural order. There was no worm large enough to create such a cavity.

Thump, thump, thump, thump.

Even if there had been, it wouldn't explain the swirling blackness he'd seen. It wasn't a natural phenomenon.

Thump, thump, thump, thump.

Though his hand... and Hugh's person had disappeared when entering the void, there was not even a hint of science existing that said one might find the means to move through time.

Thump, thump, thump, thump.

Yet.

Flattening his hand on the table, he spread his fingers wide. Staring at them for a long while. He turned back to Al, aware that she had been watching him tensely the entire time. "I beg ye, for yer own sake, dinnae repeat that tae anyone else. There are some nae as accepting of such things."

His captive turned a bit green and swallowed hard. "They still burn witches in this... time?" The last came out in a choked whisper that restored Keir's sense of humor. Such a preposterous question, yet in that instant he became a true believer.

"Nay, nae for some time, but there are some who might

be inclined to reinstitute the practice in the face of such a provocative question."

Her eyes widened marginally, and feeling the atypical urge to provide comfort, he reached out and curled his fingers around hers. They were as cold as ice, such a contradiction to her fiery outbursts, and it occurred to him that she might be afraid, nay, terrified of her circumstances. Respect washed over him. To be alone in a strange place—and time, it seemed—with such composure took a level of courage he hadn't yet considered.

Did they prepare for such things in the future? For the future it had to be for all he inclined to deny it.

Would Hugh be confronting his situation as well as she?

"'Tis the year of our Lord seven hundred and forty-six," he told her at last. "April the twenty-first."

She nodded again. He could almost see the wheels turning in her mind. Wondered what she was thinking, but overcoming the first tier of his own disbelief, another question occurred to him.

"Might I ask from whence ye came and tae where my cousin has gone?"

"He's in the year 2013," she told him. "February seventeenth was the day he got there."

So far? The time seemed almost immeasurable. Nearly three hundred years? The innate urge to reject her claim infused him once more. It was almost harder to shake it off this time but he did.

"You're taking this all very well. I'm surprised."

No more than he. But naught else could explain what he'd seen with his own eyes. Keir was astonished by the calm acceptance he felt wash through him. Even for the fate of his cousin, though it was hard to imagine Hugh in a world surrounded by women like Allorah Maines. How would he fare against them?

"I'm sorry about your cousin," she said as if she wandered the branching pathways of his thoughts with him. "I wish I could offer some hope that he'll be all right."

"Och, he'll be fine," he said with sudden certainty. "If I ken my cousin well enough—and I do—he'll find a way to escape his circumstances and live a fine life. My hope is that ye'll be able tae do the same."

"I'm sure I'll figure something out."

Och, she was a courageous lass. Brave and strong. Educated, if he understood her references correctly. Beautiful. Alluring.

Desirable.

He withdrew his hand, clearing his throat at the thought. He bedded many a lass in his life without hardly having her name, but it seemed wrong to want this one so badly knowing there was a thousand things yet to be learned of her. But where to begin?

"How?" He choked the word out and cleared his throat again. "How did ye do it?"

"Now?" she asked, with a wisp of a smile that lit her misty gray eyes and exposed even, white teeth. "Now you ask? I would have thought that would be your first question. Or that you'd demand some sort of proof."

"I saw the proof for myself, though I dinnae ken what it was at the time. I saw two men disappear before my verra eyes. Saw ye appear. A lesser man might hae killed ye on the spot believing ye the devil."

"You did call me a witch," she reminded him.

"Aye," he admitted, meeting her steady gaze, seeing the amusement there. How could she manage it in such a situation? How was she not losing her mind to fear and panic? She might be a bonny thing, indeed, but in all his days he'd never encountered anyone so courageous. Never so instantly admired another more. "Ye astonish me, lass."

><<><><

Al froze when Keir leaned toward her and lifted his hand to cup her cheek. His roughened fingertips traced a path along her cheekbone. The pad of his thumb grazed her lower lip, leaving a peculiar tingle behind.

His eyes followed and settled there. Overcome by the urge, Al ran her tongue over her lip, following his path.

He exhaled slowly. Were his fingers trembling?

Or was that just her?

"How extraordinary ye are, lass."

Look who was talking. She'd never experienced anyone like him outside the realm of fiction. Untamed and yes, a little barbaric on the one hand. Gentlemanly and seemingly cultured on the other. An enigma. A mystery she would desperately love to unwrap, beginning with that ruffled cravat.

She'd always had an overabundance of imagination. Yet the most spectacular experience of her life, real or imagined, might be finding a man like this.

He didn't look at her and see the mousy nerd, lost in books and studying. Hiding out from a world that scared her. By his own words, he saw character. Bravery. Beauty.

She couldn't remember the last time a guy had looked at her and seen any of those things. Perhaps none ever had. Certainly none of them had ever gazed at her with the blatant desire simmering in his eyes.

It tempted her beyond reason.

But for one lukewarm experience in college, she'd never

been tempted to jump into bed with anyone, preferring the passion found between pages to that she'd found between sheets.

A man like Keir, a man far more magnificent than she'd ever let even her imagination dream, might be able to rewrite the entire book of her experience.

If she let him.

If she let herself.

So tempting.

The double doors to the dining room opened then with a grainy grind of wood and hinge. Al jerked away from him as the old man who'd been manning the library doors earlier stepped in. Drawing in a deep breath as if he meant to speak, he let it out with a low whistle. His shoulders drooped and he scratched his head.

"Archie?" Keir prompted irritably, withdrawing his hand. "Did ye need something?"

"Aye, sir," the old man said. A dramatic pause followed before Archie wrinkled his nose and frowned. "Nay, sir."

A second later the doors closed again, more gently than they were opened. Al shared look with Keir before breaking down into a light chuckle. He did not appear amused. "Well, that was…"

The doors banged open once more. And again there stood Archie proudly scratching at his behind through his kilt.

"Aye, Archie?"

"Aye, laddie. Lady—"

"Oh, there you are, Keir!"

A plump, but lovely woman in her late thirties sailed through the door around poor Archie, cutting him off. She looked like she'd leapt off the screen of *Vanity Fair*. She was gowned—the only word Al could think of to credit the flamboyance of her dress—in a pink satin dress with a heavily embroidered stomacher that matched the underskirt showing beneath the parted skirt. The edges were trimmed in neat pleats of satin ribbon. An overabundance of lace flowed from the elbow-length bell sleeves, covering her forearms. She was bedecked with several long strings of pearls and wore an ostrich feather poking out of an elaborately upswept hairdo towering above her head. The skirt stood out from her hips, nearly a foot on each side.

1746, Keir had said. It did explain the clothes.

She seemed overdone to Al's eyes but also fit seamlessly in that gilded dining room with its handsome, richly-garbed master sitting at the head of the table.

She felt positively dowdy now in her borrowed plain blue dress when she'd felt ridiculously dressed up before.

He rose to his feet as the woman glided up the length of the long table. "Ceana, when did ye get here?"

"Days ago!" she drawled with a flourish of her hand. "I'd been wondering where you'd gotten to when you didn't join us in the dining room for supper."

Al frowned. Wasn't this the dining room?

Her frown deepened when the woman halted, pinning Al with an odd look as if she'd just noticed her. "Oh, you must be the one Maeve was telling me about. Tell me, did you really kill our brother?"

"Ceana." Keir's tone carried a hint of warning.

"What? I'm only asking because she doesn't look at all strong enough to have overcome him."

"And she dinnae. She had naught tae do wi' his disappearance." He lied wonderfully, Al thought. Cool as a cucumber. "She just…" He shot her an arch look. "She just happened to be in the wrong place at the wrong time."

Ceana didn't appear to be entirely convinced. "Then where is Hugh?"

Nor did she seem overly distressed by her brother's disappearance. His own sister. Keir displayed far more concern.

He only shrugged. "Taken prisoner? Many were, including perhaps my father."

The woman's expression softened and she reached out to lay a hand on his arm. "I'd almost forgotten. Have you had any news?"

"None as yet." The response was clipped, inviting no further comment. "And Braemore?"

She flicked her wrist dismissively. "He's scurried off to his hunting lodge on the Orkney's. No one will ever put in the effort to follow him there. Honestly, he may never return. I may just have to stay awhile."

He grimaced and turned to Al. "Ceana, may I introduce Allorah Maines? Al, this is Lady Ceana Sinclair, Countess of Braemore. Hugh's older sister."

A countess? She was a bit awed by the announcement.

"Oh, not much older," she chided, dropping into the chair across from Al and studying her thoroughly. "Maines? English? No wonder Maeve wants to chew her up."

"Nay," Keir was quick to answer, explaining to Al, "Maeve's only son was killed last year on the advance into Derby."

She stared back blankly. Advance?

"Into England," he added.

"Oh. I'm so sorry." She offered her sympathies to them both. "To answer your question, I'm American."

For that, she received the same blank stares in return. "I come from America. The United States. Across the ocean?" she added helpfully.

"The colonies?" Keir said at last. "Ye're a colonist?"

"Um, I guess you could say that."

"Is that where…?" He broke off, frustrated.

"How did you happen to get all the way over here?" Ceana asked curiously. "Just in time to be in the wrong place at the wrong time?"

Al cast about for an acceptable answer but Keir came to her rescue. "Now, Ceana, allow the lass tae retire tae her rooms. She's already endured a difficult interrogation this night."

Ceana's lips quirked. "Oh, aye, I could see just how terribly you were torturing her before. Very well, I'll let her be for now, but be warned, I'm insatiably curious." Her eyes slipped across the table. "Oh, how lovely! Are you not going to eat such a fine entrée? 'Tis much more appetizing than the partridge that was served up on our table. Do you mind?"

As Ceana shifted over to his chair and took up his knife and fork, Al looked to him for direction.

He merely shrugged. The moment between them, whatever it had been about to become, was gone.

Perhaps for the best. Perhaps not.

"I will return to my room. If you don't mind."

"Nae a'tall—"

But Ceana cut in, glancing up from the salmon. "Nonsense. You should join us in the drawing room, Miss Maines. We'll want to learn all about you. Do you play at all?"

Play what?

"Thank you, but it's been a long day. I think I'll just go to bed, if you don't mind."

"But—"

He lifted a hand, silencing his cousin. "Of course, I'll hae Archie show ye the way."

"Do you think he'll remember better than I?" she asked, gaining a flash of a smile for her jest. "I'll make my own way just fine, I'm sure."

"Verra well."

Keir produced another of those charming bows as Al turned away, but called her name as she reached the door. "We will continue this on the morrow."

She caught her breath at the idea of picking up just where they'd left off but he dashed away the heady thought by adding, "I will be wanting answers. Tae all my questions."

Nodding jerkily, she left the room, hearing Ceana ask sweetly before she was out of earshot, "Really? What kinds of questions, Keir? Her bed or yours?"

Al scrambled away, not waiting to hear his reply.

Chapter 11

The next morning dawned sunny and bright. Drawn to the sun after so many days without it, Al threw on one of the dresses left for her. By trial and error she found her way out to the library terrace and down the stone steps to the garden beyond. In and out of the intricate pathways she weaved, soaking up the sun and absorbing the formal beauty of neat hedgerows. The lushness of the flowers. How the variety of plants had been carefully chosen to work with the layout. The care and upkeep that had to be involved in maintaining it.

Her thoughts followed a similarly complex path. Just as they had all night. The future. The past. Her future in the past. It tied her in knots.

As did thoughts of Keir. His undeniable appeal. The startling attraction she felt for him. In contrast to her initial impression of him, he'd been remarkably sweet and caring last night. His flattery touched her somewhere deep inside.

But the implication of Ceana's taunting question preoccupied her late into the night. The insinuation that he wouldn't hesitate to sleep with her. The assumption that she would consent.

While those thoughts weren't pleasurable, they were

better than dwelling on less pleasant aspects of her situation. If she let her imagination take root, who knew what it might come up with? As she'd told him, she'd work something out. She had to.

In the meantime, she'd rather focus her energies on working *him* out. Ceana's evocative remark combined with Keir's own commentary regarding his frequent relations with women while on his Grand Tour, suggested he'd been—as her books might say—something of a rake in the past.

Perhaps he still was. Having frequent affairs with a variety of women. As much as a part of her liked the idea of joining the ranks of his lovers, another part recoiled from the thought of becoming just another notch on his bedpost.

She liked a tender happily-ever-after and assuming that wasn't going to happen with him—and she was certain it would not—she determined that it might be best to let her fantasies remain just that and let the opportunity pass.

At least that's what her mind decided.

Her body adamantly disagreed.

Not only was he the single bright possibility in this place, he might be her only chance in life at having a man who curled her toes with a single look.

"I've a shiny sterling for the thoughts going through that lovely head of yers."

Al peered up to find Keir striding toward her from across the long lawn beyond the garden. He was wet, perhaps just coming from a swim in the lake in the distance. Gone was the polished gentleman of the previous night, and in his place once more was the masculine Highlander capable of inspiring heart-pounding awe topped with a touch of trepidation.

He was wearing only a low-slung kilt of brown, gray and

black plaid with narrow stripes of red and white, flapping around his muscular thighs with each step, and a pair of leather boots laced tightly up his calves. The sight was enough to make her wonder if all the speculation about what a Scotsman did, and more importantly, *did not* wear under his kilt were true.

But she couldn't give the subject the deliberation it deserved just then. He'd slung his shirt over his shoulder leaving his broad, damp chest distractingly bare. Broad and thick with muscle, sprinkled with just the right amount of dark hair, the sight only reaffirmed the inclination of her desires.

He studied her curiously. Refusing to blush, she gave the most nonchalant shrug she could manage. Hoped he didn't notice her sudden trembling.

"Nothing interesting."

"Nay?"

"No."

He grinned at her flat denial. The flash of his white teeth in contrast to his tanned skin, the deviltry dancing in those gorgeous eyes, sent her heart rate soaring.

He knew his appeal, damn him.

Definitely a rake.

"I was just aboot tae come looking for ye." He put his hands on his hips and tilted his head back as if enjoying the warmth of the sun. He shook his head, his mop of wet hair sending out a spray of water droplets that landed like diamonds on his bronzed shoulders and chest. They glistened in the sunlight.

As if she needed to be dazzled any further.

She swallowed, her mouth dry. "Really? Why?"

He studied her intently. "Tae continue our conversation

from last night, of course."

Which one, she wondered? The flirtatious one or the serious one?

"And tae make sure ye dinnae flee intae the night."

"Of course," she responded tartly. "As if I have so many better places to be."

It was difficult to know where to rest her eyes. Meeting his gaze only aroused and aggravated her as his look was so annoyingly knowing. Scanning the rest of him... well, that was equally arousing and aggravating as well. For all his flattery, he didn't seem nearly as affected by her presence as she was by his. Parts of her body she'd never been fully aware of before were quivering.

"Will you please put your shirt on?"

"Am I making ye uncomfortable?" he asked mischievously. "Does the sight of me offend yer feminine sensibility?"

"Not at all," she responded, and hoping to divert him added, "Where I come from, shirtless men are no big deal. At the beach, both men and women hardly wear anything at all."

"Hardly anything?"

Al gave him a brief description of a string bikini, not that she'd ever dared to have her generous curves confined so tenuously.

Gratifyingly, his eyes warmed and his brogue was husky when he spoke. "I'd like tae see that, lassie. Indeed, I would."

"Well, in about three hundred years, you'll get your chance." The pert comment escaped her lips before Al had a chance to think through the ramifications, but it was too late. That serious expression was back in his eyes.

The moment—again—was gone.

Without another word, he dragged his shirt over his

head. Given only a second to enjoy the ripple of his six-pack abs before they were covered, she drank him in but lifted her eyes back up before his head emerged.

He turned, tilting his bent elbow toward her. It took her a while to grasp he was offering her his arm, but she tucked her hand in as he began a slow stroll back into the garden.

It was the first time she'd had to touch him, she realized. Keir had kissed her hand, touched her hand and cheek... even wrapped his fingers around her neck, but she hadn't actually touched him yet. His arm was solid and warm beneath her fingers. Even through his sleeve, he felt so manly.

Curling her fingers tighter, she wondered if the rest of him would feel just as nice. Ah, the wonderings of the sexually repressed millennial! Al shook away the thoughts of him and focused her attentions elsewhere.

As she'd already given the garden her admiration that morning, the castle ahead was an easy target. The morning sun kissed the exterior, giving it a fairy tale like appeal. "The castle is truly beautiful. Huge, but beautiful."

"Ye think Dingwall is large?" He chuckled. "Ye should see Rosebraugh."

"Rosebraugh?"

"Hugh's estate. 'Tis nae far away. A day's ride. Nae more."

A day's ride was not far? "Is it more elegant than Dingwall or only larger?"

"Och, 'tis like a French chateau, Rosebraugh," he said. "All white stone and turrets. Truly fitting for the dukes of Ross."

Stopping, she looked up at him in surprise. "Dukes? That man was a duke?"

"Aye."

"Holy shit," she mumbled under her breath. She'd met a duke and didn't even know it? For some reason that made her feel even worse for the man's situation.

"Holy *shit?*" he repeated, aghast.

She ignored him even though he gaped down at her. Somewhere deep inside she knew castles and dukes didn't just happen by every day. Despite the old joke about how the sheer number of Barbara Cartwright's dukes alone could populate the whole of England, they were rare and so were castles. Not just anybody owned a castle. Not one like Dingwall. If Keir were related to a duke, a cousin, he must be nobility at least, as well.

"How exactly are you related to him?"

"Cousins. My mother was Hugh's father's sister."

"So, your mother was a duke's daughter. And she married a...?"

"Interested in titles now are we, lass?" he asked, recovering his humor. "My father is the Earl of Cairn."

Al bit back a laugh. Of course he was an earl's son. Didn't that just figure? She couldn't have been any further off when she'd labeled him a barbarian. But all the blood she'd seen on both him and Hugh hadn't only been blue.

"Why were you out there that day when the wormhole opened?"

"Fighting in the battle." His look said she should have known that. But she knew nothing.

"Which battle?"

"It dinnae hae a name. 'Twas a battle fought to secure the throne for the Bonny Prince Charlie."

"Bonny Prin..." A jolt of surprise. "Culloden? Are you shitting me?"

He wrinkled his nose. "Nay, lass, wh—"

"Joking? Kidding?"

"Nay. The battle was fought nae far from Culloden."

"Holy shit," she muttered again. She was right in the middle of history in the making! How strange and thrilling.

"Ye keep saying this," he said. "Blessed excrement?"

Al blinked and squinted up at him. "What? No. It's just an expression. Never mind. Tell me more about what's happening around here."

"Nay, lass, ye've had yer turn. In all fairness, now I'll hae mine."

"A little *quid pro quo*, huh? Fine, we'll play it that way," she said, "but I'll be wanting my turn again soon."

Instead of getting angry as he'd done before, he only nodded. "Verra well."

)O(O(O(

Keir tucked Al's hand more firmly in the crook of his arm and they resumed aimlessly meandering the garden. Curiosity about her had kept him tossing and turning through the night. Part of him wanting to confront her in her bedchambers to pester her with the never-ending questions that plagued him. The other part refrained, knowing an interrogation would be the last thing that might occur between them if he came upon her with a bed nearby.

She'd been a vision of splendor when he'd first seen her in the garden after returning from his morning swim. The sun reflecting off her uncovered and unbound hair, the golden locks falling softly around the sweet curve of her rounded cheeks, over her shoulders and down her back in spiraling waves.

She was dressed informally in a bleached muslin gown with a brocaded casaca jacket over it. He'd only noticed this time because the deep V created by the jacket before a single button fastened it at her waist showed her cleavage to marvelous advantage.

Once more, she'd distracted him from pelting her with questions. He might have grown irritated with her, but it hadn't taken long to realize that she wasn't doing it on purpose. In fact, she seemed utterly unaware of her appeal.

Then she'd sidetracked him with words. Compelling descriptions of scanty swim apparel. Peculiar words of shite. Awe over noble titles.

All of it only made him more curious about her and the world she came from. So much so that the whys and hows of her arrival in this time were slipping in importance.

But he couldn't let them pass entirely.

"I want ye tae tell me more aboot this worm hole ye spoke of. How did it take my cousin?"

The lass giggled, an unusual sound coming from her, and Keir glanced down to find her usually stormy gray eyes shiny like silverplate with humor. Her pale cheeks warmed, arousing him once more, but he tamped it down.

"It's not a worm hole," she said, stressing each word. "It's a wormhole, one word."

"Verra well. A wormhole. But what was it? How did ye create it? Where did it go? Tae the Colonies? Which colony? And what's become of them in the days and years ahead?"

So many questions. His curiosity was insatiable.

"I'll try to explain it to you if I can," she said, pursing her lips. "But I'm afraid there's no chance that a man like you will be able to understand the science of it all."

Offense at her words drew him to a halt. No words could have insulted him more, though she hinted at the same again and again. It was time he explained a few things to her.

"Madam, I am a fellow at the Royal Society, the Berlin Academy, and the youngest man e'er accepted tae the Académie des Sciences in Paris. I am a learned man of science, lass. Nae some drooling simpleton who cannae comprehend newfangled notions."

✗◊✗◊✗◊✗

With each clipped word, Keir's accent grew thicker until his words were almost foreign. Certainly the string of Gaelic that rolled out after it was. But she got his meaning anyway. She had insulted him deeply.

A slap to his intelligence. Who knew that's what a man 300 years in the past might be offended by? But wouldn't she... *hadn't* she reacted the same way when someone assumed the same of her? That she was unable to grasp complex technical information just because she was tiny and blonde?

"I'm sorry," she said sincerely. "That was wrong of me. Are you really a member of all those organizations?"

"Aye." He nodded curtly. Clearly not all was forgiven.

"Okay, I'll try to explain it but feel free to ask for clarification."

Al tried to gather her scattered thoughts. Intelligent he might be but these were theories in science that hadn't even been considered at this point in time. Some of them might even get a scientist of this time imprisoned or excommunicated. Hell, his society wasn't even fully heliocentric yet much less willing to except the blasphemy of time travel.

But if he wanted it, he'd get it. Taking a seat on one of the shaded benches placed throughout the garden, she faced him when he dropped down beside her.

A deep breath. "Okay, so I suppose the first thing you

need to know is about the four dimensions."

"Four?"

"Yes, there are four dimensions to every measurement. For example, say you're riding your horse along the road, you can go forward and back along one axis." She demonstrated the line using her hands, moving them out in front of her. "Left or right." She moved from side to side. "Then up and down over a hill or whatever. Right?"

"That's three."

"The fourth is time."

He frowned but nodded. "I hae nae considered this but it makes sense."

"It's a concept that's still a couple hundred years away. So, I told you last night, a wormhole is a passageway through space. Each wormhole carries the potential to be a pathway through that fourth dimension." Simplistic and perhaps not entirely scientific, but good enough. She was sure he would ask for more detail later on anyway.

"Each wormhole?"

"There are billions of them."

"Verra well and where did ye find this wormhole?"

Al gnawed her lip. "Well, that's a little tougher to explain and maybe harder to understand. Do you know what an atom is? No, probably not that wasn't until..." She trailed off, thinking back to her most basic physics classes and searching for inspiration. Bending, she picked a flower from the garden and held it up between them. "Tell me, what is this flower made up of?"

"'Tis just a flower, lass."

"Come on," she urged.

"'Tis broken down tae the stem, petal, the stamin."

"Good but go smaller."

"The cells within? I hae seen them through the microscope, though I dinnae care much for botany. It was a favorite pastime of Euler's."

"Leonhard Euler?" she asked in distraction. "You knew him?"

"I *know* him," he clarified. "He was my mentor while at the Académie des Sciences."

Al was blown away. "Wow! Really? He's a legend in history of mathematics. His work on the wave theory of light is—"

"Lass," he warned. "Dinnae try tae turn the questions back tae yer own. I want tae understand."

"Right, right. But if you know Leonhard Euler, I might just have to become your groupie."

He just stared at her, clearly curious but refusing to be swayed from his line of questioning.

"Okay, where were we then? Oh, cells. Okay, go smaller."

"There is nae smaller."

"Yes, there is," she told him, making a circle of her hands and closing it in as she spoke. "From cells we go down to molecules then down to atoms, smaller than any microscope you have yet can see. And even smaller than that—trillions and trillions sizes smaller—is the quantum arena. This is what we call the Planck scale. So small that even the most powerful microscope cannot see it. In fact, many think it is all theoretical. But there we find what is called the quantum foam. That is where wormholes exist."

"What I saw was nae so wee."

"No, at first our project was to enlarge the wormhole just enough to slip something tiny through," she explained. "Using a burst of negative energy... I'll get to that, we were able to enlarge it beyond what was thought possible. Not just a tiny hole no bigger than my little finger but one big enough…" Al scratched at the back of her earlobe uneasily and glanced away.

"Big enough for a man."

"Yes. But the hardest part was in stabilizing it. Holding it open proved almost impossible."

"Why?"

"Wormholes are naturally volatile. Think of soap bubbles. The way they form and pop. That's what it's like in the quantum foam. Wormholes are born and die in the matter of nanoseconds. Holding one and keeping it from collapsing was the challenge. That's why I was brought in." It was a bit like bragging but she couldn't help herself. Despite the consequences, she was proud of her achievement. "The negative energy construct we developed was able to maintain it for almost a minute, which might not sound like a lot but was a pretty amazing accomplishment. After that it was a matter of being able to identify properties of the wormholes providing us information regarding its end point, harnessing those that might suit our needs, and using a massive electrical charge to steer the destination more exactly."

She could sense the wealth of questions spinning through his mind, but it was the greatest and perhaps worst that he gave voice to.

"For what purpose?"

She grimaced. "There were many applications for the technology but specifically our ultimate goal was to transport goods or troops seamlessly from one spot on the planet. Travel through three dimensions."

"But ye pierced the fourth?"

"Yes. By accident."

Keir was silent for a long while, perhaps processing all she had told him. Or trying to make sense of it. At last he spoke, looking not at her but up at the blue sky. "Some of the greatest advances in science hae been made by accident. Most accidents e'en for a prupose. I suppose I can forgi' yers since traveling through time maun be the grandest feat I can imagine."

"It would be better if we could control it," she pointed out.

"Aye, there is that." He considered her with a smile. "Tell me more aboot how ye found this quantum foam if it is so wee. And what is this negative energy?"

With a laugh, she shook her head. "No, it's my turn now. I want you to tell me how you met Leonhard Euler. And who else do you know?"

So, he told her about his studies throughout the Continent. Who he knew. Who he'd studied with. Enjoying the way her eyes would light with excitement when he mentioned names she was familiar with like Mitchell, Newton, and Hershel.

Never before had he met a woman interested in his scientific pursuits. Most ladies were lulled into boredom when he would talk of his experiments. Al soaked it all up, hanging on his every word much as he hung on hers. For hours, they talked of science, its changes and progression from his time to hers. Mathematics, physics, astronomy, biology. All of it until his mind was nearly exploding with the potential of what he might learn.

From a wee lass.

A brilliant wee lass.

Chapter 12

"I see ye've managed tae be entirely taken in by the wee witchy, hae ye?"

Al looked up to find Maeve hovering over them like a dark wraith. She was dressed much as she'd been the previous day but this time most of the dress itself was made from the tartan. A stark contrast to her elegantly gowned sister who stood by her side. With them as well were Keir's brother Oran and another somberly dressed man she didn't recognize.

The additional trio didn't speak out in agreement of Maeve's words. However, none of them appeared ready to argue with her either.

After such an enjoyable morning, the shiver of apprehension chilling her was unwelcome.

"I told ye all, Allorah had naught to do wi' Hugh's disappearance." A lie much like the one he had told Ceana the night before. Even after hearing her explanation, it seemed he didn't trust any of them to accept it with the same aplomb.

Maeve spat as she had in the library the previous day and launched into another tirade in Gaelic. This one directed more at Keir than at Al.

"English, Maeve," he warned calmly. "Lest ye be thrown tae the Butcher like so many others."

"Bah!" Maeve spat again. "Cumberland will hae his comeuppance. As will she."

Al managed to refrain from flinching when Maeve stabbed a finger in her direction, but only just. Out of all the strange and awful things that had happened to her this week, Maeve's uneven temper scared her the most.

Her diatribe continued. "When Robert returns, I will hae him cut her to ribbons for what she did to my brother."

"She did nothing."

"She's cast a spell o'er ye! But then ye've always been easily swayed by women, hae ye nae?" she continued, pausing to give Al the stink eye. "She killed my brother! She deserves to be locked up in the dungeon until she dies as he did."

Again there was no disagreement from the other three. Al wondered if she should be worried over the popular opinion of the group. Though it seemed Keir was the authority figure here.

He retained his composure well. "Maeve, ye've been in the western isles too long. Despite what some think," he threw Al a glance laced with amusement, "we are not savages here. We dinnae lock anyone up and throw away the key any longer."

"Nay, we just surrender tae the Sassenachs wi'oot much of a fight at all. We lay down our guns and e'en our language for those who would rule us."

"Shush now," the second man bit out. "Keir is right aboot one thing. Cumberland's men could be anywhere. Talk like that will get ye sent tae the tolbooth or worse."

"I'm nae afraid of Cumberland!"

"Ye should be," Keir snapped, losing both his humor and his patience. "'Tis murder he's aboot. Nae justice. Look what they did tae Frang."

Everyone fell silent, leaving Al to wonder who this Frang was and what had been done to him. She might ask now, but Maeve's zealous insistence on her imprisonment deterred her from speaking.

He sighed. "Mayhap 'twould be best if ye made yer way home and yer husband meets ye there."

"I'm nae leaving until I ken what happened tae Hugh!"

"We hae as much to explain Father's disappearance as we do Hugh's," he pointed out. "Yet I see none of ye pointing fingers and casting accusation o'er him."

"Aye, but Father has e'er been one tae act rashly," Oran said.

"He has a point," Ceana chimed in. "Hugh was never one to give into folly."

"Yet he did," Keir countered, rising to his feet to face them all. "He gave into imprudence the moment he loosed his sword and charged intae the enemy wi'oot a second thought. If he had nae been so foolish, he'd be here right now wi' us all. Whate'er his fate, 'twas of his own making and that is the truth of it."

His voice rang with conviction. It was the truth, Al supposed. Depending on what side of it one considered. Only a spacial thinker would consider it while those of a more linear logic would not. As attached to science as Keir was, she rather thought he might have made an excellent barrister.

"Enough of this now," he went on. "I ken ye're all worried for Hugh... and Father. As am I. But let's put the responsibility where it is the most logical and that is wi' Cumberland. I've sent oot men tae find our kin. To find oot if they are imprisoned or something more. Trust me to discover the truth before yer behavior descends tae that of animals." He pinned Maeve with a glare after that last statement. "This lass is under my protection and there she shall remain until we ken the truth. And e'en after that."

※※※※

The somber man lingered after Ceana took her sister firmly by the arm and led her away with Oran trailing after them.

"She does hae a point, brother. There maun be an explanation for all this." His eyes drifted over Al, down where they shouldn't be, and back to Keir curiously. "There was much speculation over the dinner table last night aboot who this lass is and what she kens."

"Her name is Miss Allorah Maines," Keir snapped and turned to her. "May I present my brother, Mr. Artair MacCoinnich."

Since the somber man kept his eyes on hers this time and bowed politely, she rose and held out a hand. "Nice to meet you."

His eyes sharpened inquisitively at the gesture but he shook her hand, seeming more surprised by her firm grip. "Despite Maeve's claims, I can hear for myself ye're nae Sassenach. From whence do ye hail?"

"The colonies."

"Which ones?"

How many were there at this time? She had no clue. "The American ones. Across the Atlantic."

"Ah, and what brings ye tae the Hielands in such troubled times, Miss Maines?"

"A sudden, undeniable urge to travel across the world," she said with a wry twist of her lips. Well, she could produce a more palatable version of the truth as well as Keir. "I just couldn't help myself."

Artair seemed unamused by her answer, though a sharp snort from Keir ended in a cough.

"Alone?" Artair pressed. His eyes drifted only a tiny bit south before lifting again. It didn't creep her out too much. His gaze was not lustful, merely appreciative and it seemed more as if he simply couldn't help himself. A family of rakes.

She nodded. "Yes, unfortunately."

"That is unfortunate. Hae ye seen much of our fair Hielands on yer travels then?"

"No, not much at all," she said, glancing askance at Keir. "A bit of the moors, your fine dungeon…"

Keir chuckled but Artair maintained a straight face.

"Enough pestering the lass, Artair," he said. "She's here wi'out family or connection. As I said, I've taken it as my duty to protect her. From all threats, including being wearied by endless questions."

She raised a brow at that.

"Except those delivered by myself, naturally."

"Of course," she agreed with open sarcasm and for the first time a full smile blossomed on Keir's lips. Again her insides fluttered and she was thankful for Artair's presence as it kept her from making a fool out of herself.

Oblivious to the flirtatious undertones, Artair only nodded. "Of course. Mayhap I can offer some more uplifting company beyond a threat, however."

"Looking for a new audience for yer preachings?" Keir asked and turned to Al. "You'll hae tae forgi' Artair, lass, he's an awful stick in the mud. A vicar, no less."

"Really?"

Like his brother, Artair was a handsome man with about

the same height and coloring. He was lean rather than muscular. While he seemed subdued in manner, he didn't possess the pious quality she'd noticed in the few men of the cloth she'd met in her life.

"Aye, wi' two parishes. One in Dingwall and another at Rosebraugh."

Rosebraugh again. The name seemed to be everywhere, the two families firmly intertwined. She felt a fresh stab of remorse for having played a part in causing them all such grief.

Odd though that they would all seem more broken up about Hugh's apparent death and not their father's. All she'd seen for the Earl of Cairn thus far was anger and frustration.

"I am sorry to hear about your father's disappearance. You must all be so worried."

Artair looked at Keir and both men shrugged. "I do hae a care for Father's fate. I should be most saddened if the worst were tae happen."

High sentiment.

"Just as I am saddened by Frang's loss," he added, looking far more aggrieved then.

There it was again. "Frang?"

Keir seemed to read her discomfiture. "Frang was our other brother, born between myself and Artair. He died in the battle."

She didn't feel like he was saying everything. Still, he also seemed suddenly sad, all traces of humor washed away as he stared blankly out toward the firth.

"I didn't know. I'm so sorry for your loss."

"'Tis a terrible blow tae lose a brother," Artair said quietly. "'Tis why we worry so o'er Hugh… and Father. Another loss would be difficult tae bear."

"I see."

The old retainer who'd announced Ceana into the dining room the previous night shuffled across the graveled path calling Keir's name. He roused himself from his mournful silence to answer.

"Aye, Archie?"

"Aye, laddie."

"Ye needed me?"

"Oh? Aye." He rheumy eyes clouded for a moment before he brightened and held out the folded paper in his hand. "A message came for ye."

She wondered how long ago it had come and how many stops and starts the obviously forgetful old man had taken on his path to the gardens.

Sending the old man on his way, Keir cracked the wax seal and read it, a frown drawing his dark brows together. "Mathilde has news, or rather nae news a'tall. Hawick has seen nae record of Father being killed on the battlefield nor among the few prisoners being held in Inverness. He is checking into those taken south."

"'Tis something at least."

Keir glanced Al's way as if he heard the silent question. "Mathilde is another of Hugh's sisters. She's wed tae the Earl of Hawick. Upon my request, she's trying tae hae Hawick find oot more when they go next tae Edinburgh." He crumbled the note in his hand. "Twill nae be easy though. He'll nae want tae help."

His brother nodded in agreement but she was baffled. "Why not?"

"Hawick supports the Sassenach king on this issue, lass."

"Oh, he's English then?"

"Nay, but he's a Lowlander so he might as well be."

"He's Scottish but he fought for the other side?" she asked. Hadn't Culloden been a battle between Scotland and England? "I don't understand."

"Och, Keir," Artair broke in, "ye cannae expect a lassie tae understand politics."

Her expression could have smote him to a pile of ashes but he was oblivious to it, just as he seemed to miss so much.

Having seen the look, Keir's lips lifted into a smile that quickly faded away. "The Hanoverian army was made up of Lowlanders as well."

"You fought your own countrymen?" She'd never heard that before. Had it been some sort of civil war?

Again, Artair piped in. "Och, lassie, the Lowlanders are nae countrymen of ours."

"You're all Scottish, aren't you?" she asked, puzzled by his fervency. She didn't turn to him for an explanation, though. He'd probably pat her on the head and tell her not to worry. Her eyes were on Keir.

"Most Lowlanders more foreign than nae. A mix of Saxon, Anglo, Norman. Some of them are e'en more Flemish than Scot," he said. "Nae like the Hielanders, a'tall. They see the Hieland chiefs as barbaric and tribal."

"I can't imagine how they could make such a mistake."

That sexy smile kicked up once more, lifting away the last of his sorrow. "A Hielander is true tae his roots, lass. The Gaels and the Celts. They maun see us as savage merely because we embrace the ways of our ancestors but 'tis a sight better than becoming like the Sassenach, taking up their ways and customs."

"Wait, didn't you say something earlier about your grandmother being French?"

He chuckled and gave her a wink. "Aye, and the other

one was English. 'Tis nae only what's in our blood but what is in our hearts, lass. And I'm a Hielander true."

She envied him his sense of place and purpose, even if it had led him into a bloody battle. She was proud of being an American but knew it wasn't in her bones like that. His nationalism was rather charming.

"I should write a reply 'ere the messenger leaves." His eyes lingered on her indecisively.

She rolled hers in response. "Go. I can entertain myself for a little while at least. I'm a big girl, you know?"

A grin tilted the corner of his mouth and he bowed with flourish. "I am put in my place. Verra well, Big Al. Verra well. I will see ye at dinner."

"Mayhap I can provide ye some company in my brother's absence?" Artair asked, as they watched Keir stride away. "Over luncheon?"

Her stomach growled, reminding her of how long it had been since she'd truly eaten.

"That would be wonderful."

"If ye care for an education in Hieland philosophy, I'd be happy tae provide that as well."

Al winced. Maybe not so wonderful.

Chapter 13

She hadn't expected to like him.

Al stood silently in the door of the library watching Keir scribble furiously across a sheet of paper. So utterly absorbed in the task, he didn't notice her presence or even the plate of food forgotten at his elbow. Pausing only long enough to jab his pen into a bottle of ink, he resumed his writing. The way he so accurately poked the nib into the tiny bottle without looking told her the gesture was a practiced one.

Yet another in a long list of surprises in the past twenty-four hours. Wonderful hours that somehow washed away the misery of the days before. He'd spent the previous night managing to make her feel beautiful, delicate.

Today, with his attention never swaying from her, hanging on her every word, he'd made her feel like the most captivating woman on earth.

She, who'd never managed more than a few lines of casual conversation with a stranger, had whiled away a shocking number of hours talking to him nearly nonstop and with ever-growing ease. That alone was most unusual for her. Over that time, she'd begun gazing more into his eyes than at his gorgeous body. Started feeling more than mere lust, but respect as well.

Yes, she liked him

Perhaps too much.

It would be all too easy to get sucked into thinking the past day would become representative of all the days ahead for her in this new world. That he would be like that every day. Attentive and interested. That it could last forever.

Fantasies and fiction might work out that way, but she knew too well reality wasn't always so generous. He'd gotten what he wanted from her. He now knew the truth of what had become of his cousin. There was nothing more he needed from her that a few more questions wouldn't cover.

Soon she would be on her way. On her own once more. She had no desire to take a love-sick heart along with her.

Gently, she tapped on the doorframe, rapping more firmly when his focus remained on the page before him.

He jerked his head up with a frown that melted away into a heart-stopping smile when he saw her in the door. "Al, lass, there ye are. Where hae ye been?"

"Having lunch with your family," she told him, entering when he motioned her forward. "You should have been there, it was wonderfully hostile. Maeve was shooting daggers at me the whole time."

He started in alarm but she raised a hand with a chuckle. "Figurative ones, not literal ones. Though I will assume from your reaction it was an actual possibility. I'll watch my step around her."

He didn't deny it but nodded. "I shouldnae hae left ye alone wi' them. I apologize. I was sidetracked by other correspondence."

"It's fine. I can take care of myself."

"So I've heard." He relaxed in his chair with a smile.

"Nevertheless, 'twould be best if ye avoid Maeve as much as possible. She's descended intae near madness since her son was killed. We will dine alone in the future."

The future? "It's all right, but about the future..."

"Please sit. Join me."

He pointed to the chair adjacent to his desk, but she shook her head. It could wait.

"No, I can see you're busy and have things to do. Really, I just wanted to thank you for defending me like you did this morning."

""'Twas naught tae be thanked for." He whisked the gratitude away with a twitch of his fingers and studied her thoughtfully. "However, we may need to find a wee bit more proof that Hugh perhaps 'died.'" He gestured to the chair once more time. "Please, sit."

Because she didn't really want to leave his company, she sat as directed. "Do you have any ideas about what to say?"

"Nay, but none of them, Maeve in particular, will accept a mere disappearance for long."

"And the truth is out of the question?"

"Aye, unless ye hae a yen tae feel the flames licking at yer toes," he joked. "Maeve isnae as enlightened as Hugh or e'en Ceana. She would ne'er rest until she saw it done."

She shuddered at the thought. "No, thank you."

"Ye're safe here, lass. I promise ye. "

His assurance warmed her and yes, made her feel secure. "Thanks, but that's the other thing I wanted to talk to you about."

As it had been this morning, his attention was completely hers. Patient, no indication that he was in any hurry to resume his writing. It was perhaps the most flattering and heady behavior she'd ever experienced in a man's presence. Suddenly, she didn't want to talk to him about leaving Dingwall and glanced around the room for inspiration. "You know, there must be thousands of books in here. Do they get read, or are they just for show?"

"Are ye asking if I can read, lass?" he jested. "I thought ye'd already satisfied yerself on the issue of my barbarism. But tae be clear, aye, I can read."

"I know... I wasn't..." She flushed. "Oh, you can be a very frustrating person sometimes."

"I'm only joshing, ye ken," he said. "Though ye're a bonny sight when yer feathers are ruffled."

If it were possible, she felt her cheeks grow even hotter under his warm gaze. Scratching the back of her earlobe nervously, she pressed on, "Listen, I was just wondering... That is, I'm not a prisoner here any more, right?"

"Of course, nae." His playful grin fell into such a deep frown, his thick black brows nearly hid his eyes. He watched her broodingly. "Dinnae think such a thing."

"I didn't... or at least, I wasn't sure." She paused with a sigh, her shoulders slumping forward slightly. "I was just thinking if I'm not a prisoner or whatever, that I should be going on my way. I mean, I can't stay here forever, right?"

Keir stared at her in silence for so long, Al began scratching at her earlobe again. "Why nae?"

Because of him. Because of the danger of living too close to fantasies was that reality never measured up.

"Ye dinnae need tae leave, lass," he said, when it became clear she wasn't going to speak. "Ye can stay here as my guest for as long as ye care tae."

"No, I couldn't possibly."

That pensive look dropped again as if she were a puzzle he was trying to work out. "Do ye want tae leave, lass? Ye've nae where tae go here."

She glanced away once more, scanning the bookshelves blindly. "I told you, I'll figure it out. And there's no reason for me to stay. You've gotten what you needed from me already."

"Hae I now?"

Her gaze shot back to him at the suggestive comment. His brow lifted a notch, his blue eyes twinkling. Heat flooded her face and she looked away. Biting her lip to keep from smiling, she pressed on. "I'm used to being on my own. It's a future thing. You wouldn't understand."

"Nay, I dinnae. Explain it tae me."

"Feminism," Al told him, mocking herself inwardly. She'd never been much of a feminist. Solitude had invariably been the result of circumstance rather than choice. "Women in the future like to be independent. Take care of ourselves." She shrugged as if it was no big deal.

"Wi'oot a man to hae a care for ye? To provide for ye?"

No, she wasn't a huge feminist but the idea that a woman in some way *needed* a man to take care of her did rankle a bit.

"Oh come on, Keir, what could a man possibly do for me that I can't do for myself?"

This time when he lifted his brow so expressively, it took a second longer for his implication to sink it. When it did, she reddened once more but couldn't help laughing.

"I know for a fact I do *that* for myself better than any man could manage."

The shock on his face was well worth the frank statement. She wasn't sure but she thought he might have blushed as well before he too smiled. Not with forthright humor but with a devilish grin.

"Ye ken, that sounds like something of a challenge, lass."

Before she could respond, Keir pushed himself out of his chair, dropping to his knees in front of her. "Shall I prove that a man can do better?"

He lifted her foot, holding her firmly by the ankle in one hand as his other slipped up her calf. Al jumped at the gentle caress, trying to kick him off before he even reached her knee. Slapping both hands down, she pinned his hand against the top of her thigh with a shaky laugh.

"Wow, you really are a rake, aren't you?"

Stilling, he stared up at her. "Is that what ye think of me?"

"Hey, I'm just going off what you've already said." She lifted her hands defensively.

"I dinnae say…"

"It was heavily implied. But it's okay. I'm sure being a rake isn't your worst quality."

"I'm nae rake!" he retorted, yanking his hand away and rocking back on his heels. "I cannae believe ye think so little of me. I've had no more lovers than any other man might."

"You must know a lot of rakes then."

"Lass," he protested in a thickening brogue, "I am nae rake."

"Aren't you?" she asked, perhaps a little wistfully as he climbed to his feet. The better to glower down at her properly, she thought. But what was wrong with being called a rake? All the books she'd read made them sound marvelous, after all. "I'll bet you're even pretty good at it."

Both brows shot up at that, then that wolfish gleam lit his eyes once more. "'Struth, a rake can gi' a woman pleasure beyond her wildest imaginings. She'll carry the memory of their night together wi' her for years tae come," he said softly, taking her hand and tugging her to her feet. "I admit, I could do that for ye."

Of course he could. Damn him. She just didn't want to be another number. But even more than that, Al realized she didn't want to be disappointed if the experience didn't measure up to her fantasies. With that in mind, she stepped away from him.

"He can make them weep for him, make them wild," he continued, closing the space again. "But he beds one woman wi'oot knowing her from the next." Releasing a shaky breath, she took another step backward, but still he followed. "Mayhap he takes her wi'oot care for her feelings." He closed the gap between them until she had to tilt her head all the way back to see him.

His warm eyes moved over her face like a physical caress. His fingers flitted across her cheekbone, her temple, and around the shell of her ear without ever quite touching her, though it was enough to set her aquiver. She longed to lean into him. To have his strong arms close around her.

And more. So much more. Brains and brawn. The whole package was undeniably attractive. She couldn't resist. She didn't want to. But she had to.

Or did she?

"'Tis what a rake does, lass." His husky brogue was close to her ear, sending spurts of undeniable desire skittering through her. "He offers naught but a quick fook and a swift goodbye. Is that the kind of man ye think I am?"

So overcome by the brush of his lips against her ear, she couldn't comprehend his words. Almost nodding before they sunk in, she shook her head.

"Excellent," he said, tracing his lips along her jawline. "Because as I said, I'm nae rake. I'm a rogue, lass. Do ye ken the difference?"

Swallowing hard, she shook her head again.

"A rogue woos his would-be lover." His mouth grazed hers ever-so-lightly, not enough of a contact to be called a kiss, but her lips tingled anyway, wanting more. "A rogue seduces his lover." His lips teased her cheek, her brow. "Seduces her wi' kisses. Wi' words of admiration and scientific discovery."

Her puff of laughter wafted between them.

"He does all this long 'ere he takes her tae his bed. He waits until she's hot and wanton with desire, longing for him. Begging him tae take her. Do ye ken the difference now?"

A jerky nod was all she could manage.

"Good. Ye'll stay here," he commanded, brooking no argument. "Where I can woo ye more wi' talk of science. It is the best option for ye now anyway."

Yes, it might be. But it might also be the worst. He was so calm and contained while she was trembling so badly, she thought her knees would give out. It made her want to hit him.

"What if I don't want to be wooed?"

That mocking brow lifted once more as if he doubted there was any such possibility. "What lass disnae?"

He was an incredible flirt. A arrogant one. How many women had he wooed? How many times had he succeeded?

"You're amazing." The words weren't entirely complimentary. "Did it even occur to you that I might not want to be wooed because I have someone already? That I'm married? You haven't even asked."

He stilled. "Are ye, lass? Are ye wed?"

"No, but that's not the point. I live alone. I take care of myself. I don't need a man to do it for me," she said. "I don't need to stay here just because you think I do."

"Yet ye will stay."

"You're unbearable," she told him, astounded by his utter confidence. "How can you be so sure of yourself?"

"Because ye are are fascinated wi' me, lass."

Cocky bastard. Yes, she was. Utterly.

"As I am wi' ye," he added quietly, turning away so quickly, Al was sure she'd imagined the admission. Or was he embarrassed by it?

"Come," he said, tugging her hand. "I've made a list of questions I want ye tae answer for me."

It was a heady feeling, being wanted by a man like Keir. Being wanted for her mind as well. Was there really anything wrong with being attracted to him? With wanting him? The temptation was strong. For all she might be able to find a physical release without a man, a part of her longed to be held in strong arms. To curl into a man. A man like him.

Maybe.

Yes, she would stay. For now. But eventually no matter what she gained from the experience, she was sure it would all end as he described. With a quick fuck and a swift goodbye.

Chapter 14

The next two days slipped away without another word being said on the subject of her eventual departure. As Keir promised, they took their meals alone and aggression-free. There were long walks through the gardens and down to the firth where he pointed out the peak of Ben Wyvis in the distance and talked about his homeland. Talks about her world and then one where his cousin would live out the remainder of his days.

Longer hours in the library reading or working their way through his ever-growing list of questions. In many ways, she felt she'd found a kindred soul in him. In all the years she'd immersed herself in science to hide from the fact that she was alone, it'd never occurred to her that she could share it with another.

His roguish method of seduction was working on her. She reveled in his company. His ability to woo her with words was undeniable. His insatiable thirst for knowledge was as sexy as his body.

But his promise to seduce her with kisses in addition to words had been coming up short. He didn't try to touch her again beyond a casual brush of his fingers or the occasional caress when holding her arm or hand. Even so she was more aware of him with each passing day.

In fact, she was beginning to think it might be fun to… well, do all the wonderfully promiscuous things she'd never had the time or opportunity to do in her life of dedicated academia.

Such thoughts only brought her closer to what she saw as the inevitable conclusion and end of her days at Dingwall.

"How did ye pass yer afternoon wi'oot me?" he asked at dinner the third night.

"After you abandoned me to actually do some work?"

With a pile of correspondence waiting for him, he'd spent a portion of each afternoon in his study. Running Dingwall and the lands attached to it took time and effort. With his father still missing, it had fallen to him to pick up the reins.

"I sobbed uncontrollably, of course," she quipped, helping herself to another portion of the delicious apple frushie they'd been served for dessert. "How could I possibly survive without your company?"

Valid question, however, as she'd been constantly by his side for days now.

He didn't seem to mind.

Neither did she.

"Did ye moan and wail?" he retorted. "Tear oot yer hair in grief?"

"Absolutely." They shared a grin. She liked their banter, too. Surrounded by engineers and physicists for the last few years, Al had almost forgotten what a sense of humor was. "Actually, I spent the afternoon with Peigi hemming a couple more dresses."

In truth, her new maid had hemmed for them both since

Al had no idea how to effectively wield a needle and thread. She'd also kept up a steady stream of amicable chatter that had helped pass the time quicker.

She didn't mention she stayed in her room in an effort to keep her interfaces with the remainder of the MacCoinnich and Urquhart clan as fleeting as possible.

Artair had asked her to walk with him a couple times. He appeared kind—as a man of the cloth, she supposed it was expected—but as their talks inevitably resulted in tedious pontification, she always felt compelled to keep them brief.

Oran seemed harmless, quiet and scholarly. He seemed more surprised than not when someone noticed he was about and spoke to him. Conversation with him often trickled away to long stretches of awkward silence, and therefore, was also short-lived. Honestly, there was little more that could be hoped for between two of the most socially awkward people born in any time.

Ceana might have been friendly enough if she weren't prone to sly insinuations with one breath and frivolous chatter with the next. Al had no idea what she truly thought about anything.

Maeve, on the other hand, clearly had it in for her, turning up whenever Al was alone to try to intimidate her into confessing to what Maeve wanted to hear. Mainly that Al really was either the witch or the clootie Maeve alternately accused her of being, and that ultimately she'd had some sort of hand in Hugh's disappearance.

As Keir had recommended, she avoided the woman as best she could.

"How would ye pass the days in yer time?"

"I told you, I worked. I had a cat."

"Come, there maun be something more."

She knew what he was getting at. He'd tried several times to turn the conversation to her personal life. To things she didn't want to talk about. As she usually did, she deflected the question. "Honestly, there's really not much to tell. I live... lived a boring, uneventful life."

"Och," he scoffed. "Surely, it wisnae so bad."

She laughed at that. "Keir, I've spent the last five years working on a dissertation about the difference between the experimental uncertainty of classical physics and the fundamental uncertainty of quantum mechanics. Does that sound like a life of excitement to you?"

His blue eyes glittered with interest in the candlelight. He leaned toward her in anticipation. God, it really did.

Another meal lost to the debate of scientific discovery between her time and his.

He didn't seem to mind.

Neither did she.

He was wooing his way straight to the center of her heart.

"Enough of this," he exclaimed some hours later, pushing away the decanter of wine they'd emptied and standing. "There's something I want tae show ye this night. Will ye come wi' me?"

She took his proffered hand and stood, a little unsteadily. "Of course." Was there any question? "What is it?"

"A surprise. Come."

In the hall, he took a branched candelabra from his ancient footman to light their way through the unlit castle passages. Through a series of dark drawing rooms they passed without any particular haste. One after another.

"Where are we going? Artair gave me a tour of the castle the other afternoon but I don't remember going this way."

"Ye'll see," he said mysteriously, leading her into a circular turret in the northeast corner of the castle. Inside, there was nothing but a spiraling staircase ascending up into the darkness. He held the candelabra high and began to climb.

"Can I ask you a question?"

"Should I brace myself?"

"Maybe." Still clumsy in long dresses, she gathered up her skirts in one hand, lifting them high. She rushed to catch up to him, reaching for his strong arm once more. "It's about your family."

"Are any of them gi'ing ye trouble?"

There was no need to mention Maeve's so-far harmless threats. "It's just that your family dynamic is so odd. You're all related but it's like living in a house filled with strangers. And I get I haven't been here long but you and your brothers don't seem to be overly upset by your father's absence."

"Is there a question in there?"

She shook her head in exasperation. "You know what I mean. I get that he was imprudent and even reckless in this whole Culloden thing, but most people tend to really care for their parents. I thought you did as well, when you left the dungeon"—and left me there—"in such a rush that day. What gives?"

He mouthed those last two words silently but a few moments later, finally replied, "Our father is a difficult man. All he cares for is appearances. He married the daughter of a duke for that reason alone... though I do like tae think he came tae care for her as she was a kind, bonny lady. Watch your step here. He had his sons for the same reason. One to inherit, one for the military, one for the church. Just as it should be. That perfection was marred by Oran's arrival. I believe Father resented him for it.

"When Hugh's parents died, Father took his nephew into his home. Just as he should. Played the perfect guardian for the admiration it gained him at court. Nae many men hae the chance tae hae stewardship o'er a duke, ye see."

If she didn't, he was painting a pretty thorough picture.

"E'en this bluidy war," he continued. "Father dinnae support the cause itself. He did it tae look good, tae gain favor because he was certain the prince had the support tae secure the throne. He recalled Hugh and me from France tae show his command o'er us. Bugger it, he probably charged intae the thick of it for the same reason. He dinnae care for anything but himself. Everything he did was for show."

From the wounded note in Keir's voice, it sounded like Cairn was also able to put on a pretty decent show of caring for his sons, in front of others at least. How it must have hurt and confused them when they were small boys if that affection didn't carry over to their personal relationship.

She knew all too well how that felt.

"I'm sorry." She squeezed his arm comfortingly.

He shrugged nonchalantly but covered her hand with his. "Dinnae be. There's no greater foolishness than living one's entire life based on how others perceive it. 'Tis difficult to like a person who does so. Or respect them. But he is my father and I would see him safely home."

"Of course, you will."

They walked up the wide staircase two flights, then three in silence. But as they began up the next, another question popped into her head. "And then what?"

"With Father back here and the conflict wi' England in ashes, I can return tae France. Continue my studies, my experiments…"

"Chase all the pretty French girls?" she added, only half-kidding.

He shook his head. "I should ne'er hae let him…" He frowned down at her. "I only just realized what ye said. Do ye still… Ah, ye're bamming me." He choked back a chuckle. "Och, ye're an audacious lass, tae be sure. I've ne'er meet another like ye in all my days. Are all the lassies in the future like ye?"

She'd never been called audacious in her entire life. But he'd made the confrontations she once avoided into an exercise of wits, an invigorating, heart-pounding experience. Their repartee did make her feel bolder, braver. More brazen than she ever would have dared.

Still, she shook her head in response. "I'm not daring at all compared to most women in my time. In fact, I've always been painfully shy." *Especially around handsome men.* She thought it but didn't add it.

"Shy? Och, lass, I find that hard tae believe. Ye're anything but. In fact, I've found ye singularly expressive in yer opinions. Especially when ye deliver such resounding set downs."

"No, it's true. I'm socially dysfunctional," she insisted. "You'd call it being a wallflower, I suppose. Honestly, I was fast on my way to becoming a regular cat lady."

He opened the door at the top of the tower and waved for her to precede him. "Cat *lady?*" he asked as she passed.

"A term for a reclusive spinster who lives alone and has no one but her many cats for company."

"Ah, your Mr. Darcy," he said, joining her on the roof of the turret. "I recall you mentioning him. Do ye think someone will take care of him in yer absence?"

"I hope so."

Shaking off the wave of sadness threatening to overcome her, Al paced around the perimeter of the tower along the thigh high parapet. She peered up at the sky, seeing more stars than she'd ever imagined existed.

"Look at all the stars! I never seen the sky so full before. You can actually see the Milky Way. It's so beautiful!"

"Nae as bonny as ye."

She cast a grimace over her shoulder but said nothing.

"Ye dinnae believe me?" he asked, moving closer. "Hae I nae made myself clear on this matter?"

With a shrug, she shied away as he neared. Slowly though, since she didn't want him to think he affected her in any way. Or that she was afraid of him. "I'm uncomfortable with men complimenting me."

"How can ye nae be? Surely dozens of men hae thrown themselves at yer feet in admiration?"

Swallowing a laugh, she shook her head. "Not as many as you might think. Most think I'm too chubby."

Scoffing at that, he strolled nearer, altering course as she continued to move. "Ye've all the lush curves any man could desire. If I may be so bold as tae make such an observation."

"You are very bold."

He grinned, his wicked smile flashing in the moonlight. He came closer still, until she had to tilt her head back to meet his eyes. He was so very tall. Even to a woman who'd had to look up at men her whole life. Having him looming over her so should have been intimidating, but it wasn't. She felt petite, yes, but protected. Safe. The idea of nestling into his encompassing embrace was alluring. But then she also felt energized and alive, even when standing in his shadow. As bright as those stars twinkling from above.

"Shall I be e'en bolder?" His brogue was low and husky.

His fingertips traced her jawline in a light caress, leaving her trembling with yearning. "Shall I offer ye my kiss and see if ye accept it?"

She licked her lips. More than anything, she wanted to say yes. For the past few days—when she hadn't been lost to the pure enjoyment of their conversation, at least—she'd been pondering how it might be to kiss him. Replaying the ever-changing fantasies in her mind over and over.

Wondering why he hadn't tried to yet.

Would he be hesitant? Would he take? Would he plunder like the rake he denied being?

Any of the scenarios might make her heart rate skyrocket. But this shameless flirtation? The way he asked in words that might have seemed uncertain yet were phrased with such assuredness, had her nearly puddling at his feet.

She wanted this. Wanted to know if it would be anything like the earth-shattering kisses she'd read about but never thought possible. Or even probable. She was dying to know.

Yet when he bent his head, his lips only hovered above hers. Uncertain what stopped him, she took a nervous step out of his reach. With a shake of her head, Al tucked her loose hair behind her ear and laughed lightly. Hoping her frayed nerves weren't evident in the shaky laugh.

"There you go, getting your rake on again. Tell me, is this one of your usual pick-up lines?"

"Pick-up lines?" Keir frowned down at her.

"I thought you told me you left such bull...er, excessive flattery to your cousin," she said with another light laugh. "Yet here you are, a veritable Prince Charming."

"Ye think I'm bamming ye now?" he asked, deciphering her words. "Look at me, Al."

Holding her chin firmly, he tilted her head back until she

was forced to meet his eyes. "I am nae liar, nor am I prone tae false flattery. If I tell ye ye're bonny, 'tis because ye are. Because I believe 'tis so." His low voice was thick with his brogue. As it had before, the gravelly tone incited a corresponding tremor through her body. The desire she'd been denying surged through her veins, making her dizzy. "Ye insult me and my intelligence by making light or assuming my words empty ones. Do ye understand?"

"Y—yes."

"Good. Do ye believe me now when I say ye're bonny?"

She believed that he believed it. Though she marveled at it, she had never doubted it. "Yes."

He nodded curtly and stepped away, leaving Al to sway unsteadily without his support. "Now, come, let me show ye my surprise."

Chapter 15

It took every ounce of his willpower to turn and walk away from her. All of his strength to even walk a straight line, but Keir did it anyway. His entire body burned with wanting, longing.

As it had been for days, without even a single kiss between them yet. He wanted badly to taste her lips, to learn their shape. To feel them against his.

But he'd be damned if he'd give her more reason to think him a rake.

True, he'd never considered she might already have a man of her own when he'd made his intentions to woo her into his bed clear. The way she looked at him, he knew she found him comely. She couldn't take her eyes off him any more than he could force his gaze from her.

That didn't make him a rake.

Nay, she would come to him first before he'd admit to being brought low by his raging lust. She'd succumbed easily to a seduction of words and the slightest caress of his fingertips. The tiny tremors racking her body told him without doubt she wanted him. He thought only that she might be shy and so had provided an easy opportunity for her to take his kiss and allow them each to expel the desire burning within them both.

Still, she denied them. It'd never occurred to him that it would take so long. Or worse. That she might not plan to act on the attraction between them at all.

Now he was becoming less and less certain she ever would. It wasn't morality or modest reticence holding her back but her own insecurity. He doubted she would ever see his true admiration for her when she couldn't even acknowledge the beauty she possessed.

How could she not see it? Be confident in her appeal? Shyness wouldn't account for it. Perhaps the men in the future were naught but blind fools? In his eyes, Al was the embodiment of womanly perfection. The generous curves were perfectly proportioned on her wee frame. Bountiful breasts that his palms itched to hold and weigh. A tiny waist flaring out to rounded hips, and her legs! Though he hadn't given them the attention they deserved in his anger in the dungeon or when she'd come to his library, the memory of those bared limbs extending from her indecently short skirt haunted him.

He couldn't imagine how men in her time kept a sane thought in their heads if all the women there dressed so scantily. Just the thought of her had kept him in a semi-aroused state for days.

There wasn't beauty in her body alone, either. Nay, she had the face of an angel. Heart-shaped, her skin flawless ivory with a perpetual blush of pink on her cheeks. Her eyes were large and gray, fringed with long dark lashes. Her most prominent feature, he'd found his gaze drawn to them over and over. They reflected her moods, her humor, her intelligence.

With her blonde hair left unbound as she liked to wear it, she'd provided yet another part of her for him to admire. The long, spiraling locks had driven him mad for days, nearly consuming him with the desire to wind them around his fingers, around his body.

Och, she might make a rake of him yet.

How could she not see it? How she enthralled him with her splendor? Even the normally stoic Artair had fallen victim to it. Yet she remained blind.

It boggled the mind.

Perhaps the perception of beauty had changed over time. It had happened before. If that were the case, Keir was glad to have her here where she might be appreciated as she deserved.

Though he was saddened for her, in losing all she might have held dear in that life, he was happy to have her here with him now. Not simply because she was so bonny to look upon, but because she held a wealth of knowledge in her head.

Knowledge he longed to explore.

Having managed to tamp down his desire, he swept an arm upward, drawing her attention to his most prized possession. "This is why I brought ye up here. I thought ye might appreciate it as few others. A better way to see the stars than merely gazing up at the skies."

※※※※※

Cursing his ability to remain so unaffected when she was shaken to the core by longing and desire, Al turned on wobbly legs and saw an enormous wooden cylinder suspended by a network of ropes and pulleys, angling outward and upward from a wood-framed support structure on top of the turret.

"What is it?"

"'Tis a telescope, lass," he said in a tone clearly implying she should have known that.

It was, she realized as she walked around the monstrous structure. Obviously it wasn't like any she had ever seen. The body of the telescope must have been four feet in diameter and at least thirty or more feet long.

"Where did you get it?"

"I built it."

Awed into silence, she listened with half an ear as Keir expounded on the device. How he'd taken an interest in the stars after becoming acquainted with James Bradley, the Astronomer Royal at the Royal Academy, but hadn't truly considered the science noteworthy until his study of light waves with Euler in recent years.

"I had it shipped from Paris when Father recalled me," he went on, climbing the stairs to the top of the platform constructed at the lower end of the mammoth cylinder. He turned to lend her a helping hand. "My men just finished assembling it this day. Would ye care tae take a wee peek?"

Nodding, Al gathered up her long skirts in one hand and took his hand with the other. His warm fingers squeezed hers before letting her go.

"This is amazing," she said, examining the eyepiece. "You did this all yourself?"

Shrugging modestly, he shed his jacket and unbuttoned his vest before loosening his neckcloth. Her eyes followed him, wishing she could put her lips on the pulse whispering along his taut neck.

Shaking away the urge, she tried to pay attention to what he was saying.

"I designed it based on other reflecting telescopes and

had a small hand in the actual construction of the housing. I employed the services of a mathematical instruments maker named James Bird who has a shop in London on the Strand to help me with the mirrors. Grinding the glass took us almost eleven months but the magnification potential far exceeds other telescopes I've seen. Look, Al," he urged. "See how far out into space its view can stretch."

She was prepared to be underwhelmed. Compared to the telescopes of her day, surely this one couldn't see very far. Even though it was so big. The moon, of course. Maybe a couple of the closer planets?

But as she peered into the telescope, listening as Keir pointed out different planets while tugging on winches to adjust the positioning, she found herself impressed by both the telescope and his knowledge. He showed her the planets, Jupiter and its moons, then Saturn. Speaking on the discovery of each by Galileo.

"I suppose you know him, too," she asked jokingly.

"Unfortunately I dinnae hae the pleasure of meeting him 'ere his death. He was verra ill when Hugh and I traveled through Italy."

She'd just been joking! How incredible it was that he had been blessed with such opportunities.

"Since I've had this telescope, I've found reason to believe Saturn has more moons than the five determined by Cassini. And even more interesting, if ye look beyond Saturn," he continued, adjusting the positioning of the instrument, "ye'll see something I believe has ne'er been noticed before."

He waved her away from the eyepiece and set about adjusting the focus before rising and motioning for her to take a peek. "See, there are more planets beyond. I've observed this one and another well beyond Saturn."

Al looked into the telescope again but hardly paid it a bit of attention. Keir pressed up behind her, his cheek just inches away from hers as if he could guide her line of sight. "Do ye see it, lass?" he asked close to her ear. "If ye'll look closely, ye'll see it has moons of its own as well. Several, I think."

How was she supposed to look when he was distracting her like that? "I can do it myself," she huffed.

"Of course, ye can," he agreed amicably enough, but he was grinning as he stepped away.

Taking a calming breath, she peered into the eyepiece once more, seeing a blue planet more clearly and far closer than she would have thought possible.

"You found this past Saturn?"

"Aye."

"That's Uranus."

His enthusiasm fell away. "'Tis already been discovered?"

She frowned, trying to think. To remember some bit of forgotten knowledge. "Yes, but…"

"And the other? The bluer one beyond it?"

"Neptune."

"Bugger it, I'd submitted my findings to the Royal Academy before I left," he said. "I'd thought I was first tae happen upon them."

"Maybe you are," she reminded him. "I'm not much of a astronomical historian. Besides, remember, what we know in my time doesn't reflect on what you know in yours, right? There's almost three hundred years of discoveries between us."

"What else will we find out there? Tell me."

"Well, there's another planet beyond Neptune called Pluto. Some say it isn't really a planet though. There's some debate on that. Then there are galaxies, nebulae."

"I ken these things."

"Black holes…?"

"What are they?"

Obligingly, Al launched into a lecture on black holes which led to a lively debate on gravitational pull and Newtonian physics. Whether his contemporary John Michell's gravitational research was truly describing black holes or not. For an outdated, mid-eighteenth century man, Keir had some surprising challenges to even twenty-first century ways of thinking.

They talked far into the early morning hours. Hours she thoroughly enjoyed both as a scientist and as a woman. There was something intoxicating about having the complete attention of an attractive man who wanted to climb into her head rather than just into bed, but in the back of her mind she was troubled.

There was something wrong here.

Chapter 16

Al slammed the thick text book shut, wrinkling her nose. She'd been through a dozen books already searching for... she wasn't sure what exactly.

Something in what Keir had said the previous night was sitting ill, though she wasn't entirely certain why. However, there was no chance of finding the answers in books leading up to this point. What she was searching for hadn't even been written yet.

Or maybe it was all in her imagination.

A byproduct of her general distress in this time. There were so many dreadful things about being stranded in the past, though most revolved around personal hygiene. Poor excuses for soap, shampoo, and toothpaste. The labor intensity of getting a bath. And she dared not dwell too long on the more sanitary issues.

The clothes were cumbersome and uncomfortable as the days grew warmer. She envied Keir his lightweight shirt and kilt so much, she'd been tempted to tear them from his back.

She laughed inwardly. Yeah, that was why she wanted to tear off his clothes.

She couldn't understand what he was waiting for.

With a sigh, she picked up another thick tome and read the spine. *De Philosophia Cartesiana* by Balthasar Bekker. With a grimace, she flipped it open to find that it wasn't written in English, which was just as well. She doubted any philosophical writings beyond those of Confucious perhaps were going to provide tolerance for the lack of innovation here.

Only time could do that.

Time for invention but also time to acclimate to it all.

In some ways, she already had. The lack of technology didn't hurt at all, much to her surprise. No phones, no alarm clocks. No TV or computers to mindlessly suck her into hours of wasted time. No social media to show her just how screwed up the world at large was. Or to body shame her into denying herself a cookie, or compel her to spend even more hours online searching for ways to exercise better and lose weight.

She liked the peace and quiet, the serene beauty of the Highlands. And the time to enjoy it.

She liked the food. The variety and freshness of the fish and gamey meats brought to the table even if they had unappetizing names like cullen skink, finnan haddie, and forfar bridie. Even haggis. The desserts were especially delightful. Fatty cutties, cranachan, and blueberry pie. Keir encouraged her to try them all without ever once implying her full curves couldn't bear an additional pound or two.

She liked spending long days among books and in actual conversation with another person without a machine or screen between them. Without a smartphone to constantly distract them.

She liked not multi-tasking and just focusing on one thing at a time. Giving it her full attention.

Most of all, she simply liked Keir. Spinning the fantasy of days like these into a life and future was dangerous business. She wasn't looking forward to the end.

So perhaps she was subconsciously searching for something else to rankle. Something to draw her from her growing comfort. To keep her uneasy, on her toes. So that when the time came to leave, she'd have a reason to go without hesitation.

"What are ye looking for?"

Al closed her eyes and prayed for strength. There was at least one part of Dingwall she'd be eager to walk away from without regret.

Maeve.

There'd been a dead sparrow on her pillow last night when she'd returned to her room. A curse, Peigi told her, that her cow's milk be turned to blood. Since she didn't own a cow, Al wasn't as worried about that as she was about how Maeve had gotten into her room.

For it had to be Maeve. The most hostile element in a house or castle inhabited by those with hostile and semi-hostile inclinations. If she could get into her room, what was to stop her from smothering her in her sleep?

"Are ye spying? Hoping tae find some way tae do more harm tae this family than ye already hae?" Maeve snatched the book out of her hands as if it held national intelligence. "I willnae let ye do it."

Al didn't even try to defend herself. It was useless. Whether it was depression and grief over losing her only child that drove her, or she'd truly had been touched by madness as Keir believed, Maeve was wholly unwilling to listen to reason.

She moved closer and Al instinctively shied to the side,

eyeballing the door as if it were her salvation. Either as an escape or as a entry point for deliverance. Unfortunately, it remained vacant and the woman stood between her and a way out.

"I don't want to fight with you, Maeve," she said slowly. "Or hurt you or your family. I would never do that. You've all been very good to me."

"Aye, ye've cast a spell o'er them all. Especially Keir. He cannae see ye for what ye are, but I can."

It was just too exhausting. Helplessly, she tried once more.

"What do you see, Maeve? What am I? I'll tell you, I'm a woman like you. A woman who's lost something and is just trying to make a new life without it." She wasn't certain but she thought she was getting through to the woman. The wildness in her overly-bright blue eyes had softened. She seemed to be listening. Perhaps understanding. At last. "You've lost the men you love. You're angry, I understand that. You want to lash out at something. But this isn't going to change anything. It won't bring them... *Ow!*"

Stumbling to the side, Al cradled the side of her head and stared at Maeve and the huge leather-bound tome she was wielding in astonishment. So much for sympathy. The woman was completely psychotic.

She lifted the book to take another swing and Al lifted an arm to shield herself.

"Maeve." A firm male voice rang out over the room, freezing Maeve in place before she lowered the weapon with one last snarl.

But it wasn't Keir who had come to her rescue. Artair stood at the door, piercing Maeve with his most solemn gaze. "Leave her alone."

"May the devil cut the head off ye and make a day's work of yer neck," she growled at Al. With one last huff, she dropped the book and spun on her heel. Her ominous words echoed throughout the room as she left.

"Ye'll hae to forgi' her," he said quietly, watching his cousin leave. "Ye're an easy target for her tae place blame upon and she has little else tae occupy her time, I'm afraid."

"Glad I can give her something productive to do." She rubbed the side of her head. Her skull was ringing but nothing more harmful than that. "What did that mean 'a day's work of my neck?'"

"Och, that," he scoffed, strolling farther into the room, hands clasped behind him. "Pay her nae mind."

"What does it mean?" she pressed.

"In essence, she was merely wishing ye tae the devil."

"Oh." She could live with that. While a part of her felt sorry for the woman, there was another part happy to wish her a cheerful journey down the same path. Uncharitable, perhaps, but so was cursing people and hitting them with books.

Artair's intense gaze rested on her until she shifted under its weight. As if sensing he was making her uncomfortable, he shifted his gaze, scanning the empty room. "Is Keir aboot?"

"No, he had business in Inverness. He said he'll be back for dinner."

He nodded. "I wanted tae discuss the eulogy wi' him. Make sure he approves of my words."

"The eulogy?"

"For Frang's funeral. Didn't he tell ye?"

He hadn't, but then he was remarkably reticent in speaking of his family. Though he was open and even verbose with his answers once asked directly, as she had the previous night, he never volunteered new information.

She hadn't decided if it was because he was a private person or if he just wasn't used to anyone showing interest in his personal life.

Over the past few days she'd begun to think it was the latter.

"When is it to be?"

"'Tis uncertain. We wanted tae postpone it until Father returned tae Dingwall, but since we've nae idea when that will be, I thought tae be prepared." He drew a roll of parchment from behind him and unrolled it. The large page was covered front and back in his tight, cramped handwriting.

It was going to be a hell of a eulogy.

"Would ye like tae hear it?"

"No," she said quickly. Too quickly. "I'm sure whatever you wrote will be perfect. Just perfect. I wouldn't mind hearing more about Frang though. Would you like to talk about him?"

His flat blue eyes lit with an inner light normally lacking in his gaze. "Ye're a fine woman, Miss Maines. Allorah. Ye show a true interest in people. 'Tis a rare quality. I find ye most amiable."

"Uh, thank you. You're very nice as well."

He rocked back on his heels, his eyes dropping to her toes before rising once more. "I've enjoyed our conversations verra much. Ye listen, truly listen when others speak. Yet ye ne'er speak aboot yerself."

"Well, I ca—"

"Frang was a serious man," he cut in.

Al grimaced. Perhaps she never spoke and appeared to be a great listener because he didn't stop talking long enough for her to get a word in edgewise. Ugh, she wasn't a fine woman at all to think such thoughts. But in her own defense, she wasn't used to socializing much either.

"He knew he was destined for the military from birth and took his occupation seriously. He fostered wi' the earl of Athol and 'twas his ranks he joined for the recent battle. Are ye sure ye dinnae want tae hear my eulogy?"

She should have stayed in her room, but no.

Al dropped down into one of the chairs and surrendered. "Sure. Go ahead."

He beamed down at her in approval. "As I said, ye're a fine woman, Allorah."

)(X)(X)(

"What's all this?"

Al's head shot up from where she'd been resting it—not at all snoozing—while Artair worked his way down the front page of the eulogy, pausing every now and then to make notes in the margin with a pencil. He'd even started over twice, after changing the wording of a sentence.

Even the old footman Archie's random but forgetful interruptions hadn't broken his flow.

Keir's arrival was her salvation. Heavenly deliverance framed in the doorway to the terrace like a sunlit god.

She wanted to run to him, throw herself at his feet. Sob her eternal gratitude into the pleated hem of his kilt.

"Ah, Keir," Artair glanced up from the paper. "Allorah was being kind enough tae go o'er Frang's eulogy wi' me since ye were nae aboot, but since ye're back, perhaps I should begin ag—"

"No!" She bit her lip. "I mean, I told you. It's just perfect. Really."

"But I hae nae e'en progressed past his childhood yet," he protested.

"Leave it, brother," Keir spoke up, striding toward them. He unbuckled his scabbard and tossed it on his desk along the way. "I'll read it o'er later."

"But I…" Artair sighed and walked over to put the parchment on Keir's desk. Moving the sword and scabbard to the side so that he could spread it over the center of the surface. He meant for it to be noticed, not forgotten. "Perhaps this evening, we can…"

Keir pinched the bridge of his nose. "Later, Artair. Please."

With a brisk nod, Artair shuffled to the door. Pausing, he looked back, his lips parting as if he meant to speak again but eventually, he disappeared through the opening.

"Thank you," she said. "You saved a life today."

"Yers or his?" he asked with a half smile, as if producing a whole one might take too much effort. "Allorah is it, now?"

She shrugged. "He's a mind of his own."

"Aye, he does."

A wave of concern washed over her. "Are you all right? You look tired."

"It's just been a long day."

"I'm sorry."

Acting on instinct, she rose and wrapped her arms around his waist, hugging him tightly. He hesitated only a second before wrapping his arms around her and holding her close. He buried his face in the crook of her neck and simply held her for a long while.

After a while, his arms relaxed somewhat and he shifted to loosen his hold enough to give her space to put her arms between them. She ran her hands up over his chest, marveling at his size and sculpted muscles. Up and up, until her arms were looped around his neck.

His hands ran up her back before tangling in her hair and drawing her head backward, forcing her to look up at him. Smiling invitingly, she complied, expecting him to take the kiss she had evaded last night.

He brushed the hair from her temple, tucking it behind her ear. "Ye're such a bonny lassie," he whispered, the gruff rumble sending a thrill down her spine. She wiggled closer.

She tightened her arms behind his neck encouragingly, but he didn't take the hint. Instead, he drew her back into his embrace, tucking her head beneath his chin.

Confused but not disappointed by his display of affection, Al lowered her arms to his waist. It had been a great many years since she'd been so well hugged. Most hugs were brief squeezes in greeting between friends. Some awkward like those she shared with her mother. Being lost in his arms was paradise.

With a sigh, she melted against him. His heartbeat was strong and steady beneath her cheek. "So what did you do today?"

"I went tae see if I might retrieve Frang's body from the mass graves there. Och, it was truly horrific, lass."

How awful! She tried to pull away to look at him but he only held her tighter. "Do you want to talk about it?"

"Nay." His chin brushed back and forth across the top of her head. "Nae now. I've other news as well. I've found us a witness who will attest tae the fact that Hugh was killed in battle on the Drumossie Muir by some unnamed Hanoverian redcoat."

Stiffening, she tore herself away and stared up at him in shock. "What?"

"It had tae be done, lass. There will ne'er be peace until he was put tae rest." He sighed heavily, dropping a kiss on the top of her head. There was a sadness in his voice Al hadn't heard in days. Another bout of mourning for the brother of his heart.

She was a piss poor substitute for an affection like that.

Chapter 17

"*Ouch!*"

"Sorry, lass." Keir peeked beneath the wadded handkerchief he was pressing to her arm, then pulled it away. "I think the bleeding has stopped. Ye shouldn't need tae be stitched."

Al twisted her arm and craned her neck to squint down at the bloody nick across her upper arm. It was still oozing slightly but didn't look too bad.

"I can't believe she came at me with a knife."

The fierce frown which had only just begun to fade from between his eyes returned with a vengeance, burying his narrowed eyes beneath his drawn brows.

"I'm ne'er imagined she would react so violently hearing the news. 'Twas meant tae ease the threat against ye. Nae intensify it."

His heart had stopped beating when Maeve had thrown herself at Al from across the drawing room. He'd gathered the family there together to hear of Hugh's death from the witness he'd bribed to deliver the news. He'd thought it the perfect solution, a way to end the animosity running so rampant in the castle. To douse the suspicion of servant and

137

cousin alike.

He'd flung himself into Maeve's path even before knowing she wielded a small dagger. But he'd been just a fraction of a second too late, succeeding in deflecting the weapon from its path to Al's heart at least. Despite his effort, the blade had sliced her arm right through the sleeve of her dress.

"Where is Archie wi' the cluidy bandages?"

"Probably halfway to China by now," she murmured under her breath. "Don't worry about it. It's just a little blood."

A little blood? The sight of her precious blood had nearly turned *him* into a madman. He'd flung his cousin away as if she were nothing more than a sack of barley. Caught her under his arm, when she shot forward again, intent on completing her task. Wrenching the knife from her so violently, he probably sprained her wrist.

Whether it was too many years living in the uncivilized wilds of the western isles or true madness afflicting her, he could no longer welcome his cousin in his home. It was only Al's plea which had stayed him from clapping Maeve in irons and sending her to the dungeon for a bit of her own medicine.

He wasn't feeling so kind. Two of his strongest, ergo youngest footmen had taken her away, to be locked in her rooms and guarded. On the morrow, Oran would accompany her home to the western isles. Gone from Dingwall, taking her threats with her.

That she would not be about to witness her own brother's funeral was no issue with him, but he'd have to speak with Maeve's husband about her troubling behavior. Her spells of madness were only getting worse since her son's death.

His witness had fled at the first sign of violence.

"Anyone else hae anything tae say on the matter?" He turned to his brothers, to Ceana who managed to appear mildly amused by it all considering she'd just had her brother's death confirmed and watched her sister attempt murder.

Oran and Artair shook their heads. His cousin tossed hers. "I might say that if you'd have provided Miss Maines with gowns more suitable to evening wear, she might have had better armor against the blade. Why, a quality silk properly pleated can—"

"Anything else?" he asked, cutting her off.

"I'll take Maeve tae Northton, Keir," Artair offered. "Oran needn't go. He's tae return to university soon."

"Nay, Artair. I need ye tae go on tae Rosebraugh, prepare for Hugh's funeral once we've had Frang's."

He nodded. "Will we wait for Father then?"

"Aye, we'll wait tae hear from Mathilde as well."

"She'll want tae hear this news," he pointed out.

"I will write her. If there's nothing else?"

It wasn't so much a question as a toll ringing to bring the discussion to an end. As one, the three of them exited the drawing room, leaving Keir and Al alone.

"You have a hell of a family, my friend," she said as he dropped down next to her.

"Al. Lass…"

How could he possibly apologize for such an appalling incident? He should have known Maeve was more unstable than he'd thought. They'd seen the signs of her madness growing over the past few months. She'd been volatile toward them all but saved her violence for Al.

"Thank you for saving my life."

"'Twas nothing."

Her tiny hand slid into his. "It was my life. And twice in one day, too. One more time and this might become a habit."

She offered a smile he wasn't quite yet willing to return.

"I wouldnae hae let her harm ye. On my own life." It was on the tip of his tongue to say something more but what exactly escaped him. Instead, he raised her hand, pressing it to his lips. Then to his cheek as he bowed his head.

"You're all worn out, Keir." Her sweet voice was soft with caring, as if her ordeal were somehow insignificant compared to a long day in the saddle. "Why don't you go to bed and get some rest?"

She truly didn't believe herself worth caring and effort. What kind of life was there in the future where one didn't know their own value?

"Nay, lass," he said, lifting his head. "I'll make sure ye're well abed 'ere I seek my own."

"Will you now?" A wicked innuendo laced the words.

Now she flirted with him? He shook his head and drew away. As if he could consider loveplay when she was injured.

"The bandage ye asked for, laddie," Archie grouched from the door, thrusting out a wad of gauze. After Keir took it from him, the old man shuffled away, grumbling and itching at his thigh.

Returning to the sofa, he folded a bit of the gauze into a square and replaced his bloodied handkerchief with it. Taking another length, he began to wind it around her arm.

Al sighed—in regret? In fatigue? "I don't suppose you have any bacitracin or an antiseptic laying around anywhere?"

Unfamiliar with the words, he only shook his head. "What do ye need, lass? Something for the pain?"

"No, it doesn't hurt too bad. I'm mostly worried about it becoming infected. I mean, who knows where that knife has been?"

"Ah." He retrieved a bottle of his best Scotch from the sideboard. Making another linen square, he doused it thoroughly and pressed it against the wound beneath her bandage.

A shudder ran through her wee body. Though she didn't make a sound, he felt her pain as if it were his own. Rewinding his work, he tied the outer bandage securely around her arm.

"I could kill her for this."

"Oh, pooh. You wouldn't hurt a fly," she responded with a short laugh.

She didn't know him at all. The rage that had swept through him would have ended with him snapping Maeve's neck if Al hadn't stayed his hand.

"I can't believe she tried to stab me," she repeated, softly now. He doubted she even knew she was expressing her disbelief aloud. "What a bitch."

Feeling the anger boiling up within him anew, he filled a tumbler with Scotch and downed it in one swallow to douse the violent rage. He refilled it then poured another for Al and held it out to her. "Tae heal ye from the inside as well."

She grimaced at the glass but didn't take it. "I don't drink hard liquor, but thanks."

"Why is that when I ken ye drink wine and plenty of it wi' dinner?"

"There's nothing wrong with a glass of wine or two, but that stuff... my stepfather..."

A vague memory nearly whisked away by the high emotion of that day in the dungeon returned to him. "Ah, aye. What did ye call him?"

"A mean drunk," she said, her voice clipped.

"That's it. Was he…?"

She snatched the drink from his hand and thanked him briskly. "I'll take it but only because I'm sure there aren't many other forms of painkillers handy."

"There's some laudanum aboot, if ye'd care for it."

A shudder ran through her body and she shook her head more vehemently than he thought the offer warranted. Just another question to put to her. Once she was in a better mood. Or if he ever managed to have an inquiry of a personal nature satisfied at all.

She sniffed the whiskey then sipped cautiously, wrinkling her nose so adorably a spark of humor returned to him. "I take it ye've ne'er been stabbed before?"

"I stepped on a nail once when I was ten," she said, taking another sip with only marginally less nose wrinkling. "My grandma had a farm with this creek running through it. She warned me I should have worn my shoes. Personally, I don't think it would have mattered. It punctured my foot all the way through. Eight stitches. Five on the bottom and three on top. How about you? Ever been stabbed?"

"Just once. A rapier through my side. Mother made nine stitches of it, I believe."

"Of course there were nine to my eight. So competitive," she teased. "What was it? A duel with an angry husband?"

"Nay, fencing lessons with Hugh," he said with a grin. Lifting the tail of his shirt, he pointed to the scar left behind. Felt her gaze on his exposed flesh like a physical caress. He dropped his shirt and fell into a chair across from her. "The tip fell off his blade. We dinnae notice until it was too late."

"Was he a better fencer than you?"

"Nay, only luckier."

"Geez," she said with a low chuckle. "You do arrogance better than anyone I've ever met."

He winked and they laughed together.

With another sip and a sigh, she kicked off her shoes and stretched out on the sofa, cradling her tumbler. "What is with your family, Keir? I'm beginning to think they're all half-cracked."

Another of her curious terms. There'd been so many over the past few days, he had half a mind to begin cataloguing them into a sort of dictionary of future terms.

"Half-cracked?"

"Nuts. Bat shit crazy," she said. "Maybe it runs in the family."

"Are ye implying I'm... er, half-cracked as well?"

A little giggle escaped her. She took another drink of her Scotch. Ah, the joys of a superb whiskey. The old Scots proverb said, alcohol does not solve any problem but then, neither does milk. Though it seemed to be working for his sweet Al just then.

"No, you're your own special brand of crazy." She pointed her tumbler at him. "The academic. The one who voluntarily cracks the spine of text books for the fun of it."

"Would yer own sanity nae be called intae question then as well?" he asked. She twirled a long lock of her hair around one finger. So distracting, he almost lost track of the conversation.

"Probably. But I don't mind. I think I would've been a professional student if I could."

"Professional student?"

She turned on her side to face him more fully. She hadn't rolled onto her injured arm, at least, though she did wince slightly at the movement. Tucking her arm beneath her cheek, she curled her feet under her skirts. In all his days, he'd never had a conversation with a woman at her leisure like this. It felt comfortable. Intimate.

Chapter 18

Relaxed by the Scotch, Al curled up on the sofa and smiled at him. There he went, poking into her personal life again. This time she didn't mind.

She nearly had her life taken away from her far more effectively than any mere wormhole could manage. Or even boredom. He'd saved her. She supposed he deserved some sort of reward for that.

"Yes. Most people I know hated school. I loved it. And would love to just stay in college forever. Go to medical school, law school, maybe. Study archeology. Oh, I've always wanted to study volcanology. That would be fun."

"Why dinnae ye?"

"It's incredibly expensive. That's why. And a girl's got to work." She sipped more of the now-excellent whiskey. "At least you've had the opportunity to study at will. Who knows, with all the research you've done and discoveries you've made, you might make the history books one day."

He shrugged modestly. "I dinnae need to make history tae ken my place in it, lass."

"What a lovely sentiment."

"Naught but the truth. What I do, I do for science but I

also do for myself. I could spend my life in learning. A professional student, as ye call it."

"And that's why most people would call you crazy. Or mad. Or whatever the phrase is here." She rolled her hand lazily, closing her eyes with a sigh.

"Ye should be abed and resting."

Al opened her eyes to find him standing over her, amusement and concern wrestling with one another for command of his expression.

"Come, let me help ye up tae yer room. Yer maid can bandage yer arm and put ye tae bed."

"I can do it myself."

"Aye, I ken ye can, ye stubborn lass."

"Why doesn't anyone here think a woman can do stuff by herself?" Her words were thickened by fatigue and alcohol. Her drink disappeared from her hand, a second later he put it on a table nearby. "Peigi doesn't even want me to bathe myself. Well, I won that one, I'll tell you."

He grinned down at her but didn't address her question. He was smart. She'd give him that.

"Up, lassie." He bent, slipping his arms beneath her and lifting her off the couch.

"Hey, I can walk, you know?"

Keir ignored her protest and carried her from the room, cradling her like a child. Except, for all her size, she wasn't one. And she'd never had a man carry her like this. Not even her father that she could remember. The feelings it aroused were not even a shade paternal either. His strong arms held her close against him. She looped one arm around his neck and cuddled closer, resting her cheek on his shoulder.

Running her hand over his bulging chest muscles, she inhaled his scent. He must have bathed before dinner.

Different than it had been earlier, he smelled of man but also mildly spicy. Still delicious.

He started up the stairs, his heart rate accelerating beneath her hand. His breathing increased as he took the steps two at a time. "You don't have to carry me all the way. I can—"

"Do it yerself. I ken."

"But it's three stories," she felt compelled to protest.

"Aye, three stories that would take an hour tae scale if ye were left to climb them yerself," he pointed out.

"I'm not drunk. Just tipsy."

"Cease yer protest."

She did. But only because she liked being held by him. And he didn't appear to be suffering under her weight too badly.

They reached her door but Keir didn't drop her there. Instead, he kicked the door open and strode right in.

And stopped.

)O(O(O(O(

He froze at the sight of the bed. Turned down.

Waiting.

He hadn't been thinking about what awaited him once he got Al to her room. Nay, all he could think of was unburdening himself of the warm, curvy body in his arms before he did something he'd regret.

Like take advantage of a tipsy, tired, and traumatized lass. What kind of animal would he be?

The rakish sort.

Och, he was such a fool. He should have never picked her up. The feel of her body so small and fragile in his arms should have evoked nothing more than the caring and concern that flooded him after Maeve's maniacal attack.

Instead, he'd felt every curve of her voluptuous form, from the swell of her breasts against his chest to her rounded hip rubbing dangerously close to his aching groin.

Rousing the passions he fought so hard to temper all week. But it wasn't only his body she roused. Holding her in his arms in the library earlier, it hadn't been mere desire but so much more. On his return from Inverness, he'd been able to think of nothing more than seeking her out.

Wearied by an emotional day, by the horrors of what he'd seen, he found relief in having her small body tucked close to him. It'd been an unusual moment for him. He'd felt a deep sense of perfection standing there. By rights, it should have alarmed him. But it had comforted him. Just as she had.

That was not to say he hadn't been aroused as well. Her arms laced around his neck, her breasts pressed against him, her hands caressing... it had been incredibly tempting.

Her lips were mere inches away, but still she hadn't taken the kiss.

Let her prove him a rake then. If she didn't soon act on the lust he knew full well simmered in her just as it did in him, Keir was going to take the choice from her and ravish her like the beast he was fast becoming.

But not now.

Now, though the lust that should have been there earlier raged through his body, he couldn't satisfy it. Not when she was injured, hurting because of the actions of one of his own. Not when she was made vulnerable by exhaustion and whiskey.

It would be another cold bath for him this day.

Just as soon as he set her on her feet. But while her legs fell when he slipped his arm from beneath her knees, Al clung to his shoulders. She just peered up at him with those dewy gray eyes. Those tempting pink lips parted. Begging.

But waiting.

Ever waiting.

"Aren't you going to kiss me, Keir?" she dared ask. "You said you were going to woo me with words *and* kisses."

"I dinnae recall," he bit out.

Grabbing her hands, he tugged them off his shoulders and stepped away before he caved to his body's persistent calling and showed her how thoroughly he longed to kiss her. She swayed on her feet and reached for him again.

Blast, of all the nights to fill a glass of whiskey to the brim! When he kissed her at last, he at least wanted her sensate enough to recall it as vividly as he would, not dulled by an alcoholic haze. And when he took her to that bed and made love to her at last, there'd be no bloody risk of her falling asleep halfway through it.

"I'll call Peigi for ye, lass," he said through clenched teeth, desperate to leave before his desperate longing overrode his sense of chivalry. "Get some sleep."

"You're a confusing man, Keir MacCoinnach," she said as he turned and walked out the door.

Nay, he was a bloody saint.

Chapter 19

The carriage jerked into motion, sending Maeve and Oran on their way.

Al watched from a window in the hallway on the second floor, having no desire to be within a book's length or knife's throw of the sad woman. Even though Keir stood on the front steps of the castle watching the carriage rumble down the lane.

She wanted to talk to him. Try to figure out what was holding him back for something surely was. Not that she'd dare to ask directly. No matter how bold he thought she was, she wasn't courageous enough for that. Maybe she could prepare some leading questions or related topic to segue into the subject.

Yes, she laughed inwardly. And simply hope he volunteered the information she was looking for on his own. She might be ignorant of most male ways, but she wasn't stupid.

He wanted her. He hadn't said it in so many words, but he had stated his intention to woo her. She hadn't misinterpreted the unspoken addendum 'into his bed,' had she? No, there was ample, and she did mean ample, evidence that he wanted her on a purely physical level if nothing else.

She didn't think she could have been any more clear that his wooing had paid off. She was available and ready to become his lover. So what was the problem?

What more indication did a rake need?

Unless she had been nothing more than a scientific case study all along.

A week ago, the thought would have cowed her into full retreat. She would have assumed the worst, slunk away, and licked her wounds. But Keir had sparked something in her as the days passed. A willingness to face confrontation without fear, to say what she wanted without worry of rejection or reprisal. To fight for something she wanted.

And she wanted him.

All of him.

And she was pretty damn certain he wanted her too, even if it was only for that one quick fuck.

"Congratulations, Miss Maines."

Al jumped at Ceana's murmured words so close to her ear. She hadn't even heard her come up behind her.

Turning on her heel, she found Ceana smiling at her ever so slyly in that way she had. Once again, she was dressed as if she expected to be called to court. Heavy satins, profuse quantities of lace. Those expansive panniers. Today her towering hair was even powdered and she wore a false, heart-shaped beauty mark at the corner of her mouth.

"Congratulations for what?" she asked, trying to calm the racing of her heart after such a start.

"Why for driving my dear, dear sister absolutely insane, of course," she drawled, flicking out a fan with the snap of her wrist. Peeking out the window, she wafted it slowly. "She was never quite like this before, you know? Angry, of course.

152

She's been forever angry since she wed Robert MacLeod. I would wager he either keeps a mistress and doesn't see to Maeve's needs properly or he beats her."

Were there no other options, she wondered? She was no psychologist, but it seemed to her Maeve was deeply depressed and lashing out rather than simply crazy or married to a bad person.

"She lost many a bairn, too, before Marcas was born."

Marcas must have been the one who'd died recently. But there had been more? Her annoyance with Maeve's behavior began the slide into sympathy.

"He was the only one to survive childhood. Sad really. I never had any children of my own but I'd think if I had, each one would have had the good sense to grow to adulthood." The fan stilled and Ceana stared down at her thoughtfully. "Have you any children, Miss Maines?"

"No, I've never been married," she pointed out. "Hence the *miss.*"

Ceana chuckled at that. "As if one needs a husband to bear a brat. But of course you've never wed. Your sense of style is deplorable. Ye'll never get a man dressing in those rags." She fingered the MacCoinnach tartan shawl Al had thrown over her plain dress. "Especially not one under this roof."

Not subtle, but she wasn't surprised. "I can assure you, I'm not looking for a husband. Under this roof or any other."

The fan began to wave once more. "Oh, la, Miss Maines! Don't sell yourself short. Why, I could dress you properly and take you to court. You could snap up a minor lord, perhaps even a baronet with the right tutoring."

"I'm good. Thanks."

"You're sure?" she asked. "After all, you can't expect to

stay at Dingwall forever."

Al couldn't help but roll her eyes. Most every conversation she'd had with Ceana—brief as they were—ended up in this direction. It was like being a teenager again with her mother and stepfather telling her she would never be pretty enough to get a boyfriend. Or smart enough to make up for it.

"I'm well aware."

"Even if my cousin is interested in keeping you around for now. For his particular amusement, I suppose."

There it was.

For a second she would have given anything for Ceana and Maeve to switch places. Either way, it felt as if there was a knife aiming for her back.

Was the whole family like this? Spiteful and mean? If they were, what kind of man had she helped set loose on Tacoma?

No, Hugh couldn't be like this. Even Keir's tolerance for such cattiness couldn't last long.

Turning away, she descended the stairs with Ceana's shrill laughter trailing behind her. She hated that she looked like she was running from the woman. Even though she was. Ceana was intolerable. It was either seek out Keir or return to the haven of her bedroom to avoid her.

One was far more pleasant than the other.

He'd disappeared into the castle after the carriage left. Seeking help in locating him, she followed Archie on a fruitless search. Briefly, she wondered if the old retainer even remembered who they were supposed to be watching for.

Surprisingly, they eventually found him in the dark-paneled study. Normally he preferred the brighter, bigger library. He sat at his desk, once more writing as if the hounds of hell were driving him. He'd shed his coat, his linen shirt straining across the broad width of his shoulders as he hunched over his work. His thick, untamed hair falling over his forehead before he shoved it back impatiently.

Her fingers itched to dive into the curly locks, comb them back so she could see his gorgeous face. Not that she would but she still hated to interrupt and tried to slip away unnoticed. Archie took it upon himself to announce her.

"Ye're up."

There was gladness in his eyes that warmed her but some surprise in his voice. Since it was almost noon, she had to wonder at it. "Of course, why wouldn't I be?"

"I only assumed ye'd need more rest following yer injury," he said, pushing back his chair and rising. As if she might need assistance. "Already ye're breathless from exertion."

Or maybe the sight of him, she wanted to counter. Would she ever be able to see him and not experience a rush of awe?

"I'm only breathless because I was in such a hurry to escape your cousin," she said.

"Hae I a need tae send Ceana away now as well?"

Oh, would he? She longed to say yes, but didn't want him to worry about her. "No, she's no threat, just annoying."

He waved her into the room and held out a chair near his at the desk, just as he'd done before. Gladly, she joined him.

"What is with her though? Maeve I get. At least a little, but even she is baffling."

"What aboot them?"

"For all Maeve's... *um*, let's call it *expressive* anger last night, she didn't seem all that sad about Hugh's supposed death. Angry. Righteous even, but not sad. And Ceana! There's no broken heart there. Not even crocodile tears. It's her brother. I don't get it."

"Are ye attached tae yer siblings, lass?"

"I don't have any."

He harrumphed, reclining in his chair. "Mayhap things are different in yer time. 'Struth, Ceana, Maeve, and e'en Mathilde hardly know Hugh. They are all older than he. Plus, he was fostered oot tae the MacDonald of Glendenning wi' me when we were only lads of eight years. By the time he was old enough tae be of interest tae them, they were married off and gone. Truly, they dinnae ken enough aboot him tae hae a caring for him."

"Yet, they were here," she pointed out.

"Aye. They were at Rosebraugh when the battle began, but both their husbands hae gone tae ground in hiding for their part in the battle lest they, too, suffer Cumberland's wrath."

"You're not in hiding."

"Nor will I be. I'm only recently returned tae Dingwall after years abroad. I had nae commanding position in the battle. Few probably e'en ken I was there," he said. "'Tis only my connection tae my father putting me at any risk."

"Maybe you should hide."

"I willnae. Should they come tae Dingwall, I will face them."

With such an answer brooking no argument, she revisited the previous subject. "So, why were Maeve and Ceana here instead of at Rosebraugh?"

"Wi' Hugh still missing, the unrest in the area, and their husbands in hiding, they sought protection wi' their nearest

156

male relative. As they should."

"You."

He shook his head. "Nay, my father. Wi' Hugh gone and nae other... "

Keir trailed off with a curse and she glanced up at him questioningly. "What? What is it?"

"Ah, bluidy fookin' hell."

"Keir?"

"I'm aboot tae be the next bluidy Duke of Ross."

Al's eyes widened. She scooted up on the edge of her seat. "You?"

"I feel the same skepticism," he said dryly, rubbing his hands over his face. "I wisnae cut oot to be a bluidy duke."

Poor Keir, he seemed overwhelmed by the realization. "You? Why you? Doesn't that whole primogeniture thing apply here? Sons, nephews, and all that?"

"Hugh wisnae married."

He pushed out of his chair and paced the shelves behind him before drawing out a thick book. A bible, she saw when he brought it back to the desk. He flipped through the first few pages to reveal a list of names. A family record, much as her grandmother used to keep.

His finger trailed over the record. "He had nae sons, nor any born on the wrong side of the blanket. Nor do any of Hugh's sisters hae a surviving male child. Maeve's lad is gone now. Ceana has nae children who made it past infancy."

Interesting. Hadn't Ceana just told her something indicating the opposite? Was it denial? Deception? Or had the loss of a child had as much an affect on Ceana as it had on Maeve, though with a difference in how it was expressed? How could it not? An unexpected wave of sympathy for them both washed over her.

"Mathilde has only lasses. My mother and Hugh's father had nae other siblings."

She could almost see the wheels working in his mind as he tried to find a way out of it. She couldn't blame him really. There was a wealth of responsibility that came with being a duke, she would imagine.

"The auld duke had only one brother who died 'ere he might wed. That leaves me as the oldest male grandchild of the auld duke." A single concise oath, then silence fell.

"Should I congratulate you, Your Grace? Curtsey?" she asked at length.

He stared at her in horror. "Dinnae do that! Are ye certain there is nae way for Hugh tae come back?"

"I've already explained that there isn't. I'm sorry."

"Ah, bluidy, bluidy hell! I dinnae want this any more than I anticipate taking on the earldom." He buried his head in his hands and tugged at his hair with his fists. His frustration obvious. "Och, I confess, that is the true reason I made haste tae discover my father's fate that day. I dinnae want tae be the earl. Nae yet. I've so much I still want tae do. Now this. An dukedom tae bear as well."

A rush of sympathy drove her from her perch. Dropping to her knees in front of him, she rubbed her hands up and down his thighs to comfort him.

"Oh, it won't be that bad, will it?" A piece of one of their many conversations leapt to mind. "Didn't you tell me Hugh had been all over Europe for the past few years?"

He lifted his head, brightening. "Aye. Rosebraugh has an excellent steward. 'Tis true."

"There you go." She beamed, happy to have been able to offer some actual consolation. Squeezing his knees, she leaned away to push herself up, but he put his hands on top of hers. Staying her.

"Thank ye, lass. I dinnae ken how I would hae borne these last days wi'oot yer company." Sincerity rang in every word. "Ye've been a bright light in an otherwise dark time of my life."

He leaned forward, his lips skimming lightly across her cheek until they rested on her temple.

"You're welcome."

With a heavy sigh, he released her and returned to the papers strewn across the desk. "Such a realization makes writing these all the more difficult."

"What are they?"

"Letters relaying the details of my cousin's death."

She winced and picked up one of the pages but after taking a moment to decipher his looping hand, saw that it spoke of Hugh's death in Paris. Not on the battlefield of Culloden. She asked him about it.

He shrugged. "Only a scant handful of men were aware of his return tae Scotland. Most of them died along wi' him. The others willnae argue a fine point such as this."

"But why?"

"Hugh ne'er publicly declared his politics," he explained. "Ne'er took a side. In truth, politics were of little interest to him. If I can keep his presence on the Jacobite field a secret, the name of the Duke of Ross willnae e'er be associated them."

She understood what he was getting at. "And the other side won't see him as a traitor or whatever."

"Precisely."

"And you? How will they see you?"

"I'm nae an overly political or religious man."

"Don't let Artair hear you say that."

His lips quirked. "I dinnae believe any king should rule merely because of how he expresses his faith in God," he told her. "This whole thing has become little more than a religious war."

"Really? That's not how I think history remembers it," she said with a frown.

"Och, it dinnae matter." Keir whisked the subject away with a flick of his fingers. "Catholic versus Protestant. Neither of our choices for king has overly impressed me. Like Hugh, I was smart enough tae ne'er voice an opinion on the matter."

"So his name will remain unsullied?"

"Aye. His name. And now mine." He dropped back in his chair. Al knew he was shaken more than he let on.

"Can I help?" she offered, trying to find a way to ease his burden. "I don't have the best handwriting, but I'll give it a shot if you want."

"Gladly, lass."

Retrieving another pen from the drawer, he spent a few minutes showing her how to use it and let the ink draw up inside of it. Her blotchy, ruinous attempts restored his ususal congenial humor.

"My grandma had one of these." She laughed. "Now I know why she kept it in a box and never used it."

"Ye mentioned her last night," he said, resuming his seat and taking up his pen. "Yer grandmother and her farm. Is she still alive?"

Constantly with the personal questions! But he'd had a bad morning and she didn't mind talking about her grandmother. So, Al obliged him. Sort of.

"You know, she hasn't even been born yet, right?"

"Ah, the time paradox ye spoke of." He grinned back

and tapped the base of his pen to his temple.

"To answer your question, no. She died when I was sixteen," she told him. "I loved her dearly. Loved being with her away... away from everything else. She encouraged me to read when—well, she always encouraged me. When I was a kid, I loved to go visit her. Her farm was my happy place."

"What did she raise?"

"Oh, it hadn't been a working farm since my grandfather was a little boy," she corrected, concentrating more on her writing and trying to make it look as nice as his. Handwriting was a lost art. "But she had a bunch of cats living under the deck and an old horse out back."

"Where was this farm? In your colonies?"

Al rolled her eyes dramatically. "The United States. That's what it will be called once they gain their independence from England in oh, about thirty more years. No more king."

He nodded in approval. "More power tae them."

He asked her what had prompted their revolution and happy with the change of subject, she told him.

Though they were interrupted twice by the absentminded Archie who ended up with nothing to say either time, the afternoon passed quickly.

Chapter 20

"What is that?" Al swallowed the bit of toast she'd been munching on for her breakfast late the next morning. Peigi was laying out a heavy-looking black dress for her to wear. Nothing like the light-weight linen dresses she had been wearing over the last couple days. It looked wholly uncomfortable... and hot.

"Master Keir... I mean, His Grace, asks that ye wear it, miss. A surprise, he said."

Yes, he was full of those.

Peigi's eyes were wide with anticipation. "Ye'll look lovely in it, I think. Yer hair will shine against the black."

"I'm sure one of the normal dresses will be fine no matter what we do, won't they? It's been awfully warm lately." The past couple days had been warm for the end of April. She'd been hot even in the lighter dresses simply because of the corset and all the other layers that accompanied them. She'd die of heat-stroke in this one.

"He did ask that ye wear it, miss," Peigi urged once more.

"Don't worry, Peigi," Al assured her. "I won't let him blame you, but there's no way I'm putting that one on today.

I want the thinnest one we've got, with the shortest sleeves and the fewest layers."

The maid giggled as she listed off her criteria.

"And I'd like my hair up and off my neck today, too."

She generally wore her long hair up in a ponytail or messy bun. While there were ribbons aplenty, they tended to slide right off her silky hair when she tried to tie it back or braid it. There was nothing else for her to use but combs or the stiff wooden bobby pins available now. Frustrated, she'd given it up after just a single attempt to do it herself.

"If you don't mind helping me again, that is?"

"Nay, miss. I'm happy tae help ye wi' it e'ery day. I told ye, 'tis my job tae assist ye."

Wincing at the reminder, Al just nodded. She'd never had help taking care of herself, not even from her mother, since she was five. It was more difficult than she thought, accepting it now. "Thank you."

Forsaking even the corset and drawers she was slowly becoming accustomed to given how warm it already was, Al opted in favor of her own bra and panties. Covering them in a linen shift, she allowed Peigi to help her dress in a light linen dress of periwinkle blue with a simple ivory underskirt and only one petticoat. Though she knew her best hope of a life here without regrets meant embracing all it entailed, there were just some things the future did better. Undergarments was one of those things. The assumption that she could dress herself was another, but the maid was just too earnest and kind to deny.

After Peigi announced her perfectly respectable, Al dropped down on the vanity bench and let Peigi brush out her hair. Trying not to squirm impatiently as she braided and twisted and pinned the long locks until they were all up and off her neck as promised.

"Ye will tell the master I did insist upon the black?"

"I will," Al said, patting the girl's hand assuredly. "He won't blame anyone but me, I promise."

Peigi relaxed, her usual smile returning to grace her round face. Bringing over a wide-brimmed but flat straw hat, she placed it at a flattering angle over Al's hair-do and pinned it securely. "I'm tae tell ye, also, Ma—His Grace requests that ye join him in the front hall as soon as ye're ready."

"The front hall?"

The maid beamed at her. "Aye, miss."

"We're going out?"

)()()()(

"Ye're nae dressed tae go oot," Keir said with a frown when she reached the front hall.

In contrast to the past several days when he wore little more than a simple linen shirt and a kilt, later adding a jacket and waistcoat for meals, Keir was once again dressed much as he'd been that first day she'd met him in the library. This time in a jacket of navy blue with a striped waistcoat beneath it. He wore a neckcloth tied in an intricate knot at the base of his throat and his thick black hair was once more bound at his nape. The only exception was instead of wearing stockings and shoes, he wore his shiny black knee boots and carried a tricorn hat tucked beneath his arm.

He did indeed appear ready to go out.

"I couldn't wear that heavy thing," she said. "It's just too hot outside and even in here for that. Please don't blame Peigi. She tried."

"That *thing* was a riding habit. I planned on us traveling today," he told her.

"Traveling on horseback?" she asked, lifting her brows in

165

surprise.

He nodded crisply to one of the younger footman hovering nearby and spoke to him in rapid Gaelic. He ran off eagerly to do his master's bidding.

"Let me guess," he said after the man was gone. "Ye dinnae ride."

"I've never been on a horse in my life."

"Never?" he asked, offering his arm and leading her outside while Archie held the door open for them. The sun was already beating down on them, bouncing off the stone of the castle for enhanced solar effect.

He might not have approved of her choice of dresses, but she was glad for the lighter gown. Though she didn't think he really minded much. He'd watched her entire descent of the stairs with hungry, hooded eyes. Though she'd never been much of a lace gal and sometimes felt silly in the overly decorative dresses Peigi plied her with, the way he watched her when she was dressed up made her feel beautiful. And wanted.

"Nae even the one on yer grandmother's farm?"

"What? Oh, no. Especially not that one."

Awaiting them were two saddled horses. One, the evil thing of Keir's who she was so well-acquainted with. The other, dainty and brown, impatiently shaking out its long blondish mane.

"I picked her just for ye," he said. "She's mild of temper, I promise ye. Ye dinnae want tae gi' it a try?"

"I don't know." Al tweaked at her earlobe and gnawed on her lip. She looked fairly nice. But... "Maybe. Someday."

With a low chuckle, he stroked his horse's head, scratching it affectionately behind the ears. "How do ye travel then?"

"You don't really want me to go there, do you?"

But he did, she could see it. As usual, his curiosity was limitless, his desire to learn everything about her time attractive in its own right.

"Well, I can give you the long or short version. How long do we have?"

As she spoke, a black carriage pulled by four bay horses came around the corner of the castle and stopped in front of them. A groom rushed forward to lead the two saddled mounts away.

Keir opened the door and turned back to her with a broad grin. "It seems we'll hae all day."

"Great," she drawled unenthusiastically, grimacing as she squinted up into the closed interior.

Archie shuffled forward to help her climb into the creaking contraption. She thanked him but he just clucked his tongue and shut the door on her.

Keir reopened it and grinned up at her. "Do ye suppose he thought I wisnae going wi' ye?"

"Going where exactly?"

"'Tis a surprise."

"You and your surprises. I think you're doing this just to have a captive audience," she grumbled.

"We might hae had a enjoyable day on horseback."

"Don't be a pain in my ass."

His laughter echoed off the carriage walls as he climbed in and sat opposite her, tossing his hat to the side. "Grieg," he called out the window at the footman as he returned. "Dinnae forget tae hae Peigi be on her way after us wi'in the hour."

"Aye, sir."

"Why that sneaky bitch," she sighed.

"Bitch? Och, lass, if Peigi has been anything other than polite wi' ye, I'll hae her replaced immediately."

"No! No, it's just that she knew about this all along. She should have said something."

"But I told her nae tae," he said. "I wanted it tae be a..."

"A surprise. I know." She glanced out the small window as the carriage jerked into motion. The sun was already high in the sky. Those little windows didn't look like they'd provide any sort of real air flow. "Did it ever occur to you that I don't like surprises?"

"'Tis only fair, wee lassie, that I hae a share of them for ye when ye provide me wi' so many every day."

"I can't wait to tell you about the space shuttle," she murmured under her breath. "There's a surprise for you."

"So, tell me aboot yer modes of travel," he said, settling in his seat and lifting one leg so that his ankle rested comfortably on his knee.

"I should deny you the pleasure until you tell me where we're going."

He nodded thoughtfully. "Do as ye will, lass. We can pass the hours instead wi' me showing ye another way for a man and his lady tae while away the time in a closed carriage such as this."

She colored at the innuendo. "I think you'd die from shock if I took you up on that."

"From pleasure, lass. From pure pleasure. I can easily imagine how the day might pass." He raked his warm gaze down her body. A shot of pure desire sent shivers down the same path. His eyes traveled up once more, and when he spoke, his voice had lowered in timber. "'Twould be a most agreeable time indeed. Would ye like me tae elaborate?"

Her eyes widened. She'd hadn't thought he would

continue to pursue this. No, she imagined he would tempt and retreat just as he had been doing for the past few days. A little verbal allusion here, a stray touch or caress there. But that was it.

Could he tell she was tired of denying the attraction between them? That she wanted so much more?

No matter the consequences?

"I'd hae tae move o'er there wi' ye, of course," he went on quietly as if she'd provided some sort of affirmation. "Tae be next tae ye, tae feel the press of yer body alongside mine.

"Then..." His eyes took her in her from top to bottom once more, full of appreciation, desire. Her breathing became shallow, as if she might not hear him if she took too deep a breath. "I'd caress yer cheek and turn yer face up tae time. I remember the feel of yer lips just beneath mine that night on the turret. Just a hairsbreadth away. I wanted tae kiss ye then. More than anything."

"But you didn't."

"Nay, I wanted ye tae want it as much as I."

"I did," she confessed.

"Yet ye stepped away," he reminded her, his eyes held hers.

"Once," she said defensively. "You stopped it several times."

He shifted, one hand coming to rest casually on his leg. His fingers tapped out a rhythm, then repeated it, before spreading out over his thigh.

"Nay, lass. I merely waited for ye tae begin."

Finally she understood. She considered throwing herself at him now, but he leaned back and continued.

"But I digress, where was I? Aye, I was aboot tae kiss ye. I've imagined the ways it might begin. Imagined even more aboot how it might end. 'Struth, I find it hard tae believe I've nae done so yet. But if I were tae come o'er there now, if we were tae nae speak of travel and whatnot, I would take the kiss I've waited for. Aye, take it. I would wait for ye nae longer, lass. I would take yer lips and make them mine. I imagine the feel of them, soft beneath mine. The taste of them. Sweet and heady. I'd explore them wi' my tongue. My teeth. But 'twould nae be all my pleasure, lass. Ye'd hae the taste of mine as well upon yer sweet lips. Kisses taken but given. I want tae feel yer tongue against mine. Kiss ye again and again until ye're moaning yer pleasure, begging for more."

Just the words slowly rolling off his tongue in that deep Scottish brogue were enough to draw the moan from her. Al bit it back, her head swimming dizzily. She'd never heard anything so sexy, been talked to so bluntly.

He shifted restlessly, leaning forward with his elbows on his knees until he was but a foot away. His hands inches from hers. His gravelly voice grew softer.

"Whilst I was kissing ye, I'd make the most of yer distraction and touch ye as I long tae. The sweet curve of yer neck, yer shoulder. Yer dress might slip off under my fingers so I might touch more of ye. Here." He gestured to a spot on his chest. Across and down the center. "Here. I'd ken at last the silkiness of yer flesh. Further down, I might slip my hand tae cup yer sweet breast. Feel its bonny weight in my palm. Or perhaps I'd forgo that pleasure for now in favor of what lies below yer skirts. I'd slip my hand up yer skirts once more. Ye've fine legs, lass. Long and strong. I'd love tae hae them wrapped around me one day. I want tae be between them."

A shudder shook her from head to toe at his confession. Her heart pounding like a drum in her chest. Still, he hadn't even touched her! What could he do to her if he did?

Whether it was because of him or the heat of the day, a light sheen of perspiration had broken out all over her body. Prickling at her skin. Beading between her breasts. She was pulsing with need and want, intensifying between her thighs.

Unpinning her hat, she fanned her face with the wide brim, hoping for some relief.

"'Tis nae a verra big carriage though. I couldnae lay ye down and hae my way wi' ye as I might like," he carried on, but his breath was heavy now as well. His eyes as dark as a stormy night and just as tumultuous. "Mayhap I could lift yer skirts away and pull ye o'er me so ye could ride me. Mayhap I'd save that for another day and merely drop down into this wee space between us and discover what's beneath them more intimately."

Gently, he pushed her knees apart and slid off the seat until he was between them. Her hat ceased waving, forgotten. He stared up at her as if she were a goddess and in that moment, Al knew what it truly felt like to be beautiful. His hands encircled her ankles, sliding slowly upward until her skirt was resting across her knees.

"If I touched ye, would ye be wet for me, lass?" Clearly he didn't expect an answer which was a good thing because she wasn't sure if she could have voiced one. She stared down at him helplessly, speechless. "Would ye be hot and tight around my finger? If I caressed ye wi' my mouth, my tongue, would ye scream for me?"

"Oh, God," she moaned aloud, unable to control herself any longer. She was all those things and more. Her heart was pounding so fast, she thought she might faint.

Lifting her hand, she ran trembling fingers along his temple and into his hair, loosening it from its confines until it was once again the unruly mass she adored. Her other hand stroked his jaw, his neck.

"Keir."

He took her hand, pressing a kiss to her palm. "Those are the things I would do o'er the course of a long carriage ride. Unless ye'd rather talk aboot travel instead."

Despite the state she was in and the arousal he seemed to share, she was suddenly uncertain which one of those he would honestly prefer. That was rich! But she wasn't sure he didn't want to hear about cars and planes and spaceships more.

"I guess I would say we can do whatever will make you happier," she said ambiguously.

A smile so broad, a dimple appeared on his cheek blossomed on his face, his blue eyes suddenly alight with roguish satisfaction. He was so beautiful, the sight tore at her heart.

"Excellent choice."

He levered himself off the floor and for a fraction of a second, she feared he meant to resume his place opposite her and ask his questions. Disappointment pierced her but quickly faded when Keir pulled down the shades on each of the windows and shifted to sit beside her.

Yes, pressed so close she could feel the heat radiating off his massive body.

He took her hat and tossed it on to the other seat next to his. Tilting her head back as promised, he caressed her jaw with the pad of his thumb as he looked down at her.

"Ye made a fine choice, lass. I was afraid ye might nae." His hot eyes searched her face, settling fleetingly on her lips before lifting to meet her eyes once more. "I've contemplated so many ways I might kiss ye, I hardly ken where tae begin."

"The lips?" she suggested a little hoarsely.

He chuckled. "The lips then."

Al held her breath in anticipation as he lowered his lips to hers. They were soft but firm, brushing lightly over her mouth. Tasting her before he settled in, kissing her more deeply. With a moan of satisfaction, she melted against him as the fireworks flared more brilliantly than she'd ever imagined.

Breaking the kiss, he glanced down at her with a grin.

"Ah, definitely the lips."

Definitely.

Parting her lips as his returned to hers, she quivered in delight as his tongue plundered her mouth, teasing, tempting. Just when she thought it couldn't get any better, it did. He retreated and advanced, nuzzled and nipped at her lips until she was awash with wanting, alternately sighing in pleasure and moaning, craving more.

ANGELINE FORTIN

174

Chapter 21

The carriage slowed and Keir brushed his lips across hers one last time before lifting his head. Eyes still closed, she sighed softly. The wanton hum of pleasure and desire stirred him even more, bolstering the already painful arousal that had been his constant companion for more than an hour. His body screamed for release. He yearned for nothing more than to bury himself deep inside Al's luscious body, to spend himself in her hot sheath.

Or at least urge her petite hand to provide the satisfaction he needed so desperately. He did none of those things, though he had fully intended to.

No, he'd known straightaway after taking her lips with his, she had either never been kissed, or at least, had never been kissed properly. Though there was no hesitation on her part, no surprise when he progressed more thoroughly into the task, she employed none of the skill one might when practiced in the art.

His astonishment that the men of her time hadn't seen to it that she'd been well-tutored returned. She was of an age where she should have been kissed, and often.

Nevertheless, it had been his pleasure to be the one to

teach her the true potential of the kiss. To be the first to coax her, guide her to such a level of rapture that she was only now fluttering open her silvery eyes to stare up at him in wonder and with unguarded desire.

Her full lips swollen and red, wet with his kisses. The sight of her tongue sweeping over them as if she might have one last taste of him, tightened his groin painfully.

By God, but he must have her! Though how could he conscionably seduce her into his bed when she was clearly a novice at such loveplay? When what she needed was a slow, thorough schooling on the matter. An experience demonstrating the finest nuances of what two bodies might achieve together.

He didn't know the extent of her experience—in truth, he didn't want to know the details—but again she was old enough that she might have taken a lover or two. If she had been as clumsily introduced to lovemaking as she had been to kissing, he'd find himself hard put not to find a way to travel to her time and pummel the life out of the man or men who'd denied her the proper appreciation.

Keir intended to be the one to show it to her. But for all his jesting, a carriage wasn't the place to do it properly. So, he kept his hands to himself, though the temptation to do more was almost beyond his control.

Easing away, he adjusted his breeches before drawing the curtains and peeking outside.

"Are we stopping?" she asked. "Are we there already? Wherever it is we're going?"

A purely masculine surge of smugness ran through him as she peered dazedly through the windows to the left and right. She hadn't a clue the time that had past.

He had done that to her.

He fully intended to do it again, with an even grander conclusion.

XOXOXOX

Al blushed under his knowing gaze and fidgeted in her seat, straightening her dress and skirts. A pointless endeavor as not an inch of it was askew or a single tie undone but she had to do something to hide her embarrassment.

Except it wasn't truly embarrassment. Rather it was something more akin to awe. For all the books she'd read, she'd never realized how thoroughly one could be kissed. How it might be ever-changing, inducing shivers of delight under the skillful touch of his lips one moment. Lifting her to electrifying heights of euphoria with the passionate stroke of his tongue in the next. Tempting her into the burning depths of pure lust until she practically begged him for more.

"Are we there?" she repeated, clearing her throat when her voice emerged husky with wanting.

"Nay, tis just a stop in Cullicudden tae rest the horses and provide us a change to refresh ourselves." He opened the door and leapt out, turning to help her down. She took the stairs slowly, hoping her knees wouldn't give way.

A crisp breeze caressed her hot skin, cooling away the uncomfortable warmth caused by the closed carriage and the more enjoyable warmth he had infused her with. She lifted her face to it with a sigh of relief and wished she might lift her skirts high for a better all-over effect. Instead, she studied around her surroundings.

They were in a bustling, small town, she saw. Or a village, anyway. People filled streets lined with short buildings, most not more than two stories. More were walking on the streets rather than any sidewalks. Some more leisurely, others carrying packages, some looked far to heavy to lift. Others pushed handcarts full of vegetables or other goods.

There were a number of armed, red-coated soldiers walking the streets as well. "What are they doing here?"

"Cumberland has troops and militia patrolling all o'er these parts. Guarding passes tae the north, warships guarding the coasts," he told her grimly. "Despite the defeat at Culloden, as ye call it, the rebellion was closer tae success than the king e'er imagined. He'll nae risk it happening again."

Al eyed the street, taking it all in. Real 18th century life. It took her a minute to realize what was missing. "Everyone's walking."

He glanced around over her head. "Aye, how else do ye expect them to get aboot?"

"I don't know. I guess I always thought there'd be lots of horses and wagons."

He looked down at her with that gleam in his eye telling her he was anxious to hear more. "Livestock is expensive tae keep. But e'en those who hae a horse or cart wouldnae use them aboot town."

"Why not?"

"'Twould take more time tae fetch the horse from pasture or from the livery and see it harnessed or saddled than the effort to walk," he said. "I take it that isnae the case where ye're from?"

She could see the conversation on travel methods that had been put aside in favor of a thorough round of kissing hadn't been forgotten.

"I've a private dining room reserved for us inside. We can talk more there." He pointed to an inn marked by the curious signage *Pig and Whistle*. "I've a room as well."

"A room?" she asked, casting him a saucy smile as he took her hand and led the way. "What for? Something rakish, I presume?"

She couldn't believe she was being so forward. This wasn't the light flirtation they'd been toying with all week. He'd driven her to the very fringe of release. She was eager to see what came next.

He only grinned down at her, squeezing her hand. "I would ne'er presume so much."

What? She was practically propositioning him. For a rake, he was slow on the uptake. He'd better catch on soon or she'd lose her nerve.

"You could share it with me, if you wanted to."

Licking her lips nervously, she watched as his gaze darkened. He knew full well what she saying. Offering.

He shook his head slowly. "Much tae my regret, lass, we hae nae the time tae employ it in any other way, nae matter how titillating the possibility. Nay, the room is for ye tae attend tae yer personal needs."

"What? Oh." The subject thoroughly changed, Al flushed and glanced away.

"Yer mortification o'er the most basic bodily needs is intriguing. I shall add it tae my list and perhaps one day ye shall explain tae me why 'tis so."

"Ha, I doubt it," she huffed.

With a grin, Keir opened the door and waved her inside. It was quieter here, dark just as she imagined a Scottish pub might be. Warm also, though windows had been opened to allow for some air flow. What she wouldn't give for an A/C.

After a word with the innkeeper, who'd rushed forward to greet them, he waved her off with a maid. She led Al up a narrow flight of stairs and into a private room. A few minutes later, another maid arrived with a pitcher of warm water and offered her assistance in undressing. Curious as to why she might need to undress to see to her 'needs,' she found she was being given the chance for a quick sponge bath to wash away the grime of travel.

As hot as she still was, she agreed, even accepting the maid's help without one modest blush so she might keep Keir from waiting too long.

Keir.

She shivered, not from the water trickling across her arms but from the memory of his kiss fresh in her mind and on her lips. He played her like a fiddle suddenly strung taught after being out of tune for too many years.

Adrift in his strong embrace, she would have been his most willing instrument. Her body ached to sing for him.

There was no doubt in her mind that he knew it well. Therefore, it surprised her that he'd tried nothing more, but merely carried on hungrily kissing her as if he couldn't get enough of the taste of her.

She supposed she was fine with that. For now. His kiss was pure delight. If the rest of it were to exceed her wildest dreams as well, she had much to look forward to.

Refreshed, redressed, and almost skipping in anticipation, she found Keir in a private dining room. His back was to her as he sipped wine and read from a folded sheaf of paper. Peeking over his shoulder, she saw that it was a newspaper though it lacked commanding headlines or colorful pictures.

"What are you reading?" she bent to whisper in his ear.

He didn't jump but turned his head to kiss her lightly. "My thoughts are so focused on ye, I couldnae read a word."

He folded up the paper, tossing it aside, and stood to

hold out a chair for her. His finger trailed down her nape when he pushed her in before returning to his own seat. The table was filled already with plates of bread, cheese, and meat pies so aromatic her stomach was quick to remind her of her paltry breakfast hours past.

"What were you thinking about?" she prompted, serving herself from the platters. Keir poured her wine and filled his own plate, but she could feel his eyes on her the whole while. Warm and assessing, like a physical touch, it had her skin tingling once again. "Something good, I hope?"

"Thoughts of ye are always pleasant." The quick response brought a smile to her lips. "My imagination regarding the future of travel hae been most diverting."

She pursed her lips, feeling a stab of self-deprecation. She kept having to remind herself that for all his gratifying attention to her person, his true fascination was for the glimpse into the future she provided him.

"Ye dinnae ride horses," he said, unaware of her disillusionment as he looked away and dug into his food. "Why is that? Has the animal population been depleted in some way?"

"No." She sighed in resignation and cut into her pie. "There are still horses and people do ride them, for sport and pleasure mostly. In about a hundred years, cars will be invented. Picture a horseless carriage. That's what they first called them. A carriage propelled by a machine, an engine."

"An engine? How did it work? Was it steam powered?"

Leave it to Keir. It was never enough for him to just know what would happen or what would change. He wanted to know *how* it worked, who had invented it. In many cases, he wanted her to draw out a schematic for the internal workings of machines she had limited or superficial exposure to. He couldn't quite accept there were things she didn't know about. It flattered her that he gave her so much credit.

Frustrating that all their conversations constantly returned to what knowledge she had to impart. That endless, insatiable thirst for more was maddening, infuriating…

Oh, she sighed. Who was she kidding? She was just the same, her entire life dedicated on wanting to know more. For all it rankled her that his keen interest in the discovery of knowledge put his more intimate interest in her person on the back burner, it was also one of the things she loved about him.

Al froze with her fork hovering at her lips. No, she had not just thought that.

"Lass? Al?"

Blinking, she shifted her eyes to his, holding her utensil aloft. "*Hmm?*"

"Are ye well? Ye look a wee bit pale."

His concern was obvious and another wave of affection swept over her but she forced it aside. "I'm fine. It's just warm in here. So, no. Though there were some early models with steam engines, most were internal combustion engines…"

Prattling on through the rest of their meal, only half her attention was on him as she struggled with the possibility of her revelation versus the probability that it was merely a slip of the subconscious.

She loved that *about* him. It didn't mean anything or imply anything grander than that. Her cat, Mr. Darcy, had a kittenish weakness for a laser pointer and she loved that about him. Albert Einstein wore fuzzy slippers and she loved that about him.

It was just a saying. Nothing more.

So all-encompassing was the inner debate, she might have been reciting her grandmother's chocolate chip cookie recipe for all the notice she gave to the words pouring from her mouth.

Chapter 22

A taste of her lips and it was as if he'd opened Pandora's Box. Releasing not the evils of the world, but opening a floodgate to the lust he'd been holding at bay these last days. Once opened, it was impossible to rein either back in.

For nearly an hour, he'd stared blankly at the latest newssheet imagining her in the room above with a large comfortable bed close at hand. The fresh, clean scent of her when she nuzzled so close to his ear... He'd been tempted to drag her onto his lap and have his wicked way with her. Thankfully, he'd managed to introduce a subject suitable for conversation while he forced his meal down his throat.

He'd have to find a way to reintroduce the topic one day as he hadn't absorbed a word of what she said. And he did want to know.

It was a good thing he'd had his driver take down the top of the carriage while they were dining. For her comfort, he'd told her in response to her curious gaze when he'd handed her up.

Though she'd assured him he hadn't needed to go to such troubles, Keir knew the opposite was true.

Chivalrous intentions might have stayed his hand for a

couple hours but they weren't dependable enough to keep him from touching her for the several more remaining in their journey. Propriety might provide him the strength of will he needed but only just.

Another turn in the privacy of a closed carriage would have provided more temptation than he could fight. He'd be damned if he'd treat any ears beyond his own to the sweet song of her impassioned cries.

And he meant to wring a bloody aria from her once he could get her alone.

XOXOXOX

"Rosebraugh, I presume?"

"Where else?"

"When you said a days' ride, I thought you meant a whole day," she said without taking her eyes off the majestic castle rising before them. "It's lovely."

The view the entire way from Cullicudden had been. Though Al had been initially dismayed to find the open carriage awaiting them, her displeasure was quickly set aside in favor of the stunning scenery she absorbed along the way.

As they rambled onward, she realized what she had told Artair was true, beyond Dingwall Castle and a brief upended contemplation of the moors outside Culloden, she hadn't seen anything of the country since her arrival. She'd always wanted to visit Scotland. To see if it was as magical in person as it was described in books.

The bright green landscape dotted with wide fields of yellow dillseed and the occasional thatched cottage didn't disappoint. Against the deep blue sky, the view stole her breath. Shortly after leaving Cullicudden, the land gave way to the shimmering waters of the Cromarty Firth on her left. It was narrow at first with Ben Wyvis on the other side. From a distance, the mountain was long and low, shaded in purple and darker greens. The terrain soon tamed to rolling hills, hazy against the afternoon sky as they progressed. The firth grew wider and wider still. But for one lone, squat castle tower along the shore, there was nothing to obscure the spectacular vista. Though they were passed at one point by a small band of redcoat soldiers.

The afternoon sun pounded down on them, making her glad for the wide brim of her hat to shade her pale skin. It was hot for April and, she gathered, Scotland in general. But where the interior of the closed carriage had been stifling before, she appreciated the cool breezes wafting in from the firth. It made the heat more bearable but she was still hot and sticky under her many layers.

The carriage turned away from the shoreline but while it remained in view, another body of water came into sight on the right. The Moray Firth, Keir explained.

Then Rosebraugh, just as captivating as he had said. It sat on the spit of land close to the southern shore where the two bodies of water met. Appearing through the haze of the hot afternoon like a mirage. The sight took Al's breath away and she was instantly enchanted.

But the heavenly looking water beyond was what drew and kept her attention. Sunlight danced off the gently lapping surface like nymphs tempting her to join them. As hot as she was, she desperately wanted to. The closer they got to the castle, the louder it called to her. The gates to Rosebraugh were just yards away. As ornate as they were, they didn't seem near as welcoming.

"Is there a beach on the firth?"

"Aye. Why?"

"Could I walk down there?"

"I suppose. But 'tis a bit of a climb and the day is uncomfortably warm."

"Yes, but the water looks so inviting."

"Invit…" He trailed off with a grin as the anticipation in her voice clued him in, and then called for his coachman to halt the carriage. He leapt down before it came to a stop and held his arms up to her. "So, ye fancy a swim, do ye?"

Al nodded eagerly and fell into his arms. "You don't have to come with me. I can go by myself. I'm sure you have business waiting for you there."

Yes, it made sense now that he would need to visit Rosebraugh after the revelation of the previous day. "And you did say back in town that we were in a hurry."

"Honestly, I'm in nae more hurry today tae be a duke than I was yesterday," he said. "Also, I'm overheated myself. It can wait an hour more."

They why couldn't it have waited before?

Before she could ask, he waved the carriage on and clasped her hand, tugging her forward. Soon they were all but running for the edge of the cliff side overlooking the Moray Firth. Then it became a race. Laughing breathlessly, she scrambled down the steep hill without incident. The lure of cool water was all she needed.

They reached the bottom and Keir shot her a wicked grin before he was running toward the surf, throwing off his jacket and vest as he sprinted. She was close on his heels though she reached the water's edge still fully clad while he wore nothing above the waist and was already kicking off his boots.

She was struggling with her ties when he stepped into the water. "Hey! What about me?"

He looked back at her, his roguish brow lifted. "I

anticipated the merest glimpse of yer ankles, lass. Do ye intend tae do more than lift yer skirts and wade to yer calves like a lady?"

"Would there be anyone around to see? Beside you, I mean?"

"Nay, this entire end of the peninsula is owned by the dukedom."

"Then absolutely," she retorted, laughing with him as he spun her around to loosen the laces of her dress. Within seconds, her bodice drooped forward. She admired his rakish skills and told him so. He took no offense this time but merely grinned wickedly and unbuttoned the front flap of his trousers.

Blushing hotly, she turned her back. She dropped her dress and untied her petticoat, but clung to both. Getting naked in front of a man was as far beyond her normal comfort zone as having one get naked in front of her was.

The lure of the water was stronger than her modesty, it seemed. Or was it Keir who made her so daring? He'd already proven that he could. She let the garments fall to the sand and stepped out of them.

A splash sounded behind her and she spun around just as he emerged from the water, shaking his head so that drops of water flew into the air, sparkling in the sunlight.

Working faster, she toed off her shoes and unrolled her hose, cursing whomever had decided women had to wear so many clothes.

"Join me," he called, splashing water at her as he strode closer.

Not naked, as she'd thought, his linen drawers hung low across his hips. The sight of that dark hair sprinkled across his broad chest then narrowing over his rippled abs stole her breath. Her gaze followed it down, down before it disappeared into the wet, clinging garment. The way it hugged *every* inch of him might have been even more tantalizing than utter nudity.

Sweet, godly perfection. She sucked in a deep, shaky breath. It was obvious why she wanted him. Any sane woman would.

With only her linen shift left over her bra and panties, she paused before lifting it over her head, but hesitated longer in reaching behind her to unclasp her bra.

Normally, she wouldn't have dreamed of even getting close to skinny dipping in the water where anyone might come across her. Where a man might be witness to her plump curves without the proper support. She just didn't have the body for it. Especially not one on par with his.

"Is this the bikini ye told me aboot?" he asked, sloshing out of the firth. Water streamed over his muscular body, weighing down his drawers until they hung indecently low on his hips. Closer he came, shaking the water from his dark hair.

Her fingers itched to curl into the hair on his chest. Rub across his flat nipples. Count the hard ridges of his abdomen.

He reached for her and she held her breath but his long fingers only slipped under her bra strap just above the cup. Over her shoulder, his finger lifted the strap before letting it fall back into place.

"'Tis scanty indeed. Intriguing." Fire blazed in his blue eyes.

He traced the thin lace edge of the cup before the backs of his knuckles slid over the navy blue satin. Even molded and formed as they were, she could feel every stroke as if it were in direct contact with her skin.

"N-no," she stuttered. "It's n-not a bikini. It's just underwear."

His fingertips dipped into the band of her panties, tugging them just a fraction of an inch away from her skin before letting them go. Oh, God, she moaned under her breath then she realized he was captivated not by her but by the elastic band. Life could be so incredibly unfair.

Well, if all he had for her right now was more curiosity, it could wait! And she'd be damned if she would get completely naked and leave the friggin' thing behind for him to play with either!

"Later," she said firmly, pushing him away. Running into the water, she gasped in surprise but the breath caught. Gooseflesh broke out from head to toe.

Her gasp turned to a squeal when Keir lifted her in his arms, laughing down at her as he strode deeper into the water. "The firth 'tis fed from the North Sea. Did ye think it wouldnae be cold?"

"N-not th-that cold," she said, stammering for a whole different reason now. The lapping water kissed her bottom, making her squeak and squeal, but not squirm. She didn't want him to drop her.

"Aye, 'tis frigid but the only way tae brave it…" He lifted her high against his chest but she suspected what he planned and clung tightly to his broad shoulders.

"You wouldn't dare!"

"Och, lassie, 'tis the only way."

And he threw her.

Engulfed by the freezing water, Al froze in shock as she sunk to the bottom. It wasn't deep, but it took only an instant for the contrast between the temperature of her skin, heated by a long day in the sun, to acclimate to the water. The unbearable chill became a soothing caress, washing away the discomfort, the grime and sweat.

Buoyancy lifted her to the top and she resurfaced, taking only a second to hear his laughter and to draw a breath before she dove under once more, pushing off from his chest with her feet. Swimming under water as long as she could, she savored the rush of the water in her ears. The calm.

It had been years since she'd been swimming. Her grandmother had paid for her to take part in a swim league while Al was growing up. She'd been determined to extract Al from her books for at least a few weeks each summer to soak up a little of the vitamin D she was certain Al was deficient in. Those leagues had lasted until her sophomore year of high school when her grandma died and her mother hadn't wanted to waste the money on it.

She'd forgotten how much she enjoyed it. Being at peace, when even the constant churn of her mind stopped to appreciate the sheer nothingness of it all.

Isolated from everything... and everyone.

She exhaled slowly, using every second she had to savor that moment before drifting to the surface. She broke through, inhaled, and rolled on to her back with a sigh of contentment...

That lasted all of two seconds before she was jerked to the side by one arm.

"Al! Lass! Are ye all right?" Keir shouted, gathering her into his arms with a little shake.

"Why are you yelling at me?"

She dropped her feet down but found nothing solid beneath them before he lifted her up once more. He dipped down in the process and she realized her swim had taken her out into water over her head and his.

If he didn't let go of her, he might end up drowning them both. She pushed away but he held her tighter.

"Dinnae struggle, lass. I've got ye now."

"Got me?" Al swept her now-straggly hair back from her face with both hands and peered up at him. "Are you trying to save me?"

"Aye. What were ye thinking going intae open water rather than back tae shore?" he asked, clearly upset, but she couldn't completely swallow the giggle building up in her throat.

"I was thinking of going for a swim. I thought you knew that when you asked if I 'fancied a swim,'" she said, imitating his brogue. Pushing out of his arms, she twirled around with a splash before treading a few feet away from him.

"Ye swim?"

"Aye, laddie, I swim. As well as ye or mayhap e'en better."

She felt freer than she had in months. Years perhaps. As if the water had buoyed her spirits as well as her body. She dropped a few inches below the surface and came up with a mouthful of water, which she promptly spouted at him.

He sputtered, wiping his face, and when she laughed again it was as if the weight of her entire life had floated away. Ignoring his outrage, real or feigned, she swam toward him and wrapped her arms around his shoulders.

He was as beautiful as he'd ever been, his dark hair clinging to his head. His eyes as blue as the sky above.

"Thank you for trying to save me," she said softly, ruffling his curls between her fingers.

"I'll always save ye, lass. Though obviously, I dinnae—"

She kissed him. Just to shut him up, of course, but in a heartbeat his arms wrapped tightly around her and he was kissing her back.

If she thought she'd run the gamut of possible kisses that day, she was wrong. It wasn't slow and sensual as some had been, nor was it hot and fervent. Meant to arouse or impassion. Even though she might have begun it with that intention.

No, it was a kiss of joy. Release.

Just plain liking.

They sank below the water before the kiss ended and broke it before reaching the surface once more. Keir smiled down at her as he wiped her hair from her eyes. As if he had gotten a glimpse of the freedom she felt. The smile was one, not of teasing or flirtation or deviltry, but happiness.

"Tell me how ye learned to swim so well."

And so she told him, opening up for the first time about her family and childhood. The loneliness in her life and the peace she'd found in swimming but had forgotten until that day. They floated along, languidly stroking through the water every once in a while, talking. Just talking. Not about the future. Not about science or innovation. Or the history of the years between them.

But about themselves. About the history of him and her and the stories that had made them who they were.

The sun began its descent by the time they swam toward shore, the water beginning to chill them both after almost an hour in it. He caught her hand, tugging her along with him. When he could touch bottom, she hugged his shoulders and climbed on to his back, wrapping her legs around his waist.

"What is this?"

"Haven't you ever carried anyone like this?" she asked, running her lips up the side of his neck. Her breasts flush against him.

He shook his head though his hands running familiarly along her thighs to cup her bottom belied his words. "Nay, nae quite like this. But I maun hae carried one like this a time or two."

He rotated her until she was chest to chest with him. Again he cupped her bottom, but this time drew her down instead of lifting, pulling her tighter against him. The rough hairs of his chest tickled and aroused but not as effectively as the rampant erection pressed between her thighs.

"You're such a rake," she said softly, teasing the curling hair at his nape through her fingers. He gave her a sharp glance but Al only smiled. "A rogue then. Tell me what would a rogue do in this situation?"

Take her in the water until there was nothing left of the firth but steam? Make love to her on the beach until they both had sand everywhere it should never be?

Fantasies spinning through her mind, she kissed him again but to her surprise, he didn't allow it to deepen as he had before. Instead, he eased her away, carrying her up to the beach before dropping her on her feet.

What was wrong with him? Or was it her?

It had always been her.

No, he wanted her. Badly enough even the cold water of the firth couldn't diminish the evidence.

What then?

"What is it?" she asked, unable to keep the hurt from her voice. She yanked on her shift, needing even that thin cloth to provide some shielding between them. "I'm practically throwing myself at you, in case you hadn't noticed. I know you want m—want to. Have sex."

"Och, lass," he groaned, hauling her into his arms. Forcing her to look up at him when all she wanted to do was look away in shame. He framed her face between his hands and kissed her gently. "I do want ye, *mo ghrá*. Ne'er think otherwise. I want ye so badly, I could hae taken ye in the firth or right here on this beach. Bugger it, I've been wanting ye since the moment I kissed ye this morn. Before e'en. Dinnae think otherwise."

"What's stopping you then?"

"This is what's stopping me," he gestured to the wide open expanse of beach. "I'll nae be taking ye in the water nor the sand like an animal, lass. Nae matter how desperately I want tae. When I bed ye, I plan tae do it properly."

"Properly?" she repeated in amazement, snatching up her petticoat. "Never tell me the Rake of Ross is a prude who only does it in a bed?"

"'Tis another challenge?" To her surprise, he laughed, lifting her once again into his arms and kissing her until she was delirious with wanting. "I'd take ye any way a man can, *mo rúnsearc*. But the first time, aye, I plan tae do *it* in a bed. Wi' a door tae gi' us privacy and the hours required tae gi' the task proper attention."

Her eyes rounded. "The *proper* attention? Would you care to elaborate?"

And he did. Verbosely. Describing every last detail of what he planned to do to her as they dressed in the essentials, carrying their stockings and shoes and Keir his vest and jacket as they headed back up the beach.

Apparently he'd given it a lot of thought, yet the description was filled with starts and stops. He broke off again and again to draw her into his arms, kissing her silly.

As if the telling alone were so arousing he couldn't help himself.

She hoped so.

Chapter 23

Only years of playing at Rosebraugh as a lad had gotten them through a maze of narrow service stairs and hidden doorways without being detected. He wasn't making a terribly agreeable impression on his first day as a duke but his mind was occupied with far more undukely thoughts.

Though he knew his new staff would be waiting to greet him—though most had known him since he was but a lad—and Cook would have prepared a feast to welcome him, Keir was more interested in the feast he was about to partake in.

At last.

It had been a day of torment, first in their long exploration of the kiss, but even more so when Al had stripped down to her bikini that was not actually one. Whatever it had been by name, by sight it was so arousing he'd been glad for the chilled water of the firth to cool his ardent erection.

At least to a level fit for her eyes.

Her body was everything he'd imagined it would be. Lush. Curvaceous. Tempting beyond hope. It had taken all his will to refrain from ravishing her on that beach. Only the knowledge that they would soon be alone had given him the strength to watch her run into the water untouched. Though the sight of her rounded bottom cupped by a mere scrap of cloth had sent him bounding after her.

As a sort of reward for resisting, he'd been given a glimpse of an Allorah Maines he might never have known existed. A water sprite, impish and playful. True joy dancing at her lips as it hadn't before.

He exalted in her open joy. Sharing it with her.

But that wasn't all he longed to share.

Truth, he didn't care to wait any longer.

Duke or not.

)O(O(O(

Honestly she was surprised they made it all the way there. There had been a close call in the stairwell with her pinned against the treads that had almost belied his insistence on seeing them to a private locale.

She hardly had a second to ascertain the room Keir led her to was in fact a bedroom before he slammed the door and trapped her to it. Tossing their shoes and sundries aside, he kissed her tenderly, so tenderly it might not have been called a kiss, but she felt the tension in his body, the tightly leashed passion.

"Are ye certain, lass?" he had the gentlemanly nerve to ask, as if the thousand kisses delaying their journey from beach to bedchamber might have relayed some doubt. "We needn't rush. There is time yet."

For what? More waiting? No, she was ready for this. She wanted this. The ultimate compendium of the thousands of novels she'd devoured in her life. No longer did she have the vaguest doubt that he would trump them all. She wanted him more than she'd ever wanted anything in her life. Whether it was rushing or not. Accelerated her departure or not.

Drawing his head down, she answered him without words. With a hot kiss, her lips parted and inviting. A kiss of encouragement.

An unequivocal yes.

With a groan—of relief?—Keir cupped her cheeks in his hands and deepened the kiss, plundering her mouth as he hadn't yet. There was not gentleness anymore, just pure need, and she answered him in kind. Her blood burned in her veins in an instant. Pounding in her temples. Nipping. Licking.

Her head swam until she felt almost faint. Still, he persisted, stealing her breath. It wasn't enough. He tasted of sin, wicked temptation. As wonderful as the kisses they'd shared in the carriage had been, she knew now they'd been little more than child's play.

These kisses weren't meant to seduce. They were meant to enflame. To bewitch. To burn. Unable to bear it any longer, Al tore her lips away with a cry of surrender.

He gave no quarter, raking his teeth down the side of her neck. He licked at the hollow behind her ear. Nipped at her lobe. Bit her shoulder.

He turned her in his arms, unlacing her dress much as he had on the beach not long before. But there was no laughter now, no teasing. Her bodice fell away. Her skirts fell to the floor unnoticed.

Turning her once more, he looped his finger under her bra strap again. As he tugged it off her shoulder impatiently, she had no doubt this time what interested him more. The other strap followed, baring her breasts to his burning gaze. When she tried to cover them with her hands, he pushed them away.

"Nay, lass. Let me look my fill."

Her body quivered under his hands as they skimmed

down her arms. Up her ribcage until his hands cupped her breasts over her bra. "Ye're so lovely."

A long sigh escaped her when he bent his head, his tongue traced the rise of her breast swelling from the satin cups.

"Oh, Keir... yes."

"Aye, *mo ghrá*, I intend tae if ye'll take this bluidy thing off," he growled.

With a strangled laugh, she reached around and unclasped the bra, letting it slide down her arms. His hands were back in an instant, scorching against her tender flesh.

"Sweet lass." His head dipped once more, his tongue circling one sensitive nipple until her knees grew weak.

"This is so *not* a bed," she whispered hoarsely, clinging to him for support. He stared at her, his blue eyes aflame with an inner fire she'd never seen in them before. "You insisted on a bed."

A wicked grin turned up the corner of his mouth. "So I did."

He lifted her, cradling her in his arms for the few seconds it took his long strides to cross the room to the bed. He laid her on it, following until she was pressed deep into the mattress beneath him. Their mouths met once more. His chest searing her breasts even through his thin shirt.

But she wanted more. She tugged at his hem and he leaned away to yank it over his head, balling it up before flinging it aside. His chest bulged and flexed, and Al couldn't help herself. Running her palms over his pecs, she gloried in the feel of his solid flesh, his hot skin.

He gave her hardly a second to enjoy it though. He covered her once more. This time, she cried out as skin met skin. It was electrifying. Her body was instantly ablaze.

She squirmed beneath him, fisting her hands in the bedcovers. Unable to resist, she drove her fingers into his hair and tugged him up to meet her hungry lips once more. He complied with a groan. Tasting her again and again as if he couldn't get enough.

She doubted she ever could. He was a feast. To her eyes. To her lips. His hands skimmed down the length of her body and up once more to close over her breasts. Then his lips did leave hers.

She flinched when they closed over her nipple, drawing on it hard. His tongue flicked over the sensitive tip and she cried out, holding him tightly to her breast as he continued to assault the tender flesh with his mouth. Each time he sucked, tension pooled more heavily between her thighs as if some invisible cord connected them.

Her other breast wasn't lacking in attention either. He fondled her nipple, rolling it between his fingers. The combination of both left her restless and whimpering. The ache in her core becoming almost painful.

Helplessly, she ran her hands over his muscular back, over his hips. Arching beneath him, seeking relief.

"Dinnae rush so, *mo rúnsearc*," he murmured against her breast. "We've all night."

Al tossed her head on the pillow in denial, panting hard. "I hope you're not planning on waiting that long."

"So impatient," he teased, trading one nipple for the other.

His patience made her want to scream. Her needy body was sprinting for the finish line already. Near bursting with need repressed for far too long. He'd been right. Her own laughable skills were nothing compared to what a man... *this* man could do to her.

And he hadn't really done much yet!

How he would laugh if he knew just how incredibly he'd aroused her with a few kisses. She'd be pleading with him soon.

God, she'd never live it down. She wouldn't beg him. She wouldn't...

"Please, Keir." She bit her lip, trying to reclaim the words. Her hips arched once more as if they had a mind of their own.

He lifted his head, gazing down at her with ardor smoldering in his eyes. "Say it again."

She shouldn't give him the pleasure. "Please."

For a man who'd never dealt with underwear, he handled them neatly. Hooking his thumbs under the sides of her panties, he slid them down her legs. Caressing her as he slowly tugged them off. Too slowly.

His palms slid up her legs, behind her knees. Up the inside of her thighs. She was quaking from head to toes, her breaths unsteady.

Up, up.

She tensed as his fingertips grazed her damp curls.

Cried out as he slid a single finger inside her.

And exploded. Her cry became a hoarse scream as she came hard. Pressing the heels of her hands to her eyes, she bit back a sob. He pushed his finger deeper inside her and she involuntarily contracted around him.

"Oh, God!" she sobbed. Over and over he pumped his finger, shallowly, somehow elongating her orgasm.

She'd never imagined it could feel like that. Her whole body had experienced it, from top to bottom. Every nerve ending was singing in exaltation. In sorrow. It had been too much, too fast.

"I'm sorry," she whispered, not looking at him.

"Ne'er apologize, lass. I willnae apologize for enjoying the sight of ye coming apart for me. In fact, I plan tae see it happen again verra soon," he said in his gruff burr, climbing over her once more.

XXXXX

He pulled her hands away from her eyes, grinning when she refused to look at him. His fiery lass was even more passionate than he'd ever imagined. It seemed he wasn't the only one surprised by the ferocity of her climax. Yet he reveled in the fact that he'd driven her to it. Indeed, he'd made her sing.

"Dinnae be embarrassed by the depth of yer passion, lass. Nae when it pleases me so much tae ken I was able to bring ye tae such heights."

"But you...?"

"Och, my time will come sooner than naught."

His assurance was laughable. In truth, he'd nearly spilt his seed when he'd felt her sweet, wet body clasp his finger. He might not require much more effort expended by her to find his release than he'd needed for her.

But he didn't intend to rush what was sure to be a moment of pure paradise. As he told her, they had all night.

Holding her hands in his, he kissed her swollen lips, running his tongue along the seam until she yielded him entry. She tasted of heaven.

"Look at me, *mo rúnsearc*," he commanded softly, rocking back on his heels.

Waiting until she met his gaze, he lifted her hand to his lips. He kissed each finger without taking his eyes off hers. Drew each digit into his mouth, worrying the pads against his tongue. He kissed her palm, the inside of her wrist where her pulse fluttered madly. The inside of her elbow, tickling the sensitive flesh there with his tongue. She drew a sharp breath through parted lips and he bit back a grin lest she lapse into misplaced embarrassment again.

She was magnificent.

And she was his.

Aye, they had all night.

Chapter 24

Seven times.

Seven times he'd taken her on the path to oblivion, wringing her out and leaving her limp before he was done with her. For all the books she'd read describing in detail how sex might feel, she'd never imagined just how truly combustible it could be when it was her person actively involved in the incineration. Words that had once been just words to her had taken on all new meaning.

Ecstasy. Rapture. Nirvana.

He had taken her to heights she'd never known existed, in ways she'd never imagined being taken despite years of fantasizing. He'd taken her on the rhapsodic flight of coiled muscles and the beguiling friction of bodies melding.

Once her initial frenzy had been satisfied, he'd shown her slow sensuality with tangled bodies and prolonged releases. Five of those times, she climbed the pinnacle of rapture with his encouragement alone.

Twice he had joined her. At first, she'd thought the joy of feeling him possess her that first time could never be matched. He'd owned her, filled her body and soul, pushing her even higher. Then higher yet, every stroke of his body into hers reaching deeper than she ever imagined. They'd come together, the rush of heat exploding between her thighs had been so overwhelming, she'd screamed into the night. He'd driven into her repeatedly as if he couldn't stop, crying out, too, at the strength of his orgasm.

But when he entered her the second time, her cries were deep in her heart. The joining so poignant, Al knew she would never forget the moment she surrendered everything to him. She'd felt raw, exposed. He had stripped her bare to the core.

She was his. A part of her always would be.

It was a thrilling and distressing thought.

He'd had his quick fuck just as he'd promised because for all his talk about the ways of the rake versus the rogue, they were one and the same.

The end for them was near.

She'd known it the instant she'd awoken in that big, well-used bed alone.

That's just the way it was.

XOXOXOX

"What else?"

Keir pinched his nose as his new steward, Stewart Neville, slid another sheet of parchment across the desk.

"Sign at the bottom here, Your Grace. Just one more and I will have the transferences filed this afternoon. I'll see to it myself."

"Thank ye, Neville. Ye've been a great help."

"My pleasure to serve you, Your Grace."

Cringing at the title, he wanted to snap at the man not to call him that. To announce to the world that Hugh was alive and well. All morning he heard the condolences from staff and retainers, read them from clan members and tenants close enough to have already heard the news. More would come.

He was tired of this farce already, but what choice did he have? The truth couldn't come out. Even if it could, Al had assured him there was no way to retrieve Hugh from the future.

And hence his own was thoroughly fucked.

He'd only been able to maintain his sanity throughout this entire ordeal by clinging to what Al offered him. Intrigue, excitement. That ever-present distraction that had so irked him a week past but now he sought like a lifeline.

After last night, she was more of a distraction than ever. If her appearance through that wormhole had turned his world upside down, their lovemaking had sent it into mayhem. She'd floored him with her passion. He was stunned by how profoundly he'd been affected as well.

Something he accredited to his genuine fondness of her person.

None of his previous lovers had sparked the honest affection he'd felt for her right from the beginning. No, that wasn't right. It hadn't really been until she stared him down in his library that day. Wallowing in her own filth for days on end and forcing him to take the responsibility for it. She hadn't backed down then.

She hadn't really since.

Aye, for a wee slip of a lass who claimed to be adverse to confrontation, she pushed him mercilessly. Challenged him endlessly. He loved it. There was no other person he longed to talk to more. Every minute spent in the company of others made him impatient for hers. Neville was a fine example.

His impatience to be away and seek her out had him tapping his foot peevishly.

In his life, he'd not been so eager for a person's company. Not even Hugh's. Beyond his colleagues and collaborators, he had few true friendships in his life. Idle chatter bored him. And like Hugh, his relations with his family were not the strongest in his life.

He'd never before realized that in a life surrounded by people, one could have been so alone. Three brothers he had and yet he'd been lonely. Even Hugh had never delved as deeply to find the real him.

Yet, Al had waltzed into his life and in a short time had become a friend unlike any other. With her, he'd been able to find solace in the arms of another, something he'd not known since his mother died. He'd also found the challenge and intellectual stimulation of his mentors and contemporaries, the camaraderie of his cousin all combined in the body of a courtesan.

Now there was even more to look forward to.

Al as his lover.

"There is one last thing, Your Grace," Neville said, recalling him from his reverie and sliding a large parchment across the desk. His eyes were drawn immediately to the bottom of the page bearing a large red seal with a gold ribbon pinned beneath it.

"What is this?"

"A proclamation from the king, Your Grace. It arrived by special messenger this morning."

"And ye dinnae think tae lead wi' this?" he said irritably, drawing the paper closer.

"In all honesty, Your Grace," the steward pushed out of his chair and stood, "I thought it best to complete our other work before you saw it. You'd be in no mood for any of it after reading this."

Curious, he scanned the first few lines. His eyes widened then narrowed. "That unbelievable bastard."

"Just so, Your Grace."

Strong condemnation coming from his Sassenach steward.

He read on. And further on. "He cannae…"

But he had.

With a howl of rage, Keir swept an arm across the desk, scattering everything with a rain of clanks and clatters. It wasn't enough. A small vase was flung into the fireplace, dissolving into tiny shards of porcelain in a more satisfying explosion as Neville slunk out the door.

Another followed, bigger this time.

"What the hell are you doing?"

Spinning around, he found Al at the door staring at him incredulously. "'Tis better than murder, lass."

"I guess that would depend on whose," she said dryly, taking a few steps into the study to retrieve a spilled inkwell from the carpet before the stain spread too far. Breathing heavily, he watched her make her way toward him, picking up a few more things on her way to the desk.

Each time she bent, her long, wavy hair would swing down until she swept it back absently. It was hypnotic, soothing as waves. His explosive rage abated a tad with each sway.

"Is this another example of your temper? I think a few choice words would be less destructive."

A bitter bark of laughter escaped him. "Sometimes words cannae express copious amounts of anger."

Her cool gray eyes studied him, thoroughly but warily. "Yes, I can see you're very angry. Why?"

"'Tis nae ye, lass."

"Glad to hear it." The words were flippant but sensing true relief behind them, he clenched his fists, forcing his temper to further recede.

"I could ne'er be so angry wi' ye," he assured her.

She huffed a single laugh. "I think we both know that's not true. What happened?"

"The bluidy king of England happened." He retrieved the parchment from the floor and held it out to her. "He's making sure the Hielanders pay for their attempt tae dethrone him."

She fumbled through the elaborate language in the first few lines of the proclamation. She remembered something about this, if only vaguely. He was right. It was a payback of sorts.

"...it should not be lawful for any person or persons, except such persons as are therein mentioned and described, within the shire of Dunbartain, on the north side of the water of Leven, Stirling on the north side of the river of Forth, Perth, Kincardin, Aberdeen, Inverness, Nairn, Cromarty, Argyle, Forfar, Bamff, Sutherland, Caithness, Elgine and Ross, to have in his or their custody, use, or bear, broad sword or target, poignard, whinger, or durk, side pistol, gun, or other warlike weapon, otherwise than in the said act..." She glanced up from the page. "They're sure covering their bases."

"The bluidy butcher, Cumberland, is behind this tae be sure. Ol' George would ne'er think of it on his own," he said. "He's outlawed nae only the carrying of arms but speaking Gaelic as well as wearing the tartan and playing bagpipes. I shouldnae be surprised that it has come tae this, I suppose. The years of my life cannae exceed the number of those marked by this never-ending feud between Stuart and Hanover. Religious nonsense. As if it has any place in the operation of government."

There it was again. The link between Culloden and religion. While she'd known the clash between religious faiths played a strong role in British history, she'd never heard so much emphasis placed on it. Could the history books have had it wrong all along?

Keir was still fuming. "Oh, for the days when the Tudors thrived and the Stuarts had only Scotland on their hands. When we were left in peace from it all. I'll ne'er ken a day of it in my life, I'm sure. And now this? Read on, lass, he's meaning tae strip the Highland lairds who stood in support of Prince Charlie of their lands and titles. As if a laird is but a title bestowed on a man. 'Tis a responsibility that cannae be swept away wi' the stroke of a bluidy pen."

She could see the fury, the violence surging in him once more. "It'll be okay, Keir."

"'Tis nae *okay*, lass," he shot back. "He wants tae do away wi' the clan system as if our way of life means nothing."

"But he can't." She hurried to his side, stroking his arm comfortingly. "It won't work, I promise you. Before too long these laws will be lifted. The customs of the Highlanders will live on long after it."

Subdued by her words, he stared down at her in disbelief. "Aye?"

"Yes," she assured him. "By my time, the world will be in love with all things Highlander. Your kilts, your brogues. Your games. All the ladies will sigh over the sheer number of Highland warriors portrayed in books. I know, because I was one of them. It's been the thrill of my life seeing it all in person."

"Has it now?" His fingertips traced a line across her jaw, the heat of anger in his eyes receding in favor of a new warmth.

It had, she realized. No achievement in her life had ever brought her such joy. Just as nothing had ever made her realize how empty her personal life was despite her full academic career.

She was going to miss all of this when it was gone.

He would never know how much.

"Yes, it has."

A slow smile lifted the corner of his lips. He caught a lock of her hair and twirled it absently around his finger. "Do ye care tae elaborate on what exactly ye've found so thrilling?" He bent, kissing her mouth lightly.

"I don't know." Warmth flooded her cheeks. "You *elaborate* far better than I can."

"Ah, should I tell ye then of the thrills I've discovered?" he whispered close to her ear. His fingers brushed through her hair. "Just those of the past day... and night might bring more than a sweet blush tae yer cheeks, *mo ghrá.*"

He murmured a few details. Heat flooded her whole face and down her neck as well. Even the tops of her breasts flushed with color before he was finished.

"You have quite a way with words," she admitted breathlessly, too aware of how close he was. How heat radiated off of him. How the room suddenly seemed like a sauna.

"*Mmm*, I've a few thoughts on the night ahead, too, if ye'd care tae hear them."

Could she stand it, Al wondered? Already she was achy, weak in the knees, and feeling a strong urge to go back to bed.

With him.

Despite her worries upon waking, Keir seemed to have a fair amount of lust for her still unspent in him, too.

"Does it involve a bed?"

His roguish grin set her heart racing. "Nary a one."

Slipping an arm around her waist, he drew her closer. Burying his face in the curve of her shoulder, he nipped lightly. Chafing the tender skin with the rough growth of his beard.

His hands skimmed up her ribs until he was almost cradling her breasts.

Almost.

Bending his knees, he rocked his hips into her, creating a delicious friction on her thighs until he was almost pressed against her aching core.

Almost.

"Och, lass, I could take ye right here."

"What's stopping you? No one's watching," she whispered in his ear, nipping at his earlobe.

"Is this the same lass who claimed tae be so shy?" he asked in a husky chuckle. "The same lass who denied being bold or audacious? Propositioning me now?"

She certainly didn't feel like the same woman. That Al would never have dared to act this way. He had done this to her.

"Do you like me like this?"

"Aye, I do," he admitted. "But I liked ye as ye always been. Yer more colorful side as well. Ye dinnae need tae play the minx wi' me, lass. There is naught tae make me want ye more."

"Nothing?" She slipped her hand beneath his kilt, running her palm up his thigh and around to cup his hard bare buttock.

"Perhaps a wee something."

"Perhaps not so wee."

She shifted her hand around to his front, cupping him until he was overflowing her palm. Keir hissed, sucking in a harsh breath.

"Och, lass, ye'll unman me if ye dinnae cease."

"That might be interesting, too."

She wrapped her fingers around his hard length, running them up his throbbing staff, marveling at the length and breadth of him. Glorying in the way he threw back his head, tendons taut in his neck, muscular body strung like a bow.

With a shudder, he lifted her and dropped her onto the desk, tugging up her skirts with a frantic jerk. His fingers found her only long enough to make sure she was ready for him—which she was—before he drove deep inside her with a hoarse roar.

Wrapping her legs around him tightly, Al clung to him as he slammed into her over and over. Cried out as he found a hard, animalistic rhythm that pushed her too quickly over the top when she longed to savor the feel of him while she could.

Winding her hair around his hands, he forced her head back and ravished her mouth with hot kisses.

Pleasure spiraled, radiating down her limbs as spasms of euphoria racked her body. With one final thrust, he came too. Collapsing weakly over her as the passion and ire that had gripped him ebbed. He kissed her neck, rubbing his sweaty forehead on her cheek.

"Och, lass, I dinnae ken what came o'er me. 'Twas the grip of uncontrollable lust. I'm sorry for attacking ye like a beast."

She raked her fingers through his thick hair with an

inward smile. She didn't mind at all. All the flattery in the world was nothing compared to a man who simply had to have you. She felt utterly desirable, cherished.

Wanted.

There were too few moments in her life when she'd felt that way. Another fantasy ticked off her list by Keir MacCoinnach.

"I didn't mind," was all she admitted aloud. "But it wasn't anything like what you had elaborated on. So shame on you. To get a girl's hopes up like that…"

He lifted his head and grinned down at her. "Then my apologies are for disappointing ye so. I'll endeavor tae do better in the future."

The future.

She couldn't help but wonder what sort of timeline he attached to such an indeterminate word.

Chapter 25

She wandered the halls of Rosebraugh the next afternoon. If she'd paused to look into one of the many gilt-framed mirrors she passed, she'd probably see a secret smile gracing her lips. But her focus was turned inward. Not out. Not on the veritable museum she was walking through, the gorgeous paintings by Huet, Rembrandt, Chardin. Nor the sculptures by Bernini and Puget.

Rosebraugh was a wonderland of art and history, yet her mind was entirely Keir's. They'd whiled away an entire day in each other's arms, scaling the peaks of carnal passion again and again. Reaching so high, they'd caught more than one glimpse of pure paradise. She'd slept in his arms, their bodies entwined. Woken this morning to his gentle kisses and his languid exploration of her body.

Reality was trumping fantasy again and again. A few days more and she'd have enough memories to last a lifetime. Memories to warm her through cold nights and long years alone.

Being alone wouldn't bother her much. She'd been alone most of her life. Life here would be no different in many ways. She didn't weep for the one she'd left behind. And at

ANGELINE FORTIN

least here, her mother couldn't call her just to find some new way to humiliate her.

Solitude was far removed from loneliness though.

She would miss Keir. Knowing he was nearby, yet out of her reach would be painful. She loved being by his side, being close...

"Ah, good afternoon, Miss Maines."

Al shut her eyes with a low groan. Perhaps, she loved being close to Keir because it seemed whenever she was away from him, things like this happened!

Turning, she smiled tightly at the man walking down the hall toward her. "Artair. I thought you were at Dingwall preparing for Frang's funeral. What brings you to Rosebraugh?"

"I thought I might come and get a head start on the preparations for Hugh's service while we awaited news on Father," he said, clasping his hands behind him as was his norm.

Rocking on his heels in that dreaded fashion that heralded the beginning of another long-winded lecture.

Why had she urged Keir to ride out to visit his tenants today? Oh, she knew there was much he needed to do for Rosebraugh but if she'd only lured him back to his bedroom, she wouldn't be an easy target in an open hallway now.

"Ye're looking rather fetching today," he added. "Ye look lovely in the MacCoinnach tartan."

Running her hands down the gown crafted of tartan and ivory linen she loved so much, she nodded. And since Keir had pointed out how rude it was to dispute the opinion of others on that topic, she offered her thanks for the compliment, if a little awkwardly.

He smiled, the severity of his features relaxing enough to

bring to mind his handsome brother. There was a definite family resemblance.

"What has ye wandering the halls today?"

"Oh, I was just admiring the artwork," she said. "I never realized that Hugh and Keir had acquired so many pieces of—"

"In truth, Miss Maines, I didn't come tae Rosebraugh only to see tae the arrangements," he burst out. "I've had it in my mind these last days tae seek a time in private wi' ye tae make my addresses tae ye. I can tell my inclination tae come ahead wisnae misplaced."

"I'm sorry?" she bit out, irritated by his propensity to constantly interrupt. "Your inclination?"

"Aye, tae make my addresses tae ye."

She was missing something here. "I'm sorry, Artair. I guess I don't understand what you mean."

"I'm asking ye tae marry me, lass."

She couldn't have been more shocked if he'd finished the job Maeve started days before and whacked her over the head with a thirty-pound tome. Speechless, she stared at him.

Was the whole family nuts?

"I've surprised ye."

No kidding! What an understatement. There hadn't been a single word in the handful of conversations they'd shared to indicate he was... what would they call it here? Courting her? His inclination hadn't even been slightly tilted from her perspective.

Marriage! She'd never even considered it. Not ever. Especially not with him. Oh, she'd had dreams once upon a time. But her personal favorites had never included marriage. Marriage, in her experience, merely tainted the story. As it had tarnished real life. Her father, her stepfather. They'd made her mother miserable and her as well by extension. No, tying dreams to marriage led to inevitable disappointment.

Her fantasies as a teen and young woman centered on the romance. The love. When those dreams hadn't come to fruition, she'd switched her goals to more practical and achievable academic ones, and satisfied herself with finding love and romance in the thousands of novels she devoured.

Lately, her fantasies had begun to revolve around a man of flesh and blood once more. A certain Scot who was not available to rescue her from this awkward moment. But even those dreams never, ever led to marriage.

Now a man who was perhaps one of the most grating she'd ever known was asking her?

"Allorah? Miss Maines?"

"*Uh*, Artair. I'm... I'm overcome, yes overcome by the suddenness of your offer. It is *umm*, most unexpected," she belatedly managed, worrying her earlobe between her fingers.

"Mayhap, but I hope ye will consider it." He rocked back on his heels. "I've a simple living but one I feel ye would complement and enjoy. Ye're quite good wi' people, I've noticed..."

Ugh, she was horrible with people. How could he think any different? She could hardly make polite conversation without discomfort. Though perhaps he hadn't realized that yet.

"...with a true interest in the welfare of others..."

Of course, she'd just had terrible thoughts about him.

"...and a charitable spirit that will make ye an excellent wife tae me and an example tae those of my parish."

She hadn't been to church in more than a decade.

Oh, but she was a rotten person. And completely uncharitable. He wasn't a bad person, or a mean one. He just wasn't his brother. Even so, he didn't deserve a broken heart more than anyone else did. If only Keir were around to save her from having to turn him down.

"I ken I'm naught but a simple cleric," he continued. "Nae an heir tae an earl, for example. I'm certain ye considered looking higher."

There was just enough of a reprimand in his tone for Al to forget her discomfort. She narrowed her eyes, unaware that her fisted hands had taken up an offensive position on her hips.

If she wasn't going to be saved, she would save herself.

"How much higher do you presume I'm looking, Artair?"

He swallowed deeply, shifting from foot to foot. "He won't marry ye, ye ken?"

"You're not the first to tell me that."

"He's the heir tae Dingwall and now the Duke of Ross tae boot. Father would nae allow him tae wed wi' someone like…"

Of all the assumptive, judgmental… She took a step forward. "Like what?"

He took a step away. "Ye mistake my meaning, lass. I find ye tae be a most agreeable… er, a woman of agreeable temperament. Normally. I dinnae mean tae imply anything other than yer compatible fit intae a lifestyle of more modest social… er, ranking."

Her brows shot up to her hairline before dropping into a scowl. "First of all, I don't give a damn about any social ranking. People are people. Period. Second: even if I cared about that, I wouldn't let anyone, including your father, keep me from *reaching* as high as I liked. Love has no rank. And third: I have absolutely no interest in marrying. Anyone. Not you and not even the freakin' heir. I am my own woman. I do *not* need a man to complete me."

He blinked, stunned by her tirade, but Al felt exhilaration all the way to her toes. She'd never really let go like that. Her only regret was that it'd been Artair and not her mother she'd finally stood up to. It might have ended up being just a tad on the rude side, but she wouldn't apologize for it.

Be it her education, gender, size, hair color or even her newly acquired questionable social status, she was exasperated by the notion she couldn't achieve any goal she set out to because of some social barrier.

When she gained her footing in this world—and she damn well would—she was going to break them all down and knock this century on its ass.

"Complete ye?"

She ignored the question. "Thank you for your offer, Artair. It was most kind and while I appreciate the sentiment and motivation behind it, I'm afraid I cannot accept."

It was as kindly said as she could manage. She could try to explain things to him, but the honest confusion written all over his face told her he'd never really understand.

"If ye should reconsider—"

"I won't. I'm sorry."

With a bow, he turned and strode down the hall. She barely realized he'd gone, marveling inwardly at herself.

)(O)(O)(O)(

"'Though she be but little, she is fierce.'"

She spun around to find Keir at a pair of double doors down the hall, his shoulder propped against the casing. A smile lifting one corner of his mouth.

"How much of that did you hear?"

"That's Shakespeare."

"I know who it is. How much?"

"Most of it," he told her, pushing off from the door frame and striding toward her in long, confident steps, kilt swirling around his calves. "Ye put him in his place quite nicely. He's long been a pompous ass."

"He thought he was being kind." Shrugging, she stared blindly at what she was sure was a fabulous portrait of the Madonna if she were capable of taking closer note. Humiliation of being caught in such a rant burned through her. "I shouldn't have been so mean."

"I think we need to refine yer definition of *mean*."

"I was too harsh." She paced down the hall, running her fingers over the head of a marble bust.

"He was too forward."

She shrugged again. She couldn't argue with that. The proposal had been premature.

"So, ye dinnae need a man, eh?" he asked, stepping into her line of vision, if she were to look up. "Ye said as much before. I confess I thought ye only teasing tae some degree. Deep down, I thought ye were like any other lass wi' dreams tae wed and hae a home of her own. Bairns on her hip."

"And barefoot in the kitchen?" she finished without anger. No, her anger was spent. She felt invigorated. As liberated from her past as her swim in the firth had made her feel.

It would be difficult to explain it to him though. Her sentiment, while she'd never shouted it on the rooftops quite so vehemently before, was centuries beyond his time and understanding. Maybe she'd never really understood what it meant before either.

For all her protests on feminism and independence, there'd still been a part of her thinking she lacked some achievement in her life because she hadn't married. Didn't have a man of her own. Even in her time, society viewed her lack as some sort of failure. A pie missing a piece. Perhaps she had as well.

But she had her own achievements to be proud of. She was a whole pie. She really didn't need a man to complete her.

Tossing her head, she met his gaze straight on. "No, Keir, some women dream bigger than that. Maybe not yet. But they will."

"For what purpose?" he baited her. "Ye're a woman. Ye've naught more tae wish for in this world we live in now."

"Then I will change it."

He displayed none of the confusion Artair had. Or even the amusement she expected to see. No, his blue eyes shined with pride.

For her.

"Aye, I wager ye will, Big Al. I wager ye will."

He tilted up her chin, his thumb tracing her lower lip. As always, his touch brought out feelings in her which aroused not feminism but feminine delight.

"Come here, lass."

With a sigh, she leaned into him. His arms closed around her, drawing her close. She could feel the heat of his body radiating through his shirt and the tartan thrown over his shoulder, hear his heart beating strongly beneath her cheek. Smell the masculine combination of sweat, sunshine and him.

It was at once comforting and exciting. Even knowing whatever was growing between them couldn't last forever, she hoped to stay there for a good long time.

Not because she needed a man to complete her but because a scoop of ice cream was always nice with pie.

Everyone knew that.

Her lips curved up in a smile. No, there was nothing wrong with a little dessert.

He brushed her hair from her temple and pressed a light kiss there. "Ye quite impressed me. I'm glad ye dinnae accept Artair's proposal."

Why, she wanted to ask? But she didn't. Instead, she sighed and snuggled deeper into his strong arms.

"Of course, I didn't. How could I?"

How could she, indeed. She could never think of marrying another man when it was Keir who held her heart.

Chapter 26

It wasn't only his brother who'd come down from Dingwall. Ceana had joined Artair on his journey.

Both joined them for dinner.

Cook, determined to lay a table worthy of a duke whether he be a night or two late in finding his way to it or not, had outdone herself. Seven courses in the French style— something she knew he and Hugh had enjoyed while abroad—from *l'entrée* (which he'd had to explain to Al didn't mean main dish but appetizer) to *le digestif* (a healthy dose of cognac he was in desperate need of by the end of the meal). All of it served with the pomp and plodding speed typical of the French court by his new, liveried footman.

He'd far preferred the seven sensual courses he'd enjoyed privately with Al the other night. Each one more delightful than the last.

None of them involving the unwelcome company of his family. He'd come to Rosebraugh not only because his new duty to the title and clan demanded it, but simply because he wanted to have Al for himself. Away from them.

He'd not have an evening alone in any case. Somehow it'd slipped his mind that a fair portion of Hugh's clan lived at

Rosebraugh. His mother's sister, cousins both close and distant. Having kept to his rooms the previous day and night, he had forgotten all about them. Where they'd hidden themselves all day, he had no idea.

Sharing every meal with every one of them in the days and years to come, made him cringe. He wanted Al all for himself.

At least someone had warned her to dress for dinner. The first time she'd done so since being set free of his dungeons. Her maid would gain an extra sterling in her pay for this. He'd have hated for his bonny lass to be uncomfortable if she weren't dressed for the event.

Instead she outshone them all, looking as resplendent as any lady in the courts of Europe. Dressed in silk and lace, her glorious bosom straining above the low, square neckline. Though he preferred her blonde locks loose and long, they were upswept into a high, elegant twist with the same curls that had so tormented him before bouncing once more against the swell of her breasts like the sweetest caress.

She was splendid. He doubted after witnessing her set down of Artair that afternoon she'd ever not stand tall again, in any situation. Despite her self-doubt, she was as brave and bold as any person – man or woman – he'd ever known.

How far she'd come from the stuttering lass he'd chained in a prison cell. From mouse to lioness. From shy to siren. From waiting for his kiss to seducing him in his own study.

She continued to astonish him.

She might always astonish him.

)(O)(O)(O)(

There might have been a lot of things Al could say to Ceana but that night there was only one.

Surprisingly, it was thank you.

Ceana had saved her from making an utter disgrace of herself. Impossible as it seemed. She'd brought a fancy silk gown of sage green with a large print of flora and fauna to her room earlier. A *robe à l'anglaise*, she'd called it, with wide panniers holding it and a fine ivory silk damask under skirt out to the sides. She'd demanded Peigi help Al into it for dinner. At first, she'd been sure the woman was playing some joke on her but when she entered the dining room to find it filled with a half-dozen women dressed as over-the-top as Ceana tended to be and men in all their complementary formal jackets, she'd about hugged the woman.

Odd enough. But when Keir—though still in his linen shirt and kilt—looked her up and down slowly, his eyes blazing with open admiration, she'd almost been tempted to kiss Ceana, too.

He'd seated her at his right hand, taking the opportunity—she was sure—to peer down her daring décolleté as he pushed her in.

All through the interminable meal, his hungry eyes had been fixed on her. Mostly on her eyes but often enough on her bosoms being practically thrust right out of the low-cut bodice to feel hot anticipation rolling over her like lapping waves through the whole meal.

He liked it. As ridiculous as she'd felt when she'd looked into the mirror, she felt like a freaking goddess under the promise in that burning gaze.

She couldn't wait for the meal to end.

"Miss Maines?"

Someone nudged her from the other side and she tore her eyes from Keir and turned to the woman beside her who immediately pointed across the table. An older gentleman, some sort of uncle or cousin's uncle to Hugh, was regarding her expectantly. He was portly with white hair, a drooping white mustache, and a florid face. But he had kindly eyes that sort of reminded her of a benevolent St. Nick.

"I'm sorry?"

"I said, I hear ye're a colonist, lass. I served there with Saunderson's 1st Marines on the attempt to take Quebec back in '12," he said.

"Take it from whom?"

"The French, lass. The French!" he blustered. "I take it ye're nae from the northern colonies then?"

"No, sir."

"Ah, makes sense," he said. "Plus a wee lass like yerself probably disnae worry her head o'er history and such."

Keir's hand covered hers and the knife she held in her hand. "I wasn't going to stab him," she whispered.

His eyes danced. "Just making sure. I'm rather fond of Uncle Ranulf."

"Where do ye hail from then?" Uncle Ranulf asked, demanding her attention.

"Maryland originally, sir," she answered politely. "Though I... er, traveled far to the west as I grew older."

"Maryland?" he frowned. "Can't say I've heard of it. Is it far tae the south then? Tomas!" he called down the table. "Ye e'er heard of a colony called Mary-land?"

Both men frowned. Tomas scratched his head. They turned back to her expectantly.

She didn't know what to say. She'd never heard of a battle fought three hundred years before her time, it made some sense that the names for all the colonies might not be exactly as she knew them. But the revolution was only thirty years away.

"It's just north of Virginia."

"Virginia?" Keir repeated and she turned to look at him. He was frowning. A chill washed over her. There it was again. That sense that something wasn't quite right here.

"Yes. The colony named after Queen Elizabeth."

"Auld King Henry's queen?"

"No, his daughter."

It shouldn't be that hard. It was Virginia. The largest British colony in America. She glanced around the table. Everyone was staring at her curiously. Even Ceana's eyes were glittering with interest.

"Lass, Auld Henry had no daughters named Elizabeth, certainly none who became queen," he told her, his frown deepening.

Dread prickled at her flesh. A terrible foreboding. First his discovery of planets that shouldn't have been able to be seen for almost a century more. Then the references to Culloden as a religious war.

"Henry the Eighth," she said, almost desperately. "His daughter. Elizabeth."

"Bah, his bastard, ye mean." Ranulf chuckled.

The room spun around her. Or was it her head that was spinning? She stood, pushing her chair back until it tumbled backward. A strong male arm reached out to steady her. Not Keir but one of the footman. But then he was there, concern in his eyes, leading her from the room.

"A map," she gasped. "Let me see a map."

"*Mo ghrá...?*"

"*Please,* Keir."

With a terse nod, he changed directions. Taking her up a flight of stairs and down a hall, before he opened the door to his study. Leaving her by the door, he walked to a set of shelves and contemplated the spines before selecting a thick tome more than a foot across and two feet in length.

As the sun was beginning to set, he carried it over to a table near the window and opened it. She trailed behind numbly, reaching his side just as he laid the book flat.

"The American Colonies," he said, pointing at the page.

Steeling herself with a deep breath, she looked down at the page.

Oh, Dr. Fielding was going to be so disappointed when he finally figured it out.

Chapter 27

She began to laugh. A little hiccup of a giggle at first that worried him beyond measure.

"Lass?"

"Oh, this is fantastic." There was an edge to her voice. Pitched high somewhere between excitement and hysteria. "I mean, I knew we'd failed in executing our goals, but this…"

She studied the atlas, running her fingertips over the scrolling print of the Kingsland colony.

"What? What is it?"

"Who ruled England after Henry the Eighth?"

"I'm sure ye ken it well enough, lass." He caught her hand, stroking her fingers lightly. "What is it? Ye ken ye can tell me anything."

She couldn't tell him this. Without a doubt, no matter how openminded he was, he'd never understand. Hell, there were people in her own time who wouldn't understand. Who would freak out if they thought such a thing were possible beyond the realm of science fiction.

She should have known, of course, what was happening. Looking back, there'd been signs enough. Animals coming through the portal none of them could identify. An odd bear. That cute little monkey as tiny as the palm of her hand she'd assumed must have been a lost species from Madagascar or something.

To her, it was a thrilling discovery even if it did herald the end of Fielding's success for all time.

In Quantum Mechanics, it was called the many-worlds interpretation. In sci-fi, it was called an alternate reality. The birth of a new dimension for every yes or no, success or failure in the history of the planet. Another reality existed for each scenario. Millions and millions of versions of history coinciding in the same space, but veiled from each other.

Their project hadn't only cast her through space and time, but had also pierced a dimension she hadn't considered when explaining them to Keir. The portal had crossed the plane of reality, sending her to a version of history where Elizabeth the First had never ruled.

A part of her wanted to share the excitement with Keir, see his eyes light up with discovery as they invariably did, but she was fearful this one might go too far afield for him.

The idea that there were other realities happening, multiplying and existing where one was standing, was too much for the people she knew to accept. Scientists who rejected the idea, unable to take a theory like that as fact.

It would be worse than telling him about time travel or ships flying into space. There was a colossal chance he wouldn't be able to wrap his head around the idea that other realities coexisted along side his own. That if the veil were to be pierced now, a dozen more versions of him might be pacing the room as he was at the moment. Or Hugh would be, having never left. He might be gone instead.

Al might never have come.

Such a shocking revelation might alienate him completely, no matter how progressive he thought he was.

She didn't dare tell him.

But she had to tell him something.

He was gawking at her as if she'd grown two heads. She couldn't have him think she was growing a third. Become inhuman in some way.

"I-I've just never realized before how utterly uneducated I am in the history of the world," she said, once more glancing down at the map where the French colony of Quebec extended all the way down to New York... or New Amsterdam as the map said. The English only had the central Atlantic coast and the Spanish still held the Caribbean coastline.

Was all of that because Elizabeth hadn't ruled? Or had it been something else?

"Ye're lying tae me," he said flatly. "Why?"

"I'm not," she insisted. "I just never knew what a dunce I am in the liberal arts. It's... embarrassing."

God, she hoped he bought it. She didn't. "I must have been thinking of a different country, I suppose. Who... *um*, who succeeded Henry the Eighth as king?"

"Al..."

"No, truly. I'm curious." She turned to him, curling her fingers around the open collar of his shirt with a smile. A very forced smile. "Maybe it's time for a little more *quid pro quo*. Your turn to become the teacher."

He studied her silently for a long while. She was certain he was going to reject her explanation and demanded a better, more truthful response. Then much to her relief, he sighed and stepped away. Drawing her along with him, he sat in one of the wingback chairs and pulled her into his lap.

"Henry the Ninth, the son of Henry and Catherine of Aragon," he said at last.

"Didn't they have a daughter, too?" she couldn't help but ask.

"Aye, Princess Mary," he nodded. "There were other children as well. Many stillborn, a few who died in infancy. Henry had many mistresses, 'tis nae rumor but fact. And a number of bastards including another Henry and the Elizabeth I believe ye were referring tae."

"There weren't... *uh*, I thought I read something about Henry the Eighth divorcing Catherine of Aragon."

His blue eyes were sharp, piercing. "What is amiss, *mo ghrá*? 'Tis nae like ye tae disremember anything ye've read."

"We all have our failings," she shrugged, "but being here now, I really feel as if I should know more about the recent history of the area."

He knew she was lying. He knew she knew that he knew it too. Still, he gave her what she wanted, detailing the succession of the English crown from Henry IX down to the current George I. Not the second but the first. The Stuarts hadn't claimed the crown until just fifty years past when King Charles III died without an heir just before the turn of the century. Scottish king at the time, James VII, had succeeded becoming James I of England more than a hundred years after the one she knew about.

It was a tumultuous time in the nation's history. With Catherine of Aragon alive at the time of Henry VIII's death—from a peptic ulcer in his leg caused by an injury he'd taken years before (some things didn't change)—the Catholic queen regent had raised her son and daughter in her faith. There was no Church of England, just the growing discontent always broadening the gap between the Catholics and Protestants. Rather than accept the Catholic King James VII of Scotland to the throne, many had lobbied for George of Hanover to take the throne. It had been a civil war of sorts, lasting as Keir had said, more than the whole of his life.

Culloden had only been the last in the bid to return the Stuart line to the throne.

No Virginia. No Maryland. Or Annapolis. Charlottesville. Williamsburg or William and Mary. The entire history of her country had changed. Given the path it was following in this reality, it might never become the future she knew.

She was well and truly lost here without even a future she could count on to comfort her. She'd lost everything.

Still she wasn't sorry for it.

She'd had him.

"I hope that someday ye might tell me what ye're hiding from me, lass," he said as the early morning hours gonged on the mantel clock.

There was hurt in this voice. Hurt she had put there. But she couldn't risk alienating him entirely. Couldn't risk losing the one good thing she had here any quicker than she already would.

He was hers. For at least a little longer and she meant to make the most of it.

◊◊◊◊◊

"You know we've been down here for hours, talking away." She stroked his hair back, curling it around her fingers. "Have you forgotten all the lovely things you promised to do to me tonight? Though your legs are probably asleep from me sitting here so long. In fact, all of you is probably completely numb." She brushed her lips along the shell of his ear before whispering in what she hoped was a seductive voice. "Is that why you haven't taken me to bed yet?"

"Ne'er tell me Allorah Maines is a prude who only does it in a bed." He raked his teeth down her neck, chuckling at her mock outrage.

"Is that a challenge?" She laughed, looping her arms around his broad shoulders. "This time you might win. I don't see how I'm supposed to manage anything in these skirts and with these buckets on my hips."

"Och, so 'tis true. My fair lass disnae ken everything."

Picking her up, Keir turned her about in a swift motion. Lifting her skirts, he set her astride him. The broad panniers collapsing into themselves and folding up under his direction.

She was impressed by his rakish skills and told him so.

He grinned and drew her down to meet his kiss. Tender, teasing. He parted her lips with his. His tongue stroking her lips languidly, gliding across her tongue. She felt her bodice slip and noticed that while he'd been kissing her, he'd managed to tug her gown off her shoulders and loosen her it enough to bare the swell of her breasts above the corset Peigi and Ceana had insisted upon.

"My talented rake," she sighed, holding his head to her breast as his lips whispered across her flesh, spreading goose bumps in their wake.

The same gooseflesh spread up her legs as he ran his rough palms over her thighs and around to cup her bottom and pull her closer. His long fingers parted and teased, finding her swollen nub, circling lightly. With a gasp, she shifted, giving him better access. He circled once more before sliding his fingers up inside her.

Her moan was matched by his. "Ye're fore'er hot for me," he growled in a thickened brogue. "Wet. Begging for me. Do ye want me, *mo ghrá?*"

He thrust his fingers deep inside her. "Yes!" Her response was strangled by a cry of pleasure.

Pushing aside his kilt, he lifted her, gliding her along his rigid erection, letting her feel the turgid length.

"Do ye want this?"

"Y-yes…" she stuttered hoarsely, trying to lift herself into position for him to take her but he'd not give an inch.

Instead, he thrust slowly against the juncture of her thighs, rousing her to a fever pitch. Until she was tugging at his hair and sobbing for relief. Her head was reeling, overcome by the blood pounding like the tolling of the clock through her with every slow stroke.

Their mouths met again, his tongue sliding across hers, mimicking the carnal motion of his body. Tension built low in her belly, spreading like fiery tendrils down the insides of her thighs. She gripped his hips tightly, her soft cries caught by his lips.

"Keir. Keir!"

"Let it go, *mo ghrá. Mo rúnsearc.* Let it take ye."

"No." She gazed into his flaming blue eyes and stroked his whiskered cheek tenderly. "Not without you. I want you to take me."

His eyes flared even hotter. Turning his cheek into her hand, he kissed her palm. Then lifted her and let her slide down his thick staff. She threw back her head with a moan that shook her entire body. He held her hips, grinding her down until he was buried deep, stretching her almost painfully.

"Nay, lass. Look at me. Come wi' me."

Once their eyes met, he lifted her again. Driving his hips up as he pulled her down. She wasn't about to let him do it all on his own. Holding tight to the flaring wings of the chair, she set a motion that pleased them both. Changing angles and rhythm to wrench growls and moans from him she'd never heard before.

And Gaelic, a stream of indecipherable words, roughened by his thick brogue, but tender. The tender sounds tore at her heart.

The torment building in her was getting harder to fight, but she was determined to make it last, make it the best she could. For him. For them.

The pleasure he was giving her, the pleasure she saw in his eyes was so pure, so poignant her chest tightened painfully. Tears filled her eyes.

"Ah, *mo rúnsearc. Mo stór lómhara. Conas tú teagmháil liom.* Come wi' me now."

He clasped her hips in his big hands and urged her on, faster still until he bowed beneath her. With that final surge, Al fell apart in his arms, the force of her orgasm so powerful blackness swirled before her eyes. Her head spun dizzily.

And dizzier still when he drew her to him for a tender kiss.

Lifting her in his arms, he carried her to his bedchamber. Setting her on her feet only long enough to strip her bare, he laid her on the bed, and shedding his kilt, stretched out next to her. He drew her close until they were touching from chest to toe. His legs wrapped around hers until their bodies tangled together.

His rough hands swept over her body from shoulder to hip, holding her even closer. She clung to him tightly. Ran her hands down his back and butt. She would never be close enough. Never have enough of him.

Never feel so deeply as he made her feel. She longed to

tell him what was in her heart.

She knew it would be the most foolish thing she could do. Such an admission would drive him away even faster than telling him that her reality was not his.

Yet this… what she experienced with him was the most real thing she'd ever known in her life. It'd only taken an accident of science to make it happen.

His lips found hers once more, tender. Lingering. Trailing down her jaw and neck lazily. Yet she felt him stirring anew against her belly, as if he couldn't get enough of her. His hand swept down her back. Kisses trailed farther down until he was nuzzling the valley between her breasts. Lower and her heart accelerated. Rolling her over, his lips grazed over her belly sending a shiver of pleasure down her spine.

Then he cupped her bottom in his hands, lifting her hips and Al tensed…

His lips hovered just over the apex of her thighs, his deep breaths teasing her damp curls. His hot tongue parted her, drawing slowly upward over her throbbing nub, and that little shiver became a long shudder. He probed lightly once more, eliciting a low keening from deep within her.

She felt his smile, his pleasure.

He laved her ever-so-lightly, circling with the merest flick of his tongue. She tried to arch beneath him, to deepen the contact, but he held her hips tight, keeping her in place. Taunting, teasing. Tasting. Just enough contact to leave her panting in desperate arousal. Wound tight. On edge.

His name was a desperate moan on her lips. His dark curls crushed in her fists. He continued to toy with her, taking her to the brink over and over. Until she was weeping for mercy. Body and soul.

He tongued her one last time, leaving her hovering on the pinnacle. She cried out in pain as he left her. Cried out again in exaltation as he slid his body up the length of her own.

Drawing her legs around his hips, he probed her with his hard member and pushed inside. Her body pulsated around him, drawing him deeper. Aching for his possession.

"Yer sweet body is crying out for me, *mo mhuirnín*. As mine is begging for yers." His lips met hers, drawing on her lower lip as he filled her completely.

Then he withdrew so deliberately the keening wail built within her once more. He was wreaking havoc on her body. Ravaging her soul.

"Ah, lass, ye maun be the witch I first accused ye of being for ye've bewitched me as I've ne'er dreamed possible."

He thrust harder, deeper. But unhurriedly. Over and over until an agonizing throbbing began deep inside her. She trembled at the power of it. Her release when it came was not explosive as it had been. It didn't wash over her. The force of it expanded inside of her until she felt it with every fiber of her being.

It owned her.

Just as he did.

Chapter 28

"Good morning, *mo rúnsearc.*"

Finding Al at his desk hunched over a piece of paper, Keir moved behind her and tilted her head back to kiss her tenderly. He meant for it to be nothing more than a brief peck. A greeting. But the taste of her soft lips roused the memory of their passionate night and he couldn't resist lingering, drawing it out much as he'd elongated their lovemaking. He hadn't wanted it to end.

She ran her tongue over her lips with a beguiling smile, one he would never have dreamed seeing on her face.

She would ever surprise him.

Looking over her shoulder, he took in the rudimentary sketch she was working on. "What is this?"

"Well, there's one thing about being in your time I just can't get used to," she said, retrieving her fallen pen and drawing another curved line. "They never talk about it in the novels and it didn't take me even a day here to figure out why. It's just intolerable. And I was thinking to myself this morning, hey, I don't have to live like this. I may not be a sanitary engineer but I am a quantum physicist. Surely I can figure it out."

"Figure what oot?"

"Indoor plumbing," she announced with a triumphant smile and holding up her drawing. "Believe me, it's going to be big!"

"Plumbing?"

"Yes! It was supposed be almost a hundred more years before it really caught on but I figure since this is a whole different rea... well, why wait?" she continued, drawing a few more lines here and there and muttering under her breath. "I think I have a fair idea, if I can just figure out how to build enough water pressure."

"Al... I dinnae ken what ye mean."

"Water closets. Necessaries. Whatever you call them."

"They are already indoors."

"But they can be better." She grinned up at him, delight sparkling in her gray eyes. "This is it, Keir. This is how I'm going to make my fortune in this time. Believe me, it'll be a revolution. And hot showers, too!"

She was nearly dancing in her chair, excitement evident in her every movement, but he didn't have any idea what she was getting at.

"Yer fortune?"

"Well, yeah. I have to be able to support myself somehow, right? There's not exactly much call for professional scientists yet so I'll need to use the skills and some marvelous futuristic ideas to make my way."

He was thoroughly baffled. "Make yer own way?"

"Is it that confusing?" Her grin broadened and her eyes danced impishly. She reached up to lightly chafe the scruffy growth of beard along his jaw. "A person might think you didn't get a lot of sleep last night."

"Mayhap I dinnae because I hae nae idea what ye're

speaking of."

"I'm talking about a way for me to support myself when I'm on my own," she said, her winsome smile slipping away.

He was frowning and he knew it. Stealing away her joy and enthusiasm. But he couldn't provide the enthusiasm she was obviously hoping for when he was so stunned by her words.

"We talked about this, remember?"

Aye, he remembered talking about it. Talking her out of it and convincing her to stay. To stay at Dingwall. To stay with him.

He'd thought that would be the end of it. Yet here she was, making plans for a life without him.

She truly meant it. She intended to leave Dingwall. Or Rosebraugh.

To leave him.

As if the incredible passion they'd shared being thus spent had put an end to it all.

His blood roared in his ears, drowning out the slapping rain against the windows, the thunder rolling in the distance. Everything but the deafening beat of his heart.

"I have to think about the future." Her voice was dim, shaky, losing the verve and confidence she'd gained over her time in the past. With him. "And now that we've... you've..."

"What, Al?" he bit out. "Now that I've what?"

"Gotten some."

"Some? Some what?"

"Oh, come on, Keir! You're not so archaic that you don't know what I mean. You've gotten some. Yo—you've had your fill. Or slacked your lust. Whatever you call it," she blustered, flushing so scarlet she was surely red to her toes.

"You know you're not going to want me around here forever," she added in a soft voice just above a whisper, glancing back down at her sketch.

He wouldn't?

It hovered on the tip of his tongue to say, "but what if I will?"

He didn't even flinch in surprise at the thought.

He'd never been one of those hardened bachelors who claimed he'd never wed. Nay, he'd only determined in his thirty-four years he'd never find a woman to suit him. One who cared about his interests, could handle his moods. Who would never bore him.

Allorah Maines was that woman. She fascinated him in every way. Intellectually, physically. His beguilement transcended the mere knowledge she could impart, what she might teach him. Though keeping up with her mentally was a challenge he relished. Nay, her wee quirks had their own allure. The way she scratched at her earlobe when she was nervous. Bounced on her toes when she was excited.

The way she cared for the feelings of others even when they had given her no reason to.

Even her own insecurity tugged at his heartstrings. He wanted nothing more than to be the man who would make sure she was confident in her appeal. That she was worthy of love.

But how to tell her all of that without frightening her away even faster than she already planned to go?

She was indefatigably certain she needed no one in her life. He knew her well enough by now to know she didn't think herself worthy of true affection. No one had ever cared for her unconditionally before.

All that nonsense about being her own woman when no

one, no one truly wanted to be alone in life. It was nothing but fear talking. Fear of rejection.

However, he knew well enough her feelings on marriage after hearing her response to Artair's hasty proposal. Had seen for himself firsthand how she responded to a proposal of the decent sort.

Perhaps he needed to make one of the indecent sort.

"There's but one problem wi' that, *mo rúnsearc*," he said flatly. "What makes ye think I've had my fill wi' ye?"

✕〇✕〇✕

"Excuse me?"

She blinked up at Keir in confusion. A burst of thunder had nearly drowned out the last of his words. Surely she hadn't heard him right.

"I'm nae near done wi' ye, *mo mhuirnín*. We've only just begun, ye and me."

Elation shimmied down her spine. Damn, but he made that sound like a promise. One she was anxious to find out how he intended to fill.

"So, it might take more than a night but eventually—"

"Or perhaps nae," he cut in. "Are ye in some hurry tae set oot on yer own? Because I am in nae hurry tae be done wi' ye. Stay at Rosebraugh, lass."

"And do what?"

"Be my lover."

So simple. So tempting. It was what she wanted more than anything. "I-I can't just…" Al sighed in exasperation. "I have to look ahead, too. I'll need a job. Some employment to earn my keep… And don't say I can do that as your lover or mistress or whatever. I'm not a whore. I can't feel like I'm being paid for that. Like I'm being *kept*."

"Ye dinnae think it would be a mutually beneficial arrangement?" he said, wondering how he was ever to get through to her.

She saw nothing of value in what she had to offer of her self and her heart. There was nothing he could say in words to convince her. She would believe nothing he said. Nay, he needed the time to show her what he felt. Demonstrate how much she meant to him.

But he couldn't do that if he couldn't keep her with him. "I can assure ye it would. I've much tae learn from ye, lass. I want what is in yer mind."

Bloody hell, he was going to start sounding like a lad desperate enough to grovel at her feet. But what was the alternative? Clapping her in irons again and keeping her chained in his dungeon? Though the idea had some appeal, he doubted it would keep her desires stoked even if it would keep her close at hand. "If it is an occupation ye desire, I can offer ye a position as my tutor."

Al rolled her eyes, shaking her head. "That has no more security than being your lover, Keir. Both positions are useful only for so long. You'll tire of me and then someday not far down the line I'll have told you everything I know on every subject. Then I'll be in the same boat. I've got to think and plan further than that."

Bloody, bloody hell. She was without a doubt the most stubborn, obtuse woman he'd ever met in his life. If all women in the centuries to come were like her, he wept for the future of man.

She sighed sadly. "I have a whole lifetime to live here, Keir."

She was leaving him with little choice. Either he kidnapped her or...

"Then live it with me."

"I just told you—"

"Be my wife."

"What?"

"Live your life wi' me, lass. Be my lover, my teacher, my partner. For the rest of our lives."

ХОХОХ

Surely he didn't realize the *permanence* of what he was saying, she thought, gaping at him.

He couldn't possibly be serious.

He was talking about *forever*. No one had ever wanted to keep her around indefinitely before. Not even her mother. He must be as half-cracked as the rest of his family to ask such a thing.

"Keir…"

"Your Grace," the butler called from the doorway. "You have a visitor."

"Nae now, Hastings," he barked, never looking away from Al. His eyes were raging with a storm of emotion that echoed the one brewing outside the windows.

"I'm afraid she insists, Your Grace."

"Who the hell thinks they can insist upon anything in this house?" he snapped.

"Oh, I think you'll want to see me, Keir."

Chapter 29

The woman lowering the rain-drenched hood from her head was utterly beautiful. She was probably in her mid-thirties but was so riveting with her rich, russet hair highlighted with shimmering strands of auburn and dark arching brows, she seemed younger at first glance. Her brown eyes were rimmed by thick lashes, her lips wide and red. Her skin flawless.

And she was tall, practically statuesque and willowy.

In short, she was the complete antithesis of Al. The sort of woman she'd always envied, who had overshadowed her in the eyes of every man she'd ever liked.

A quick glance at Keir told her he wasn't likely to be any different. There was real affection in his eyes when he observed at her. Who was she?

"Mathilde!" he said in surprise, crossing the room in long strides to take her hand.

This was the other sister? She gaped in surprise. She looked nothing like either Maeve or Ceana. Nor did she have the blue eyes that marked all the rest of them as blood.

"Where is Hawick? Did he come wi' ye?" he asked, taking her cloak.

"No, he doesn't know I'm here," she said, eyeing Al curiously. "No one does. I couldn't say a word when he refuses to accompany me."

"Refuse? Why would he nae come tae Rosebraugh? Did ye ride all this way alone?"

"I had two men-at-arms wi' me. And only them because Hawick has said he will not help Uncle Camran."

Keir stiffened visibly. "Hae ye found him, Mathilde?"

"Hawick found him," she said. "He's being held at the Canongate Tolbooth just as you feared with more than a hundred others. Hawick spotted him there, touring the prison with Cumberland."

"And he willnae help us see him released?"

Mathilde shook her head. "He says the Jacobites need to learn their lesson thoroughly to prevent more incidents like this."

⋊⋉⋊⋉⋊

Dread snaked through Keir. Hawick had been to Rosebraugh dozens of times. They all considered him family. If he refused to come now, there must be more to it than just an unwillingness to help them free his father.

"What are they planning tae do?"

"Cumberland means to see that the lairds who had a hand in rousing the rebellion are made an example of. The prisoners are being transferred to Carlisle to stand trial," she told him. "It'll be a mockery, of course. They intend to execute them."

"Them?"

"All of them."

"That's a hell of an example," Al couldn't help saying aloud. "Surely this guy couldn't be so evil."

"They call him the Butcher, lass," Keir said. "Nothing is too bad tae be believed of him. He has already proven there is nothing he willnae do."

"He's right," Mathilde agreed, walking farther into the room with her hand extended. "You must be Miss Maines. I've heard so much about you."

Al's brows lifted in surprise and tentatively, she shook her hand. Heard about her from who? Ceana? Maeve? Would this Urquhart sister end up being at nuts as the other two? "Nothing good, I suppose."

"Some," she slanted a glance at her cousin, "but no, not all. I want to thank you for being so kind to comfort my cousin during this difficult time. He and Hugh were quite close, admittedly closer than my brother was to any of us. Nevertheless, I loved him dearly. I am incredibly saddened to hear of his passing."

Unlike Maeve and Ceana, Mathilde did appear genuinely aggrieved. Al felt a tug of sympathy. "I'm truly sorry for your loss, for your whole family's loss."

Would she again be accused of having a hand in it? Should she be wary? Expect a knife to be thrust her way? No, Mathilde only wiped away a tear and braved a smile.

She liked her.

She turned back to Keir. "To answer your question, aye, Keir. They mean to execute all the prisoners at Canongate. Including your father. According to Hawick, the Marquis of Tullibardine is also being held as well as the Earls of Derwentwater, Kilmarnock and Cromarty, and Lord Balmarino."

Keir swore under his breath. "Cumberland means to murder them all? How can he justify such a thing?"

"I told you, he means to set an example so harsh no

other will dare take up arms against the king."

"As if the murders in the aftermath of the battle were nae enough?" he asked bitterly. "As if hanging women and children who dared speak in opposition to him or hide those who fled him were nae enough? As if grinding our entire culture beneath his boot heel were nae enough?"

Tears burned in Al's eyes at his impassioned speech. It was as if the words were being torn from his soul, this man who claimed to have no political ties. Clearly, he cared for his clansmen and his countrymen deeply.

"They must be stopped," he said. "The king has got tae ken what is happening."

She rushed to his side, slipping her hand into his. He squeezed it hard. "Is there anything that can be done?" she asked Mathilde.

"I don't think so." She shook her head. "But in all honesty, my husband believes no one beyond Cumberland and a few others are aware of the identities of the higher ranking lairds being held. Hawick recognized your father straight away, of course. Uncle Camran told him of the others."

"Yet he supports this?" Keir asked. "He willnae raise a hand tae stop it?"

Mathilde shook her head once more. "No. You know he has always supported the unification of Scotland and England. He might not agree with Cumberland's methods, but he stands with him in making an example to dissuade others from rising against King George in the future."

His sharpened gaze slid to Al. "Is this how it will be then? Do ye lie tae me aboot this as well?"

As if anything she might have known of the future mattered at all in this reality. For all she knew now, the

Highlanders were truly lost for all time. Everything she knew of their evolvement over the past three hundred years might not ever happen. Yet it might. So what purpose would it serve to tell him that now? Any more than admitting to what she'd withheld from the previous night would?

No, some lies were for his own good. He needed to believe there was a future for him. She couldn't let him down. But neither could she say anything about it in front of Mathilde who was already eyeing them keenly. So, she shook her head infinitesimally, hoping it would be enough.

His shoulders sagged slightly. "But there was nothing of this?" he pressed.

Biting her lip, she shot another glance at Mathilde. "No."

"What is this?" his perceptive cousin asked. "Are you a soothsayer, Miss Maines? Do you know the future?"

Now that would have made an excellent excuse. Hokey, yes. But decent enough. But Keir didn't give her a chance to jump on it. "'Tis naught, Mathilde, merely a conversation on a different subject. She's merely a lass wi'oot a home right now."

Mathilde shrugged. "Too bad. There's more than one thing I'd like to know of my future."

"I certainly can't help with that," Al said honestly. "Sorry."

"Don't worry yourself, Miss Maines," the woman said. "What we do need to worry about is seeing dear Uncle Camran set free."

"But how?"

"Nae," he said. "The greater question is what tae do wi' him after he's freed. Will Cumberland admit who he'd taken prisoner and hope for the support of the king in recapturing him? Hound him for the rest of his days? Or will he let it go?

I'd wager on the former."

"It'll all be moot if he's taken to Carlisle, Keir," Mathilde pointed out. "I came here on my own, opposing my husband so you might have a chance to save your father from sure death. Because that is what awaits him. I overheard Cumberland telling Hawick last night that he will see the prisoners each hanged, disemboweled on the block, and beheaded before their viscera is thrown to the flames."

Al grimaced at the bloody image.

"Is that the fate you want for your father?" Mathilde pressed.

"Nay," he said, then stronger. "Nay. I willnae stand for it. Nae just Father but any of them. I'll bluidy well see them all freed and face the Butcher myself for what he's done tae my clan. Tae Frang."

Fear skittered through Al. His conviction was strong, undeniable. But she couldn't stand the idea of him getting hurt, possibly killed.

"I'm glad to hear my efforts in reaching you weren't in vain," Mathilde said with a satisfied smile. "The real question will be in how to release them."

"Aye, that might be a problem."

Silence fell over them. Evidently the problem was obvious to the two of them but she had no idea what might impede them. "Why?"

"Canongate is the largest tolbooth in Edinburgh. A prison, lass," he told her. "The most heavily guarded."

Flipping through the atlas still sitting on the table from last night, he opened the book to a map of Edinburgh and showed it to her, pointing to a building right on the Royal Mile near Holyrood. Granted the map didn't show Edinburgh to be as large as she knew it was in her time, but the thing was smack dab in the middle of it.

"'Tis a fortress centuries old. Four stories wi' a single entry kept locked at all times wi' even the guards sealed wi'in. Our only saving grace would be that it is nae far from the edge of the city if we approach from the south around the Salisbury Crag's and Arthur's Seat."

He shot a sharp glance at his cousin. "Do ye ken how heavily it is guarded now?"

"In addition to the regular city patrol, there is a platoon of Cumberland's dragoons camped in the square behind the Canongate Kirk."

Both winced. Al wondered how big a platoon was.

"You can gather the men to take the camp," Mathilde said quietly. "I know you and Hugh had connections everywhere for all you practically lived abroad. You know enough men to do it."

"Aye, honest men I can trust." Keir examined the map, scratching his jaw. "Och, the guards are nae the problem. 'Tis the bluidy jail itself. The cells wi'in present nae problem. There will be nae more than a dozen guards inside. All will hae keys. Any one will open all the cell doors. Nay, 'tis the main door. 'Twill be but one man carrying that key and he'll be inside."

"That's ridiculous," she said. "One door? One exit? And only one key? That's an awful safety hazard."

Mathilde appeared interested about her phrasing but he wouldn't allow her a breath to ask. "'Tis why it's so secure a gaol, lass. There's nae been a breakoot from the Canongate since the 1500s."

"Well, I hope they never have a fire in there."

"You must know someone who can pick the lock,"

Mathilde jumped in. "Someone who could pry it open?"

He half-nodded without committing. "Mayhap, but 'tis nae wee thing easily done. "Twould need tae be done quickly 'ere the alarm is raised and the platoon reinforced by the burgh's garrison. I dinnae ken how tae assure 'tis done quickly."

"Why don't you just blow the lock?" Al asked. They both turned to her inquisitively.

"Blow the lock?" Mathilde repeated. "Whatever do you mean?"

She shook her head uncertainly and looked at Keir as if he might truly be able to read what was in her mind.

"Blow it up." She curled her fists together before spreading them out to simulate the boom with a whooshing noise to accompany it. "Explosives. You do have them, don't you?"

"Like black powder?" he asked. "I ken 'tis been used for mining excavation but mostly just used as a propellant for cannon and musket fire."

She pursed her lips, thinking. "Could you get some?"

He was curious. She could see it in his eyes, that same vivid fire that burned whenever she talked about something new. "How much? We've muskets in the armory."

Her mind was working furiously, trying to mentally construct some mode of delivering an explosion of only gunpowder on a focused area. They needed to take out the lock and the jamb area next to it. Everything she knew about blowing things up with just gunpowder involved a coyote and barrels and barrels of powder marked Acme.

Too small, it wouldn't work at all. Too big, they blew through the prison wall and took down the innocent people inside he meant to free. Working their way through the rubble would take time.

It had to be just the door.

Then even if they managed the right amount, the ignition would be the problem. A cartoonish trail of gunpowder that might fizzle out before it could get there wasn't going to work. It would hardly be reliable in the best of circumstances. And if this pouring rain continued…

"Do you have safety fuses?"

He shook his head. He didn't understand what she meant. But she could see by the expectation on Keir's face, he was counting on her to come up with something.

"There's no dynamite…" Al left off the 'yet.' He shook his head. "No nitroglycerine?"

Her eye roll was all for herself. She knew full well from her chemical engineering classes it hadn't come around until Nobel's time after the Civil War and hadn't been employed for demolition purposes until later in the 19th century. This was only the 18th.

But there must be something here they could use. Something small but that packed a big, focused punch. Enough of a blast to take out a lock.

Tapping her lip, she paced the room searching for inspiration.

"What is she doing?"

"Thinking," Keir answered his cousin softly.

"Is there anything that can be done about it?" was Mathilde's droll reply.

"Nay, she's a brilliant lass, my Big Al. Ye just wait, she'll come up wi' a solution for us."

Warmth spread from her heart at his proudly spoken words. Bursting like the bomb she was determined now to produce for him.

No one had ever had such faith in her before.

She wouldn't let him down.

Chapter 30

Al paced the perimeter of the room, running options through her head. Best case was to make a plastic explosive for size and ease of use. Unlike nitro, it was far more stable and without the unfortunate side effect of randomly exploding if dropped. She could mold it right into the lock.

She'd even made it before in a weapons engineering class she'd taken for fun and to meet guys before she'd given up on ever finding one. Surprisingly, it wasn't hard. If she could get the ingredients.

"Do you have bleach?"

"What is she talking about, Keir?"

"Perhaps, I can have Hastings show ye tae a room, Mathilde, where ye might rest," he suggested. "Ye've had a long journey. Ye maun be neigh exhausted."

"I am to the bone but I cannot imagine leaving just now. This is fascinating. Tell me, Miss Maines, what is bleach?"

Al wandered closer to Keir and spoke softly. "It's a cleaning liquid. I'd need potassium chloride, too…"

"Nay, lass, whatever it is, we dinnae hae it."

"Any chemicals? Anything?"

He shook his head. Biting her lip, she resumed her

pacing. Not that it really mattered, she realized. She would've needed petroleum jelly for the plastic explosive as well. Something the source of wouldn't even be discovered until the next century.

She was pretty sure they couldn't wait so long.

"How long do we have?"

"Not long, I'm afraid," Mathilde answered. "The transfer of prisoners is to begin next Thursday."

"That's six days," Al said. "That should be no problem."

"Edinburgh is nearly three days of hard riding," Keir told her.

She cringed. So assuming they wanted to do this under cover of night, they had only two to three days to get this done. It wasn't long enough to get creative.

No chemicals meant no plastic explosives, so there was really nothing she could make herself. So what else was there? Back home she could have just Googled how to make any number of different bombs on her phone. Barring a handy stick of dynamite to throw at the door, a pipe bomb might do the trick. There were thousands of sites on the internet just waiting to show aspiring terrorists how to do it in a thousand different ways.

Just type, type, click and she could have the answer in the palm of her hand and ultimately use her phone for something more productive than watching cat videos on YouTube.

Not that it mattered, even if the battery in her phone weren't dead, there was no wi-fi or cell coverage here in the...

Her steps slowed along with her thought process. She scratched at her earlobe as an idea began to take form.

Maybe.

Possibly.

She looked up and found Keir staring at her. His eyes alight with something she couldn't identify but thrilled her just the same.

"Ye thought of something?"

She grinned. "I thought of something."

Chapter 31

"I cannot begin to understand what you're about."

"Go tae yer room, Mathilde."

"I will not," she said firmly. "There is something intriguing going on here. I don't plan to miss a minute of it."

"Then just shut it."

Silence fell as they hurried through the halls of Rosebraugh to the bedchamber Al had been given for her use. She hadn't spent much time there, as he'd kept her pleasantly occupied the last few days. But her clothes were kept there and among them, the scant personal items she'd carried with her from the future.

The knowledge of which was going to save more than one life. Soon.

His cousin retained her silence for all of five seconds.

"Ceana told me there was something different about you, Miss Maines," she went on. "I can see now she wasn't wrong."

Al, smart lass, ignored his cousin and dug through the small trunk Peigi had brought from Dingwall. Inside was a bundle of the green silk she'd been wearing when he first found her at Culloden.

"I told Peigi when she first asked about it that it was very important to me but not to touch it. Ever. I'm glad she remembered half of that at least and thought to bring it along."

She untied what turned out to be sleeves of the bodice she'd worn that day. Inside it were the miniscule excuse for a skirt, the flat, rectangular badge that had adorned her white jacket—which was not among the items—and a shiny black item, nearly flat and also rectangular but with no markings upon it at all.

That was what she pulled out, setting the rest aside.

"What is it?"

Al glanced at his cousin uncertainly.

"Have no fear, Miss Maines. My lips are forever sealed, but I beg you, don't deny me the first bit of intrigue I've had in an age."

Al had been right. His whole family was half-cracked. There was no denying it. But since he'd never known Mathilde to lie and because he didn't want to waste the time carrying her bodily from the room, Keir only shrugged.

"Yer solemn oath, Mathilde."

"Oh, you have it. Now what is it?"

Good bloody question.

But Al didn't seem to want to be as forthcoming as he hoped. As she had the previous night she refused him an explanation. Why? What could she say now that would serve him ill? He'd been oddly hurt by her reticence the night before, but he knew his lady well. If she were keeping something from him, she wasn't doing so to harm him, but perhaps to spare him harm.

Though he intended to delve more deeply into her reasons at a better time, he let the matter lie now and watched as she cracked the object in half to reveal the interior. Dominating it was a block of black surrounded by a geometric maze of green squares with wires and dots of finely crafted silver.

He couldn't imagine what purpose it was meant to serve. Yet he knew it must be of some importance as it had been on her person when she'd come to him through the portal. Questions hovered on the tip of his tongue but he put them aside. Not only because of their company but because there were matters of more import to focus on now.

She pried out the black piece, holding it up triumphantly. "This is what's going to set your father free, Keir."

"That?" That innocuous piece of nothing? Surely she was jesting? "How? Is it an explosive?"

"No, it's a battery," she said as if that explained it all. Obviously she knew it wouldn't because she carried on immediately. "It's a power source. Do you know what electricity is?"

"No."

"Aye," he answered at the same time as his cousin. "Charles Francois du Fay has presented on his experiments in Paris following Stephen Gray's discovery of the conduction of electricity some years ago."

"Okay, so a battery is a container to hold an electrical charge."

"Why?" Mathilde asked. "How? For what purpose?"

"I said shut it, Mathilde, or I will hae ye removed."

Had Al found his constant questions as annoying as he found Mathilde in that moment? If she had yet continued to display such boundless patience and enthusiasm all that time, his admiration would grow tenfold.

"But electricity is nae explosive," he said to Al after

Mathilde moved aside to pout near the foot of the bed.

"No, but what this battery is made out of is. The biggest problem with lithium ion batteries is that they react badly... explosively to heat. All we need to do is superheat it until the cell goes thermal. It should be enough to blow the lock."

"How does it do that?" He winced even as the question left his mouth.

"The battery should begin to break down at about two hundred degrees Fahrenheit. That will spark a chemical and thermal reaction inside the battery. The gases will expand, leading to higher temperatures and more gas. It will have nowhere to go but out, spewing hot gas and molten material of what's left at about two thousand degrees. I've seen video. It's very cool."

Despite the seriousness of their endeavor, he could see the excitement coiled within her, the tension radiating from her. She loved all of this.

God, how he loved *her*.

His heart tripped over a beat.

Keir cleared his throat and took the simple block from her, turning it over in his palm. "So how do we superheat it?" he asked, wondering if the answer were one he should already know.

"That's no problem at all. Any continuous heat source would do it. A flame or some such. Really, the easiest way will be to just short it across the leads. That will allow us time enough to get away. But..." She peered out the window and his eyes followed, watching the rain slap the panes. "But the burning question," she started, then pursed her lips, "no pun intended. But the problem is we need to charge the battery. It's dead... I used all the electricity it contained while I was waiting out my time in your dungeon. I need to fill it up again. Somehow. All of this is useless if I can't figure that out."

"But that's simple enough," he said, wondering at her bewilderment. "I assume you ken how we can put the electrical charge intae it, aye?" She nodded. "Then 'tis simple. I can create the electrical current ye need."

"You can?"

He might have felt a twinge of offense at the disbelief in her voice. Aye, he might have if he weren't having a flash of inner triumph. At long last, he knew something she did not. So for a change, he would be the teacher and she the student. "We'll use a Leyden Jar. Pieter Van Musschenbroek presented it to the Académie des Sciences two years past."

"I don't think it matters right now who invented it, Keir," Mathilde said from her perch at the end of the bed. "What matters is whether you have one and whether it will do whatever it is Miss Maines needs it to do."

Al's lips twitched but her eyes were bright as she looked at him. "You have one?"

"Nay," he disappointed her with a grin. "But I ken how tae make one. The silver foil might be a challenge but nae impossible tae overcome wi' the materials available here at Rosebraugh."

XOXOXOX

Al stared at him in amazement. The one thing she hadn't been able to puzzle out and the 18th century man, who by all rights shouldn't have known a thing about creating electricity, was the one to provide the answer.

As if it were all elementary.

A lifetime wouldn't be long enough to enjoy him. His company, his incredible mind. His tender sensuality.

Not that she had that long.

Or did she?

He asked her to marry him, hadn't he? If he'd actually been serious—could he have possibly been serious?—he could be *hers* for the rest of her life.

Hers.

To have. To hold.

To love.

Did she dare begin to dream again?

Keir clapped his hands, rubbing the palms together eagerly. "This might actually work. Shall we begin?"

She darted a glance at Mathilde, her brown eyes dancing with excitement and perhaps approval as well.

"This is the most fun I've had in years."

How could Al argue with that?

She was right.

Chapter 32

"Ye're nae coming, lass."

"I am."

"Ye're nae!"

"Yes, I am!"

"Your lovers' quarrel is charming, but if we want to save Uncle Camran, you'll have to wrap it up." Mathilde critically eyed her manicure as her droll remark landed on deaf ears.

"I willnae allow it, lass!"

"You're still arguing with me," Al said, crossing her arms stubbornly. "Why are you still arguing with me?"

"Because ye're being ridiculous, lass," he retorted. "I willnae hae ye risking yer life o'er this. One misstep and ye could die oot there!"

"So could you. Do you see me trying to hold you back?"

"Argh! Ye stubborn wee... It willnae do! We need tae move quickly. And ye dinnae even ken how tae ride a horse."

Al ground her teeth. "I'll figure it out. Besides, you need me. You might have managed to get this battery charged..."

And he had. He'd even rigged up a series of Leyden Jars in parallel to do the job quicker. She'd been impressed but he'd been smug. Washing the look off his arrogant face when her phone had lit up had been a true pleasure and a bit of a wicked amusement.

"…but you haven't any idea how I figured out to safely short the leads."

"As ye say, I'll figure it oot."

"No, I have to go."

"Nay!"

"My battery, my choice."

It was Keir's turn to grind his teeth. She could see his jaw fairly popping from the force of it.

"Three days, lass," he ground out, jabbing a finger so close to her nose, her eyes crossed. "Three days of riding hard tae get tae Edinburgh."

"Might I be the one to point out you've been arguing about this for nearly as long?" Mathilde asked.

"Will ye nae go tae yer room, woman?" he shouted, turning on her. "And leave me some peace?"

"And miss all this?"

Mathilde's glance slid around him to Al. She winked.

Al appreciated the support.

Keir turned back to her, gripped by the temper that exploded with each of these arguments and had kept their sheets ablaze for the past two nights. Oddly enough, she'd enjoyed both.

"Think what ye're getting yerself intae, *mo ghrá*. Three days on horseback. There'll be nae plush carriages and speeding automobiles wi' yer bluidy *A* and *C* tae comfort ye. Ye'll ne'er make it."

Her eyes narrowed. No one would ever tell her again she couldn't do something. She'd ride his *bloody* horse all the way to Edinburgh with a smile even if her ass was chapped off by the time she got there.

"I, for one, will be glad to have you join us, Miss Maines," Mathilde joined it. "It's been such an interesting experience, I couldn't bear for it to end. And if you're worried about how well she can handle a mount, I've a simple solution. She can ride with me. See! I've finally contributed positively to our little project."

What a nice way to refer to a treasonous activity.

There had been a brief instance of uncertainty for Al when she figured that out. But she already knew there wasn't anything she wouldn't do for Keir's sake. Apparently that included laying down her freedom and possibly her life for him.

If only he'd stop arguing and let her.

Difficult since that was *exactly* why he didn't want her along.

"Thank you, Mathilde." She smiled sweetly at the woman. For all her officiousness, it was hard not to like her.

Her smile for Keir was far more saccharine.

With a menacing growl, he turned and stomped away, his kilt flaring as much as his anger.

"Don't forget to change out of that before we leave," she called after him, feeling smug in her unspoken victory. "You don't want to get arrested for wearing a tartan before we even make it to the prison!"

"My cousin has always had a bit of a temper," Mathilde said when he'd gone. "Makes me tremble in my boots. Yet there you are, so calm. Butter wouldn't melt in your mouth. You impress me, Miss Maines."

She smiled. "Please, call me Al."

"Al? Very well, you can call me Tildy," she offered. "It's been a fair while since anyone has but then, there are few I like well enough to allow them to. And I do like you, Al."

"Thank you."

The compliment warmed her through. If boyfriends had been hard to come by in life, true girlfriends were even harder. And she got the strong feeling she might have found one in Keir's cousin, even if she was losing him in the process.

The thought made her heart ache. But it would have eventually in any case.

Turning back to the battery, she concentrated on making the connections she'd need to short the leads. She'd peeled off the hard plastic, outer casing to expose the inner wires and trio of long batteries covered in their black rubber coating. And more importantly, she'd figured out a way to trigger it that could be quickly done.

And easily. Despite her argument, Keir could manage it without any trouble at all. She simply didn't want to be left behind to wonder and worry about what was going on.

And then there had been another part of her that wanted to strike against 'The Butcher' for what he'd done to the Highlanders. What he was still doing to them. The more stories she heard about the atrocities he was committing against the people here, the more incited her humanitarian side became.

She'd felt the same anger when Dr. Fielding had begun his little zoo but had felt helpless to raise more than a verbal complaint in opposition. Even when human freedom was at stake. It had eaten at her, pained her until it burst upon Hugh's arrival.

What Cumberland was doing was even worse. The tales she heard about torture and hangings weren't just violations of human rights. They were unacceptable war crimes. Crimes against humanity that would have gotten him called before a

UN tribunal in the future. They didn't have that here to help these people. There was only men like Keir to fight back. And she wanted to be a part of it.

Even if her contribution didn't go further than the detonation of a small IED. And it was extremely improvised.

Mathilde was twisting long lengths of silver thread she'd produced from her mother's old sewing basket into wires. Al would use them to short the battery by attaching an end of each to the leads within the battery and the other ends to silver butter knives. With few things handy made from copper, silver would have to do. It was just as conductive even if her end product looked ridiculous.

"How is this going to work?"

"Once the two wires connect the knives to the battery, we can lay one knife across the other with a piece of straw between them. With that in place, we set the straw on fire. The connection will be made when it burns away between the two, allowing the current to pass through them, short-circuiting the battery which we'll string up as close to the lock as we can."

"It's quite clever really," Mathilde said. "Did you learn this in boarding school or from an eccentric governess?"

Al grinned and shrugged. "Neither."

"I wouldn't think so, governesses are so rarely interesting," she replied. "My lasses would love you though. Their governess cares only for painting and etiquette and they are bored silly. My youngest especially, she always reading from journals and such. Just like Hugh always did."

Her voice caught, just a hitch.

"Tildy, I'm so…"

"Oh, pish!" she said, straightening and holding her wire up triumphantly. "That's neither here nor there. It's only that he would have enjoyed this all immensely. He would have liked you, I think, as well. Though perhaps not as much as my cousin."

A blush painted Al's cheeks and she ducked her head to hide it.

"No, don't be shy," she chided. "'Tis plain to see he likes ye well enough and you like him. The way he looks at you tells me there is something more as well. Is he your lover?"

Her face reddened to a full flush and a low moan escaped Al. Had she just thought it might be nice to have a girlfriend? She couldn't talk about him. Not about what they were doing with each other, particularly when she had no idea where it was all going.

And most especially not with his cousin.

Mathilde laughed. "Bold as brass with him yet shy with me. It does make my imagination soar. But I won't press you... for now, at least. Tell me instead, how is it you don't know how to ride a horse?"

✗O✗O✗O✗

Al stared up at the beast in the stables. She'd had one of the stable boys point out the horse she would be riding— assuming she really meant to contradict Keir's wishes and do this crazy thing. It didn't seem so bad. Its brown eyes were kind. Other than a brief glance, it seemed pretty disinterested in her.

Which was fine.

But it was so big. No, compared to the others, it was small. It was just big to her.

"I'm an animal lover," she told it quietly, reaching out to stroke its forehead. Jumping aside with a start when it shook its head. "No, really, I am. I love animals even if I never had much of a chance to know any as big as you."

She shook her head. She was talking to a horse.

"I have a cat. *Had.* I worry about him. I hope someone found him and is feeding him. His name is Mr. Darcy. Keir hasn't asked yet why I named him that. I wonder if he ever will. Maybe he'll make fun of me for idolizing romantic heroes," she laughed under her breath. "Maybe, for my sake, he won't figure out he's one of them."

"He wants to save me, you know?" She tried to stroke the horse's nose again and this time it allowed the contact, even leaning into it a little bit. "He already has. More than once. I wish I could save him, too, but I've never really been the heroine type. I just want to try, even if it makes him angry. I want to help." Al sighed and scratched the horse between the eyes.

It nuzzled her hand and she felt herself melt a little. She really did have a soft heart for animals, and for charmers who claimed they weren't charmers. "Really, I just want to be with him. To love him... God, that sounds so stupid. So much for feminism—Oh! *Whoa*!"

The fickle horse, so happy under her touch one second, reared its head in the next. Knocking her under the chin and sending her stumbling back. Kicking over a pail, she careened to the side, taking down a pair of shovels and somehow managing to tip over a trough filled with oats.

Attempting to save it, she fell headlong over the top of it and into a pair of arms.

"Oh, my gosh! I'm so sorry!" she cried, steadying herself on the surprisingly stable arms of the ancient-looking man who'd come to her rescue.

He was not much bigger than her really. With graying hair and big ears showing from beneath his cap. He had a deeply wrinkled face, though his twinkling blue eyes were remarkably youthful.

He somehow looked familiar but she couldn't place him. He set her back on her feet with ease. She had none. She could only imagine how much he'd heard if he'd been standing there for a while!

"I'm so sorry," she repeated, flushing scarlet.

"Dinnae fash yerself, lass." He chuckled, thrusting his fists into the deep pockets on his trousers. "Accidents happen, dinnae they? In fact, some of the best things hae come from a wee accident here and there."

It sounded so similar to what Keir had said about accidents and how the greatest advances in science had come from them, Al could only gape at him.

He dragged off his cap and scratched his balding pate. "Truth be told, I've made a few of my own. Wee slips that dinnae come oot as expected. A door left open too long, for example. Sometimes things slip through ye might nae hae intended, ye ken?"

Tilting her head, she narrowed her eyes on the old man thoughtfully. Aye, she did ken, but why did she get the feeling they were talking about the same damned door. "I'm sorry...?"

"Donell, lass," he supplied at the unspoken prompt. "Do ye think mayhap that sometimes whatever gets through might be better off on the other side? E'en if it were an accident that got them there? As if it were all fated somehow?"

Her lips parted, then closed. That was the most confounded question she'd ever been asked before. "Donell, have we met somewhere before?"

"Och, nay, lass. I'm sure I'd remember." He turned away. "I should be going now... aboot my duties."

Al watched him amble into the darkness, feeling a spark

of panic. "Donell!"

He paused, glancing over his shoulder. "Aye, lass?"

"Sometimes accidents are exactly what need to happen to find real happiness." It was awful and cryptic but she felt like it needed to be said. "I'm just saying, it'd be a shame to try to undo something that turned out all right in the end. Right?"

He nodded slowly. "Just so, lass. Just so. Ye'll be ha'ing a care for yerself in the days ahead, then?"

"Yes, I will."

With another nod, he carried on, disappearing into the darkness. Who was he? He did seem awfully familiar.

"You do have an odd way with people, Miss Maines," Ceana said from behind her. "Everyone from Duke to stable hand."

"Is that who he is?" Al asked. "Do you know him?"

"Old Donell's been around Rosebraugh off and on since I was a child," she said.

"He reminds me of…" Honestly, he looked a lot like the old janitor who'd worked at Mark-Davis when she'd first been hired there years before. She used to talk to him in the cafeteria when she worked late and the place was practically deserted. One of those long conversations had sparked the idea that led to the construct she'd developed for the wormhole stabilization.

She peered back to the shadows where the old man disappeared. In fact, he looked just like him… Wasn't that strange?

"Reminds you of who?"

"My grandfather," she lied. "He seems nice."

Ceana shrugged. "He always had a particular fondness for Hugh. Heard him say to my mother once that he thought

Hugh was meant for better things. What could be better than being a duke?"

Al hoped she wasn't expected to answer that question. Instead, she changed the subject, but was determined to find the old man when they returned from Edinburgh.

"I wanted to thank you for lending me your dress the other night. It was very kind of you."

She seemed surprised by the gratitude. "You know, I'm not sure what to make of you, Miss Maines."

Well, that made them even. Clearly, there was more to Ceana than met the eye. What more, she wasn't sure.

"At first, given what Maeve said about you, I was certain you'd had some sort of hand in Hugh's death. Then I was certain you were angling after my cousin. Working to rise from whatever hole you climbed out of to a countess's coronet. Clearly, you're hiding something. Your behavior is just too... odd for you not to be."

Look who was talking.

"But Mathilde has taken a real shine to you and she's normally quite discerning and Keir... well, he does seem to care for you to some measure. I cannot really tell."

Welcome to the club.

"And you care about him. For more than his wealth and position, I mean. But again, to what degree I cannot say."

She waited, her eyes glittering in the light of the lantern, but Al wasn't going to say either and she must have guessed it. With a sigh, her rigid shoulders slumped marginally. "I heard old Donell telling you to have a care for yourself but do have a care for my cousin as well. Not just his heart but in these days ahead. Keep him safe."

Wow, maybe Ceana really wasn't so bad after all.

"Of course, if anything happens to him, I might just

have to finish what Maeve started."

Or not.

With a wave and a laugh that left Al feeling uncertain whether she was serious or not, Ceana patted the now-staid horse on the nose and left the stable.

Nut jobs or not, the many members of the MacCoinnach and Urquhart clans were certainly interesting. They'd keep her on her toes, that much was certain.

She just wished everything else was as assured. If Keir really cared for her as much as both his cousins seemed to think he did.

And more importantly. Would it last?

Could it?

Accidents happen for a reason.

Chapter 33

Three days later

Dusk was almost upon them. And then they would be on the short final leg of their journey into Edinburgh.

Al wasn't quite certain how she was going to find the fortitude to walk into the town when every muscle in her body was screaming in pain.

Three days, Keir had said. Three days of pure hell, he should have said. It might not have changed her mind about coming along but it would have at least prepped her for the reality of what she was getting herself into.

Oh, she'd managed to find the rhythm of riding the horse after the first several hours when it was either that or a continuous pounding to her rear end. But nothing could be done to spare her the desperate cramping on the inside of her legs.

At least now she knew why Ceana had looked so self-satisfied three days ago when she'd first mounted her horse. When she got back to Rosebraugh—*if* she got back—she was going to kick that woman in the teeth.

And there'd been little to comfort her since they'd

departed other than such heart-warming thoughts. Keir was still stewing in the simmering in the juices of his bad temper. Leaving her to experience the misery of riding in the pelting rain on her own.

Leaving her to Mathilde and Artair's company rather than providing his own. Leaving her plenty of time to wonder about accidents and doorways and fate.

Such abstract thoughts weren't really her forte at all. It was the sciences that had always drawn her. Hard-core fact. She'd saved her fairytales for fiction not Platonian philosophies.

She wished she could talk to Keir about it all. But he was giving her the silent treatment, repeatedly making his point that he hadn't wanted her along.

Hadn't wanted her in harm's way.

His point might have been more effectively made if he hadn't come to her at night and curled beneath the blankets of her pallet with her. Massaging away the ache in her thighs and bottom for her. Warming her against the chill of the dampness that lingered. Then holding her so tightly she couldn't breathe. Whispering sweet Gaelic in her ear that might very well have been scolding but sounded far more loving.

How could the words be anything else as he made love to her under the cover of his tartan?

She'd loved sleeping spooned alongside his hard body but she'd been surprised and perhaps a wee bit mortified when his wayward hands had first found their way to her breasts, then between her thighs. His warm lips nuzzling the nape of her neck with Artair, Mathilde, and a handful of his clansmen not more than twenty feet away.

But he had plucked her nipples until her body sang for

him as always, played her with his skillful fingers until she was wet and throbbing, helplessly grinding her bottom against his groin. Without hesitation, he'd pushed up her skirts and entered her from behind, sliding in and out in a sensual dance. Silencing her with a kiss when she couldn't stop herself from crying out as the cataclysmic crescendo struck.

Only to ignore her the next morning, leaving her alone to blush under Mathilde's knowing smiles and Artair's reproachful glares.

Last night, she'd only fallen to sleep in his strong embrace, exhausted from the journey. From the worry and apprehension of what lay ahead.

She'd woken in his arms this morning, legs twined with his. Her cheek resting on his chest. Listening to his heart's steady beat as the sun began to rise. Pink whispered across the canvas of purples and reds. Lightening. Brightening.

Not nearly as beautiful as that steady rhythm.

Birds called in the distance, sweetly heralding the new day as if it were to be a fine one. The weather might be. Al could only hope their mission would shine so bright.

Keir stirred beneath her, his arms tightening around her. Wakening drowsily, he nuzzled her hair. His fingers finding the long braid she'd been wearing for the past few days and unconsciously winding it around his fist.

As if she were a part of him. An extension.

As he was already a part of her.

Live your life wi' me, lass.

Oh, she wanted to. Wanted to be a part of his always. But did "always" ever last? She'd never known anyone who'd stayed together before. Not when things got rough. Not when they should have clung to each other even more tightly in times of adversity.

As she was clinging to him now.

For the rest of our lives.

As he was holding her?

"Tell me ye'll stay here, lass," he whispered in her ear.

Her heart leapt at the thought that he meant for her to stay in his arms.

"Tell me ye'll nae go tae the tolbooth."

Her heart sank.

"I'll do what must be done, Keir. Just as you will."

Pushing aside the blankets, she rolled away from him. Ignoring him when he reached for her braid.

He disappeared after that. She hadn't seen him all day. Disappointed, a little heartbroken, she'd traveled with Mathilde, Artair, and the rest of the men to an inn just outside Edinburgh. There she'd spent the day checking and rechecking her wiring, wrapping them in waxed parchment so they wouldn't touch until she wanted them to and accidentally blow up the inn.

They would need to be leaving soon.

Where was he?

Chapter 34

"Ride ahead then, but wait for us ootside the borough. We'll move in together, keeping tae the shadows. Once ye hear the signal, we'll attack the guards and Sassenach platoon as one and drive them away from the tolbooth until the escape is made good."

Keir scrutinized the group of men assembled in the stable behind the inn. Sixty men, one and all who'd lost dearly to the battle at Culloden, gathering at his call to free their clansmen.

Each one a true and loyal Highlander.

Each one eager for a bit of revenge against the Butcher who'd ravaged the countryside and their homes giving no quarter along the way.

No quarter. He had begun to revile the term and the unconscionable carnage committed under the auspices of Cumberland's act.

Aye, he was eager for a bit of revenge himself.

"We'll need tae move quickly, lads," he warned. "As the prisoners are freed from the prison, take one up wi' ye tae hasten our retreat. The fewer left afoot, the better off we'll be. Aye?"

"Aye!"

He nodded at their enthusiasm. "We've brought a fair arsenal wi' us from Rosebraugh. Available tae ye if ye dinnae hae arms. See yerselves ready and ride. I'll follow shortly."

The group disbanded, murmuring among themselves. Hopefully they would have enough men to accomplish their mission. To free, not just his father, but all those men about to cross through the valley of death.

What would happen to them after, he had no idea. Hopefully with a clean get away, the foot soldiers and militia being held would be forgotten. Their insignificant political importance making the effort to retrieve them improbable.

As for the others, the title lairds and men of rank, Keir wasn't sure what would become of them. Openly arresting them would be inadvisable even for a man of Cumberland's rank. On the other hand, he might defy logic and pursue them even in the public eye. So, would his father be able to return to Dingwall? Take up the reins as its laird once more? He didn't know.

Perhaps it didn't matter.

Freeing them, making as big an example as Cumberland intended when it came to proving that a Highland laird was more than just a title to be taken away.

That's what mattered.

Keeping Al safe in the process. Aye, well, that mattered even more. He'd thought he could wait her out, give her plenty of time to think about what she was planning to do. Time to change her mind.

She had not.

In all his days he'd never met a female so bloody stubborn. He didn't just weep for the future of men any longer. Nay, he despaired for them.

How was a man supposed to protect his own if she didn't allow him to do his duty?

Nay, she had to be right in the thick of it without thought to her own frailty. One misstep, one confrontation with a Sassenach soldier, might see her cleaved in two.

Her plan—even though it was a bloody fine plan—didn't sit well with him. But she had a point, bugger it all. The men guarding the prisoner wouldn't give a look beyond the salacious to a pair of women. If they were questioned, they'd only have to say they were on the way to visit the redcoats camp to sell treats from their baskets.

Aye, unlike an armed man, she'd be able to walk right up to the prison door. No one would consider a wee, delicate woman like her a threat. A danger. She might even linger for a minute or two before she was questioned.

Al assured him it was all she would need.

Bloody hell, he couldn't bear to let her do it. It was those who might assume they were selling more than just their wares and press them for even sweeter delights that he worried about. What might happen to her if her purpose was discovered. He longed to hold her back, even knowing the benefit that might come from her participation.

"Are ye nae going tae ask me tae come along, brother?" Artair asked after the other men had all wandered away. "Do ye nae think I can raise arms against my enemy?"

Keir slapped his brother on the shoulder. "Nay, brother. I ken ye could. But I need ye tae be here tae minister tae the injured who might return. And...," he paused with a heavy sigh, "see tae it Al returns safely if something should happen tae me. It may nae be a war, but 'twill be a battle in any case. I am nae delusional enough tae think we will achieve the whole of our goal wi'oot some loss of life. Mayhap my own."

"Ye've ne'er lost a fight in yer life," Artair teased uneasily.

"There's a first time for everything. No one can live forever."

Silence fell between the brothers.

"I would ne'er let any harm befall Miss Maines," Artair said at length. "I care for her."

"As do I."

His brother shifted uneasily, rocking up on his toes. "Do ye plan tae keep her then?"

He almost laughed. As if Al were some simple creature who could be kept. He could hardly keep *up* with her.

"I plan tae wed her, Artair. I hope ye will wish us happy."

His brother grimaced. "Truly? Ye hae nae showed much kindness tae her these last few days beyond..." He flushed and glanced away.

"That isnae yer concern. Know she has my heart. I'm merely uneasy aboot her role in our plan for the night and she willnae let me dissuade her from taking part in it."

"Aye, I'd thought her a biddable lass, but..." Artair's lips tightened in an exaggerated grimace that made Keir want to laugh. Aye, Al had too much spunk for a staid man like his brother. Though he'd never mention it, he was surprised Artair had even thought to try to make a preacher's wife out of her. "Keir, I like the lass... but Father. Ye ken he'll nae like it."

He rolled his eyes. "If Father survives this night, he should be grateful enough tae let it pass but I dinnae care for his opinion on the matter one way or the other. Al will be mine."

"Unless ye die."

"Aye, only that would keep me from her."

XOXOXOX

"Ye're leaving then?"

Al peeked up from the ties of her cloak, her heart rate accelerating. "In a few minutes."

Darkness had already fallen. She'd been afraid she wouldn't see him again before she left. Wondered if he would continue to give her the cold shoulder and then never have the chance to berate her once more, if that's what he wanted to do. She'd take even that if it meant seeing him again just in case...

Tears burned at her eyes but Al blinked them back. She knew what they were about to do was dangerous. She wasn't a fool. But whatever he thought, her part in it was minor. She was just a player not the hero.

It was his neck on the line and damn it, she wanted to hug it one last time just in case it was the *last time*.

If only he didn't seem so foreboding, much as he had down in the dungeons. His arms crossed over his chest, his blue eyes gleaming in the darkness. But with what emotion she couldn't say.

Vision clouded with unshed tears, she tucked her head down and fumbled with ties at the neck of her cloak. A second later, warm hands covered hers. With a soft squeeze, he pushed them away and finished the job himself.

His rough fingertips caressed the line of her jaw and tilted her chin up. "Lass, ye dinnae hae tae do this." His brogue was thick, husky.

"Of course, I do."

"*Mo rùnsearc...*" He trailed off and sighed heavily.

"What *is* that?" she whispered, running her fingers into the curling hair clinging to his neck. "What does it mean?"

291

"It literally translates as *my secret love*," he admitted, looking away. "It means beloved."

"Oh, an endearment then?"

"'Tis nae merely an endearment, lass," he corrected, his voice low. "I've ne'er used it before. But perhaps it isnae entirely correct either."

A poignant ache gripped Al's heart. No, of course it wasn't. She'd never been anyone's beloved before.

"I might hae better said *mo shíorghrá* or *m'fhíorghrá*. Either would be more fitting. More true tae what I feel." He gazed down at her, stroking the hair back from her temple tenderly. "Do ye ken what that means?"

She shook her head. He knew she didn't.

"It means my eternal love." He lifted her hand to his lips, pressing a gentle kiss to her fingertips. She was riveted by the intensity of his vivid eyes. "My true love."

She shook her head and tried to look away but he wouldn't let her, holding her firmly.

"Ye dinnae think ye deserve love. Nay, dinnae try tae run away. I ken all too well how ye think, lass. What ye dinnae realize... what ye willnae accept is ye already hae it. Ye dinnae hae tae do this thing, risk yer life tae earn it. I love ye already, lass. My heart is yers."

It was incomprehensible. There wasn't a thought beyond denial running through her head as she stared up at him blankly.

"Ye think I lie?" he asked perceptively. "That I make it up tae keep ye from going? Can ye nae see in yerself what I see in ye? A beauty of heart? A brilliant mind? Ye stole my heart from the beginning, lass. Ye give of yerself so fully. Did ye ne'er think anything would e'er be given back?"

"I don't know..." God, he scored her heart with his

words. Never had she heard anything so soul-wrenching. But here? Now? Turning her head, she stared down the street. If only...

Damn, if only they were alone. A handful of his men were waiting not far down the street. Far enough away to be out of earshot but not so far they had any real privacy.

"We don't have time to do this right now."

She pushed on his chest but he took her by the shoulders and held her tight.

"What? Nae time for me tae tell ye I love ye? Nae time tae hear the same from yer lips?" He gave her a little shake. "Do ye hae nae love for me, lass?"

God, he couldn't be doing this right now! His words had flooded her to the edge of her limits. If he continued to press her, she'd end up bawling all over him, clinging to him in desperation and begging him never to leave her.

She'd never had a man tell her he loved her. Lay down his heart like that. Certainly not in a way that skyrocketed past every far-flung fantasy she'd ever had or any narrative she'd ever read.

Couldn't he see she just didn't know how to respond to something like that? How to deal with her heart aching so painfully in her chest it must have cracked open inside of her and spilled out? Couldn't he see it leaking out in her tears?

Her throat was so painfully clogged with emotion she could hardly breathe. Her chest burning. Her head reeling...

"Good God, Keir, is she about to faint?"

ANGELINE FORTIN

Chapter 35

Mathilde stepped out of the inn pulling on her gloves, studying Al's... aye, near-faint, with an expression bordering on amusement.

"Go away, Mathilde," he barked, sweeping Al off her feet and into his arms. Brushing past his cousin, he carried her into the inn.

"We don't have time for this!"

Ignoring his cousin, he made his way toward the stairs with his curvaceous bundle.

"Keir, stop," she whispered, regaining some tension in her body. "Stop."

"Ye're ill."

"I'm overwhelmed," she murmured so quietly he barely heard her. "Please stop."

He didn't but he did veer into one of the private rooms off the tap room and close the door.

"Will you put me down?"

"Nay."

Her soft chuckle tickled his ear. A moment later, her arms wound around his neck and she nestled her cheek against his chest with a sigh.

"You sure do know how to sweep a girl off her feet."

It sounded quite complimentary but he wasn't entirely sure what to make of her comment. "I dinnae mean tae overwhelm ye, lass. I only meant tae speak of what is in my heart 'ere ye put yerself in harm's way."

She leaned back in his arms and eyed him seriously. "To keep me from putting myself in harm's way, you mean." Her wide gray eyes narrowed. "You said that to keep me from going."

Unwilling to let her go, he sat in one of the chairs by the table, keeping her in his lap. "I will admit I hope tae talk ye oot of taking part in our ooting, but I dinnae say what I did merely tae convince ye."

"Then why?"

"Because I dinnae want tae go tae my death wi'oot saying it aloud."

Uncomfortable now, perhaps the heat of the moment had passed. She was staring at him so oddly, he might have thought he'd grown another limb. He lifted her off his lap and stood.

Pacing the small room, he felt a hint of uncertainty. True, he thought he knew her well already despite their short affair. Could he have been wrong all along? Perhaps she did not reciprocate his feelings with the same depth. Or perhaps, not at all? He knew she was fascinated by him, attracted to him. Was he some novelty to her? A man beyond her time?

Keir ran his hands through his hair, fisting his fingers around the wild locks. Tugging as if he might be able to draw the answers from his head. Or restore his confidence. He'd never been so impotent in all his days.

Och, what this wee lass had done to him. "Mayhap, I dinnae want tae go tae my death wi'oot hearing the words from yer lips. Alas, I cannae force from yer lips what ye dinnae feel, can I?"

Deafening silence. Then...

"Oh, *my God*, is that what you think?" Her high-pitched disbelief rang from the rafters of the small room. In a heartbeat, she was out of her chair, her hands wrapped around his arm, tugging until he looked down at her. Gone was the panic darkening her eyes. They shined like silver coins. "Do you really think...? Can you possibly be so...? Are men idiots in every century, or is it just me?"

"I dinnae ken what ye..."

He could say no more as she dragged him down and stole his words with her kiss. Hot, open-mouthed. Fervid. She'd never approached the task with such... enthusiasm.

"Does this mean?"

"Shut up for a minute."

※※※※※

The minute spun into many but Al couldn't stop herself. It had taken awhile, probably too long, but she finally realized he meant it. It wasn't just words spouted off to coerce her into doing what he wanted. Drivel to get his own way.

He *meant* it, heart and soul.

And her brawny, burly, gorgeous... *brilliant* Highland laird was stupid enough to think she wasn't in love with *him*?

What a topsy-turvy past she was living in!

Draping her arms around his neck, she lifted herself against him, wrapping her leg around his thigh. He'd recovered from his surprise and was hungrily kissing her back, plunging his tongue past her lips to parry hotly with her own. Desire heated her flesh, the humidity rose. Panting against his mouth, she caught his bottom lip between her teeth, drawing on it until she felt the quiver of his chest and his arms banded so tightly around her waist, her breath was again taken away.

Tilting his head, he took his turn sucking on her top lip then the bottom. Running his tongue along her lips before kissing her roughly. When he pulled away, she was left breathing hard, dizzy. Panting.

He held her snugly to him until she could feel every hard plane, every bulge, every ripple she pressed against. Lifting her, he turned, backing her to the wall with a thud that stole her breath even more. Gasping, she threw back her head. The raspy burn of his whiskers trailed down her neck along with his lips. She cried out as his teeth nipped the curve of her shoulder. In pain. In wanton craving, she wrapped her legs around his hips. His huge erection was throbbing, burning through the layers between them.

"Keir!' she cried out, desperation igniting every pore of her body.

"Aye, *mo ghrá,*" he growled in his deep brogue and fumbled at the buttons of his trousers.

"God, I like kilts so much better than pants," she breathed, loving the heave of his chest and shoulders as he silently laughed.

Then the laughter was gone. He drove into her, slamming her against the wall, their cries of passion and joy intermingling.

A fist banged on the door. "Children, there's a rescue waiting to be had," Mathilde called. "We don't have time for this."

"Aye, we do," Keir whispered, grinning down at her with love in his eyes. He kissed her answering smile away and began to move.

With a sniff, Mathilde turned away from the door. "If the rest of the night is this explosive, we'll be assured of our success."

ANGELINE FORTIN

300

Chapter 36

"You fret too much."

"And you're surprisingly calm for a woman who just got groped by a complete stranger, Tildy," Al muttered under her breath while Mathilde just laughed.

"You think that was groping?" she scoffed. "My cousin must not be doing a respectable job of it. Och, Al lass, I should think you'd be far more relaxed now that you…"

Her wicked grin had Al blushing even more than she had been when she and Keir had left the inn to find his men, Artair, and Mathilde waiting on them, each with a knowing smirk on their faces.

Well, except Artair.

She'd never been so embarrassed in her life, but she wouldn't have traded it for the world. She was loved. Thoroughly completely. Heart and soul.

She'd felt like she could conquer the world.

Unfortunately, that feel-good moment had only lasted until Keir was out of sight, parting from them at the edge of the city. He called orders to the men, directing them this way, and disappearing into the darkness.

It was like her light had gone out with him. Her

confidence leeching away. She was so strong with him but reverted to her old inhibited self the second she was apart from him.

It had pained her to leave him and she knew from the hard pressure of his hand around hers before he'd determinedly let her go, he felt the same.

It wasn't until they were some blocks away, she realized she hadn't told him. At least in so many words. The temptation was strong to say 'screw the mission' and run back to him and assure him she felt for him every ounce of the love he so eloquently described and more.

No chance with someone as headstrong as Mathilde tugging her along.

"You should come to court someday if you want to know what it truly feels like to be groped. Why, I could tell you some stories about King George that would make you blanch. There was this one time…"

Mathilde carried on with her atrocious stories of having hands thrust down her bodice and up her skirts in the dark staircases and back halls of Windsor Castle, as they wound their way through the dark streets of Edinburgh with only the light of a single lantern to guide them. Al cringed for womankind, and desperately missed for just a instant, a world where a woman could walk in safety.

Well, at least in a palace.

She doubted the Queen put up with bullshit like that in Buckingham.

The walk wasn't a long one but there were miraculously no direct through streets in the handful of city blocks they needed to cover. They were forced to turn this way and that. Thank God for Mathilde's company and lead. She would have never found her way through the maze on her own.

Would have chickened out long before they reached their destination.

Cutting through a dark alley, they found themselves on Canongate Road. What Al knew as the Royal Mile.

Mathilde covertly pointed to the prison. As Keir said, it was a fortress. Four stories with more than a half-dozen gables tenting up from the slanted roof. In the center, a circular turret arose from the central block. An arched opening hollowed it out at the bottom.

"That's where the door is. It's sheltered from the street. No one should see you once you're in there."

The problem was, there were several people on the street, despite the late hour. Two red-coated men patrolling together near the western corner of the building. Another flirting with a woman across from them. Just a block away, Cumberland's platoon thankfully hidden from sight beyond the Canongate Church.

As she stood there worrying her earlobe, Al's eyes darted up and down the street. She was losing her nerve despite overwhelming moral cause. She didn't know if she could summon the courage to get the job done.

Then she saw him. Keir, farther down the street, leaning against a building across from the gaol as if he had nothing better to do.

Of all the ballsy...

"Go distract those two down there," she whispered to Mathilde.

"How?"

"Flirt. Swish your skirts." Al rolled her eyes. "I'd bet you know exactly how to befuddle a male mind or two. Get to it."

With a saucy grin, Mathilde took off, sauntering straight down the middle of the street. Swishing her skirts as if she hadn't a care in the world. She walked right by the pair of guards, even caught the eye of the other man as she passed. And kept going. The three men couldn't look away.

Heartened, Al crept down the street keeping to the shadows until she was directly across from the prison door. Taking a deep, bracing breath and a page from Mathilde's book, she strolled casually across the street. Hoping she wasn't attracting the same attention as Mathilde, but she hadn't wanted to catch anyone's eye with a sudden movement of her lantern either.

Safely in the shadow of the door, she drew the battery/bomb from her basket and began to unwrap it. The lock itself was a broad metal plate across the right-center portion of the door. That was it. Nothing but a notched out keyhole to upset the clean aesthetic.

Luckily, the keyhole itself was so large, she should be able to wedge the battery right into it. To her pleasure, it fit. Tightly enough she needn't worry about wiring it in or about it slipping out. Close enough to the mechanism, the heat of the blast should crack the bolt without trouble, allowing the door to be pushed open by Keir's Highland men waiting to storm the building.

Unwrapping the two wires from the wax paper, she made sure to keep them far apart and she stretched the wire down to the ground. With the straw she included in the basket, she made a cushion on top of one knife and laid the second diagonally across from it.

That was it.

Removing the stub of her candle from the lantern, she held it near the straw but hesitated in lighting it. Thoughts of the butterfly effect staying her hand. Everything she'd ever heard or read about time travel said any change to the past could have disastrous effects on the future. Surely she hadn't made much of a ripple so far, but this was big. A game changer. She was about to change history by setting the people inside this prison free.

Or was she?

This wasn't her history. The days ahead weren't her future. It was a different reality and by lighting this straw she'd only be creating another.

Accidents happen for a reason.

Keir had said. That funky little man, Donnel, had said it.

Maybe this was the reason. Casting her lot, hoping fate truly did have a plan, she lit the straw. Making sure it was burning steadily and wouldn't go out, she blew out the candle and darted away from the building.

Dashing into the shadows on the other side of the street, she saw Keir inching along, coming closer. Though she longed to have him with her with every fiber of her being, she waved him back. He sank into the shadows out of sight.

Across the street, the little flame flared like a beacon then flickered. And died.

Any minute now.

She waited. Nothing.

Another armed soldier rounded the corner on the east end of the prison beyond Keir's hiding place. He was coming closer and there was no way to warn him without alerting the patrolman.

Damn, why hadn't the battery exploded yet?

Still nothing.

The knives must have shifted or something. She chewed her lip. It had to be that or the battery hadn't taken enough of a charge from the Leyden Jar to short circuit at all.

Another glance down the street told her the soldier was

almost straight across from Keir now. Surely, he would spot him any second. Their chance might be blown even if the battery wasn't.

Her confidence built again. For Keir, she needed to remain strong and get this thing done. Sucking in a breath, she waited for the guard to turn away and ran across the street into the archway once more.

Damn, the straw hadn't burned through! To hell with it. Snatching up the two wires, she twisted them together above the dangling knives, wincing at the static snap zipping through her.

"Shit that hurts," she muttered under her breath.

She didn't run immediately but waited to make sure it worked. How far away was the soldier? Did she dare peek around the corner?

Desperate, she glanced back at the bomb.

With a sigh of relief, she saw the rubber casing around the battery begin to swell with the gasses heating within. In just a few seconds...

Shhh-foomp!

Chapter 37

The explosion hadn't been at all as he thought. Not the boom of a musket or the blast of a cannon. More a hiss followed by a bang that might have been a door slamming.

No one paid it any mind. Not the soldier passing by. Not his men.

No, it wasn't the blast that snared Keir's attention, it was Al's cry of pain. Not even knowing what it was, the sound had yanked him like invisible chains from his hiding place. She was crouching near the archway cradling her arm. Heedless of how he might be exposing himself, he ran to her side and dropped to his knees.

"Are ye hurt, *mo ghrá?*"

"No, I'm fine. It was just a bit of plastic that hit me when it blew." Twisting her arm around gently, he saw a charred hole in her sleeve, burned straight through to the angry wound on her upper arm. "I had to pull the plastic off. It stuck to me." Her thumb and forefinger were blistering already. "You know, I think it actually hit me in the same spot as the knife. Nice, only one scar, huh?"

Foolish lass. He wanted to berate her for being near the explosive when it went off. For being here at all.

"Let me get ye oot of here."

"No, you have to—Watch out!"

Whipping around, he found a burly, red-coated soldier looming over them, the bayonet extending from the end of his long musket wavering dangerously close.

"Oi! Who are ye? What are ye doing here abouts?"

He hadn't heard the blast, or at least identified it for what it was, Keir realized. Dashing a glance at the prison door obscured by the dark, he saw there was no visible damage showing. The guard hadn't any idea… yet, what they were about.

Rising slowly, he held up his hands. "Just oot for a walk. My wife fell. Can ye help?"

The moment the soldier's gaze moved to Al, he acted. With both hands, he grabbed for the musket and tried to wrench it from the redcoat's grip. He began to holler an alarm, so Keir jerked the musket down, dragging the soldier down as well. Releasing it, he thrust a hard right punch up, catching the soldier in the jaw and snapping him backward. Laying him onto his back in the street, groaning but conscious.

Putting a boot down in the center of the man's chest, he loomed over him and used all his body weight to hit him once more. With a grunt, the soldier's head lolled to the side.

He was out. The sounds of a scuffle had heads popping from the shadows up and down the street. His men. With a wave of his arm, the shadows began to move down the street toward them.

"I hae tae get ye oot of here," he said to her, dragging the soldier deeper into the archway and out of sight.

"I'm fine. Check the door."

He pushed on the door but it didn't give. If they couldn't

get the door open, this was all for naught.

"Try again," she urged, getting to her feet. "Harder. It might have only torqued the bolt."

Rattling it a second time, he felt enough movement to give him encouragement needed to put his shoulder to it. With a steely whine, it swung inward.

"Go!"

She was once again trying to spur him into action but he knew before anything else, he needed to be assured of her safety.

His men were nearing. Waving them to gather in, he gazed around the eager group. "Quiet now, lads. Seems the company yonder disnae yet ken we're here. Let's keep it that way and get everyone oot quickly. Aye?"

But then, from within the prison, a voice rang out. "What's going on? Who's out there?"

Bugger it, he'd forgotten the guards inside. "Nay time tae waste, lads. Get tae it!"

They didn't mind the brusque order. They'd come expecting a fight. Some of them were probably looking forward to it. Enthusiastically, they stormed through the door and almost immediately, muffled shouts of alarm and a scuffle sounded within. The clang of swords.

He scooped Al into his arms, and carried her quickly across the street. Saying, before she could bother, "Ye can do it yerself, I ken. But I'm taking ye back tae the inn."

"No, you need to make sure your father is safe. I'm waiting here for Mathilde," she hissed at him. "For God's sake, go!"

Bloody hell, the sounds of battle coming from within the gaol were getting louder. Shouts of alarm. The clang of swords. Fortunately, there was no musket fire yet, but the alarm was sure to be sounded soon.

Kissing her hard, he did as she asked. As his loyalty to his clan and country demanded.

XOXOXOX

Her heart was pounding in her chest as Keir ran from her and into the jailhouse. She'd never known such a flash of utter panic in her life. Not when her father had left her and her mom, not when her stepfather would get drunk and rage at them. Not when her grandmother had died. She wanted to run after him and throw herself into his safe, secure embrace and beg him to come away with her.

But Keir MacCoinnach wasn't that kind of man. One who could deny his obligation to his men. It was what had drawn him to the field at Culloden that day they'd met.

Besides, Al was fast discovering she wasn't that kind of woman either. She could be strong, confident. For him. Because of him.

"We need to hurry," Mathilde called, running up the alleyway behind her. "The guards are returning. They'll be sure to sound an alarm."

It was sure to be sounded anyway. Men were pouring out of the narrow prison door like a river delta. Fanning out across and down the street. Some limping, wounded. Some carried.

Some scattered, making the most of their escape. Others stayed, ready to help. A few minutes later, Keir emerged supporting an older man who was limping along beside him.

"That's Uncle Camran," Mathilde said and ran out into the street to help.

"He's injured. I need ye tae get him back tae the inn."

Mathilde nodded and looped her uncle's arm over her shoulder but Al shook her head.

"Mathilde can do it, I'm staying here with you."

"Go. I'll be along shortly. As soon as I ken every man has been freed."

"I'll wait for you."

Down the street, shouts rang. Then from the Highlanders, shouts of alarm. Catching Keir's attention, they pointed down the street. Al, Keir, and Mathilde all stepped out to look to the east.

Damn, their luck had run out.

The redcoats were coming.

She could see now the reason for the notorious words of warning. They were an impressive sight in the those red uniforms, black belts crossing their chests, high black hats, white pants, and muskets held at the ready.

There were only about three rows of ten or so men. Only, she qualified in the way that a tsunami was only a wave. Real fear sank into her chest, setting her heart aquiver.

"Go!" Keir's command brooked no argument but Al couldn't help it.

"Come with us."

"Nay, lass. I will nae leave these men and I cannae be worrying o'er ye. For my sake, go now." He strode out into the street, pulling a pair of pistols from his belt. He stood there, brass and balls in front of an armed foe, and waved his men to assemble. "*A MacCoinnach!* Wi' me, lads!"

"*A MacCoinnach!*" they rallied, joining him in the street.

It was a magnificent sight but one that froze her in terror.

"Al!" Mathilde tugged at her arm, rousing her forgotten pain. With a wince, she turned. "We've got to go. Now!"

For Keir's sake, not her own, she did.

Musket fire thundered from behind them, reverberating down the alley, and Al's heart stopped. Turning to look back, she tripped and fell. There were screams from the street behind them, cries of pain.

Boom.

Another volley.

"Keir!" she cried in alarm, picking herself up and scrambling toward the fighting. She shouldn't have left him there.

"No!" Mathilde caught her arm and dragged her back.

Al fought her, trying to free herself. Every fiber of her being urged her to return to Keir. "I have to help him!"

"Don't be a fool! You go back there, you'd only get in the way and maybe get him killed in the process." Al continued to struggle but unfortunately, Mathilde was bigger and stronger than her. She held her tight and hauled her along, even while helping her uncle.

Behind them, the sounds of war escalated. The cries of the wounded multiplied. Terror shook Al's body until she was quivering from head to toe.

"Oh, God."

Mathilde's lips thinned grimly. "Aye. There's nothing you can do for him now but pray."

Chapter 38

Funny how religion could suddenly come to someone, because she began praying on their way back to the inn and hadn't stopped since. The sounds of the struggle had faded with each step. The anxiety gripping her had not.

"Och, lassie, can ye nae be more gentle?"

Al bit her lip and refrained from berating Keir's father. He'd complained the whole journey to the inn about his wounded leg, which had turned out to be nothing worse than a long scrape down the side of his ankle and perhaps a slight sprain. Yet he carried on and on about it as if he were bleeding in the streets while the men they'd left behind might have been.

Perhaps she was being uncharitable, but for all his complaining about his own discomfort, he hadn't yet given even the slightest mention about his son who might, at this very moment, be wounded or worse.

She couldn't take it. Any compassion she might have been able to dredge up had slipped away with the hours that passed without a word from Keir. She had no idea where he was. How he was.

The uncertainty was pure torment.

She would've gone back already if Artair and Mathilde

weren't actively barring her from leaving the inn. She couldn't overpower them based on size alone. But when they wanted to start out for Rosebraugh as well and leave Keir to find them there, she'd become a lioness. She didn't care if they wanted to get out of Edinburgh before troops began searching for the escaped prisoners. She wasn't leaving unless they bodily forced her. Thank God they didn't try.

Artair had negotiated a bargain where he would go out to find Keir as long as she stayed at the inn.

She agreed but that left her with nothing to do but wait and listen to Cairn complain while Mathilde nursed his minor wounds. She paced the room and stared repeatedly out the window for sight of the men. Fear was plaguing at her and yet Cairn seemed unconcerned. He did nothing but bitch and moan about the pain and Mathilde's technique the entire time.

"Nae so tight, Mathilde!"

"Sorry, Uncle."

When did Mathilde become so meek? If she were wrapping that bandage she'd be telling him what he could do with his complaints. For a grown man, he was the biggest baby she'd ever known. She didn't care if he was the Earl of Cairn, after all, and Keir's father.

"Oh, my God!" she burst out. "It's not that bad!"

"Listen here, lassie—"

"Please," Mathilde interrupted as if she hadn't heard the miraculously renewed strength in his voice. "My uncle is a man of sixty years. He is too old to suffer such an injury."

Al shook her head. She might not be able to say a lot of complimentary things about her stepfather, but at sixty-six, he'd knock anyone on his backside who said he was too old for anything. But then again, sixty might be considered old since the life expectancy was probably shorter. It was a different time. She'd only assumed from the example Keir had set that it was a tougher one.

"No, he's too old to act like a child," she argued, then glowered at the man upon the bed. "Haven't you even thought to ask about your sons?"

"Impertinent, lass! Who are ye tae question me?"

"I'm someone who actually cares about what's going on out there," she told him. "You should be grateful for what Keir's done for you. If you can't manage that, you should at least be concerned. Worried that he hasn't returned."

Cairn harrumphed but didn't say anything else. But this time when Mathilde tightened the knot, he only hissed and shot Al a venomous glare. "He would nae be in this mess a'tall if I'd stayed where I was."

"In prison?" If he wanted to go back, he could be her guest.

"Nay, I've nae e'en been here a full sennight. I was safe and comfortable in the home of my," he shot a glance at Mathilde, "er, a certain lady friend. She convinced me I should return tae Dingwall. That is when I was captured. Shouldn't hae happened a'tall."

Al and Mathilde both gaped at him.

"Uncle, you'd been free all the days following the battle and didn't think to let Keir or anyone know you were well?"

"I dinnae dare send a message. It was in my best interests—"

"*Your* best interests?" Al questioned in amazement. Fear for Keir and anger over his unbelievable apathy bubbled up inside "Yours? Your family has been worried sick about you." Perhaps an overstatement but at least now she was getting a clearer picture of why none of the MacCoinnach men seemed to be genuinely worried about their father. He wasn't only selfish, he was uncaring of their feelings, too. "Do you even know Frang was killed in the battle?" she asked. "Do you even care?"

Cairn only blinked. Surprise, but no remorse. "Aye, well, 'twas the lad's duty tae serve his clan."

"Oh my God. You don't care at all, do you?" She looked up at Mathilde who seemed equally taken aback by her uncle's indifference. "One son dies because you command him to fight, your nephew is lost as well. Keir is out there fighting right now because he was determined to save your life."

"I dinnae expect it, but 'tis good to know I raised sons who know their duty."

Yes, Keir did know his duty. Somehow this man had managed to instill that in him.

"You don't deserve a son like him. He's the finest man I've ever known, even dreamed might exist. He's smart, brave, and loyal even when his loyalty isn't deserved, I can see," she choked the words out from the tears clogging her throat. "You, sir, are a horrible person."

Cairn lurched up in the bed. "Just who do ye think ye are, lass, tae talk tae me like that? I am the Earl of Cairn."

"I don't care if you're the king of the world!"

Hot tears fell then, splashing on her cheeks. It was as if letting them fall unleashed a torrent of emotion as well. Her body stiff, hands fisted at her sides, she screamed at him. The words were ripped out of her, from her very heart.

"I love him. Even if you don't care, I do. I love him! God, I love him more than anything. More than I ever imagined. And you just lay there not giving a damn. You bastard, don't you realize he might have given his life to save yours?"

"I dinnae."

Whirling around at the rumbling burr, she saw Keir in the doorway being supported by Artair. There was a small trickle of blood running down his temple, another spot on his shoulder, but overall he looked sound and wonderfully alive.

With a sob, she ran to him, falling into his arms as he lifted her against him. Her feet dangling inches above the floor as he hugged her tight. His warm lips brushed her brow, her temple, then her cheeks. Kissing away her tears.

"'Though she be but little, she is fierce.'"

A watery laugh escaped her and she buried her face in his neck. "How long have ye been listening?"

"Long enough." He chuckled near her ear. "I seem to learn a lot lingering in doorways."

He leaned back and kissed her so tenderly her heart ached even more.

"I've learned much about Father as well."

"Are you sorry you saved him?"

He shook his head, glancing over her shoulder. "Nay, but I'm glad I dinnae have to live with him. I'm the Duke of Ross now, ye ken?"

Her lips quirked. Releasing her, he turned to Cairn who was pushing himself out of bed.

"Father, ye should know I'm getting married."

He started to protest but Keir went on.

"Whether ye like it or nae." Glancing over his shoulder at her, his lips kicked up in the corner. "Whether *she* likes it or nae."

He strode to Al and took her in his arms once more. "Tell me ye'll marry me."

Tears burned in her eyes. "I will."

"And say again how ye love me."

"With all my heart."

With a grin, he bent his head and kissed her.

"We're not going to go through this again, are we?" Mathilde asked dryly.

"It's been some time since I've done a wedding," Artair spoke up. "I shall hae tae prepare a sermon."

Groaning under her breath, Al kissed the man of her dreams and thanked God for accidents.

Epilogue

The redcoats hadn't offered much of a fight, Keir told her later. The Highlanders didn't fight like the Sassenach who lined up just so before taking a shot. They had attacked en masse and broken through the enemy formation by the time the second line had taken their shot.

It was only a stray bullet grazing his temple that had delayed his return. The way it sounded, adrenaline had energized him through the fighting. He hadn't even been aware of the injury until he'd been on his way to the inn and briefly fallen unconscious in an alley where Artair found him.

She'd wanted to stay at the inn and nurse him, but he'd insisted they start straightaway back to Rosebraugh to avoid any other encounters with the soldiers.

But the redcoats hadn't come after them. Nor did they in the days following. Cumberland had recaptured a few of the men and had his trial in Carlisle. Following Keir's example, a mob of angry Scots had stormed the building and freed them. Holding Cumberland and his senior officers as leverage, they were petitioning King George, who was also Cumberland's first cousin, for peace.

When he hadn't responded straight away, others had

taken up the standard and attacked the prisons in Inverness and Carlisle and farther south in York and Kennington Common. Even the prison hulk on the Thames had been struck. An accord between England and Scotland was being negotiated.

Part of the terms laid out by Scotland was for Cumberland to face punishment for his 'crimes against humanity,' a term newly coined for the time in a long letter by the Duke of Ross to King George detailing the atrocities Cumberland had heaped upon the Highlanders after the battle at Culloden.

History had a way of changing.

So did families.

Oran returned from the Orkney Islands with news that Maeve's husband, Robert MacLeod, had died from an infection from a minor wound he received in the battle. In her grief, Maeve had thrown herself from the cliffs on the southern coast of the island of Hoy.

Mathilde and Ceana were grief-stricken. Al, too, felt a true sorrow for how unkindly life had treated Maeve.

Mathilde was fast becoming her dearest friend besides Keir. Though she was to return to the Lowlands and her husband soon, she promised to bring her daughters to Rosebraugh soon to visit and be tutored.

Having bet on the wrong side, Cairn's perfect image with the English monarch was soiled. His place in court lost, he left Scotland for Paris.

Without a word to anyone.

But he did send a note days later.

Ceana and her Earl of Braemore had gone as well to wait out the reprisal of the English king on those who had stood in opposition to him. She would return someday soon, Ceana promised and Al would welcome her back. At least life would never be boring with her around.

Nor would it be in general. Keir had plans for them, both romantically and academically. Having received word that his discovery of two new planets and their moons was being duly noted, he was determined to see what else he could find. No cheating, though, she was only there for confirmation after the fact.

Fortunately, Dingwall didn't suffer heavily under the land seizures of the Highland lairds. Not because the sins of the father hadn't descended upon the son, but because Keir had made friends over the years in some high places.

He might suffer some retribution in the days ahead though if he continued to flout the new laws against Highland customs, Al thought. They might also be negotiating with England to change them as well, but they weren't gone yet.

Keir didn't care. Dressed in full Highland regalia, from his kilt to his sporran, he stood in open defiance of the law at Hugh's graveside.

The wind was blowing from the south off the Moray Firth, tugging at the long length of tartan flung over his shoulder, lifting the hem of his kilt. He wore the outlawed broadsword hanging from his hip, too.

The banned bagpipes wailed mournfully as Hugh was laid to rest. Artair's eloquent but lengthy eulogy kept them standing there for a long while.

Al stood by Keir's side, his hand tight around hers as they waited out the speech patiently.

She was to officially become the mistress of Rosebraugh and Dingwall in just four days, though by the traditional Highland customs, they were already wed having publicly stated their intentions in a handfast ceremony. She would be

Duchess of Rosebraugh, eventually Countess of Dingwall, but most importantly, Keir's bride. His wife.

Forever.

She'd probably never read another novel. She'd never need to dwell in far-flung fantasy again. Reality—or alternate reality—provided everything she'd ever need to be happy.

Someone to love.

Someone to love her in return.

And a purpose.

If at some point over the years she just happened to "discover" the light bulb a century early...

Well...

Accidents happened for a reason.

Authors Note

I wonder if you recognize Hugh and Keir from *A Time & Place for Every Laird*? I've gotten many emails since it was published asking about the American Indian who'd been imprisoned with Hugh and escaped at the same time but also a few inquiries about the cousin he left behind on the battlefield at Culloden. I got to thinking, since a wormhole is a two-way street, it would be interesting if someone traveled back through it at the same time it'd been opened for Hugh.

And since Keir is, after all, Hugh's friend and cousin, he couldn't be anything less than brilliant and in need of someone to push him and challenge him on that front. A bit of a change to the typical Highland tale but I hope you enjoyed it.

Culloden was of course, one of the most famous and bloody battles in Scotland's history. To my surprise, I learned something new in reading about the Duke of Cumberland and how he earned the moniker 'The Butcher'. By giving 'no quarter' (a term hated among the Highlanders at the time) he became the most reviled man of the era.

His treatment of prisoners afterward was appalling. One passage I read summed it up rather well.

When we had filled all the jails, kirks and ships at Inverness with these rebel prisoners, wounded and naked as they were, we ordered that none should have any access to them, either with meat or drink, for two days. By this means, no doubt, we thought at least the wounded would starve, either for want of food or clothes, the weather being then very cold. The two days being passed, there was a quorum of officers pitched upon to go and visit them, in order to take down their names and numbers, which was diminished pretty well, without having the least regard to order the remaining part either meat or drink to support nature. Amongst the number I was myself; but oh, heavens! what a scene opened to my eye and nose all at once! The wounded weltering in their gore and blood... Their groans would have pierced a heart of stone; but our corrupt hearts were not in the least touched; but, on the contrary, we began to upbraid them the moment we entered their prison.'

Even so, the Highland spirit never died. The laws banning Highland customs and tradition were lifted within fifty years and still lives proudly today.

Obviously for the purposes of this book, I changed a few historical facts here and there.

Keir's telescope is modeled after one built by Willaim Hershel in 1789. It had a 49" (1200 mm) lens and was 40 feet long. With it in 1781, he discovered Uranus and was appointed Court Astronomer by George III. He discovered its moons not long after, as well as a wealth of other discoveries. Neptune wasn't discovered until 1846. You can see why Al was a bit confused.

I had a bit of fun playing with history and thinking about what might have happened if Elizabeth I hadn't ever been queen of England. Catherine of Aragon did get pregnant many times during her marriage to Henry VIII. Though there were several sons among her unfortunate miscarriages and still births, one son, named Henry and titled Duke Cornwall, was born on New Year's Day in 1511. He lived for fifty-two days. But what if he'd never died at all? No necessity for Henry VIII to divorce Catherine. No split and excommunication with the Pope. No Church of England.

Perhaps Ann Boleyn would have still entered the picture, perhaps Elizabeth would have still been born but she would not have been Queen. Think of her long reign, the battle against the Spanish Armada. Maybe England would have never become such a worldwide power. And perhaps those English colonies in the Americas wouldn't have grown so large.

Maybe none of us would be here at all.

I think I could write a whole book just about the possibilities.

Angeline

ANGELINE FORTIN

About the Author

Angeline Fortin is the author of historical and time-travel romance offering her readers a fun, sexy and often touching tales of romance.

Her most recent release, Taken: A Laird for All Time Novel, was recently awarded the Virginia Romance Writers 2015 Holt Medallion Award for Paranormal Romance. Her first release in May of 2011, the Highland time travel novel *A Laird for All Time*, has steadily ranked in Amazon's Top 100 in Time Travel for the past four years with more than 100 five-star reviews so far.

A Question of Love, the first of her Victorian historical romance series Questions for a Highlander, was released later that year and quickly followed by series additions *A Question of Trust* and *A Question of Lust*. The series primarily follows the siblings of the MacKintosh clan. Ten brothers and their lone sister who end up looking for love in all the right places.

While the series continues on with familiar characters well known to those who have read the entire series, each single title is also a stand-alone tale of highland romance.

With a degree in US History from UNLV and having previously worked as a historical interpreter at Colonial Williamsburg, Angeline brings her love of history and Great Britain to the forefront in settings such as Victorian London and Edinburgh.

As a former military wife, Angeline has lived from the west coast to the east, from the north and to the south and uses those experiences along with her favorite places to tie into her time travel novels as well.

Angeline is a native Minnesotan who recently relocated back to the land of her birth and braved the worst winter recorded since before she initially moved away. She is a PAN member of the Romance Writers of America, Midwest Fiction Writers and Romancing the Lakes. She lives in Apple Valley outside the Twin Cities with her husband, two children and three dogs.

She is a wine enthusiast, DIY addict (much to her husband's chagrin) and sports fanatic who roots for the Twins and Vikings faithfully through their highs and lows.

Most of all she loves what she does every day - writing. She does it for you the reader, to bring a smile or a tear and loves to hear from her fans.

You can check out her website www.angelinefortin.com for summaries off all her books, companion information and for news about upcoming releases. Email her at fortin.angeline@gmail.com.

Or you can follow her just about anywhere!

Facebook - http://on.fb.me/1fBD1qq

Twitter – https://twitter.com/AngelineFortin

Google+ - http://bit.ly/1hWXSGB

Tumblr – https://www.tumblr.com/blog/angeline-fortin

Pinterest - https://www.pinterest.com/angelinefortin1/

Made in the USA
Charleston, SC
17 October 2015